"Liking y ocean?" Jack asked

"I wish I'd tried it before," Chloe replied, her voice a dreamy whisper.

He smoothed his hands over the arch of the bottom of her feet and Chloe sighed. Her toenails were painted a bright plum color, he noticed, smiling. "Well, you're trying it now." He kept his voice soft and soothing, hoping it matched the way his fingertips were working her silky skin.

Jack let go of her feet, assuming his massage duties were over. "And if there's anything else I can do to make your stay more relaxing, just let me know."

"I will. This is wonderful," she said, turning onto her back.

He blinked, his body throbbing painfully. She was waiting. And she expected more....

Blaze™

Dear Reader,

Strangely enough, I usually come up with titles before I come up with stories.

I thought of the title *Jack & Jilted* and knew that I had to write a romance to go with it—but first I had to figure out who Jack was, and who exactly got jilted. Meet hot "Captain Jack" McCullough, owner and operator of the pleasure cruising yacht *The Rascal,* and his passenger Chloe Winton, a blushing, sexy bride who was abandoned at the altar and decides to take her honeymoon cruise alone.

Writing about Jack and Chloe, and about the ship and their adventures, was a lot of fun. I hope you have as much fun reading about the two of them as I had writing about them!

Enjoy,

Cathy Yardley

JACK & JILTED
Cathy Yardley

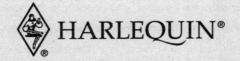

HARLEQUIN®

TORONTO • NEW YORK • LONDON
AMSTERDAM • PARIS • SYDNEY • HAMBURG
STOCKHOLM • ATHENS • TOKYO • MILAN • MADRID
PRAGUE • WARSAW • BUDAPEST • AUCKLAND

If you purchased this book without a cover you should be aware
that this book is stolen property. It was reported as "unsold and
destroyed" to the publisher, and neither the author nor the
publisher has received any payment for this "stripped book."

ISBN-13: 978-0-373-79304-4
ISBN-10:   0-373-79304-9

JACK & JILTED

Copyright © 2007 by Cathy Yardley.

All rights reserved. Except for use in any review, the reproduction or
utilization of this work in whole or in part in any form by any electronic,
mechanical or other means, now known or hereafter invented, including
xerography, photocopying and recording, or in any information storage
or retrieval system, is forbidden without the written permission of the
publisher, Harlequin Enterprises Limited, 225 Duncan Mill Road,
Don Mills, Ontario, Canada M3B 3K9.

All characters in this book have no existence outside the imagination of
the author and have no relation whatsoever to anyone bearing the same
name or names. They are not even distantly inspired by any individual
known or unknown to the author, and all incidents are pure invention.

This edition published by arrangement with Harlequin Books S.A.

® and TM are trademarks of the publisher. Trademarks indicated with
® are registered in the United States Patent and Trademark Office, the
Canadian Trade Marks Office and in other countries.

www.eHarlequin.com

Printed in U.S.A.

ABOUT THE AUTHOR

Cathy Yardley needs to get out more. When not writing, she is probably either cruising the Internet or watching movies—those featuring pirate captains and those not. Her family is considering performing an intervention for her addiction to pop culture. She lives in California.

Please visit her at www.cathyyardley.com.

Books by Cathy Yardley

HARLEQUIN BLAZE
14—THE DRIVEN SNOWE
59—GUILTY PLEASURES
69—WORKING IT

HARLEQUIN SIGNATURE SPOTLIGHT
SURF GIRL SCHOOL

Don't miss any of our special offers. Write to us at the following address for information on our newest releases.

Harlequin Reader Service
U.S.: 3010 Walden Ave., P.O. Box 1325, Buffalo, NY 14269
Canadian: P.O. Box 609, Fort Erie, Ont. L2A 5X3

To my husband, Joe,
the love of my life

1

FEELING SHELL-SHOCKED, Chloe sat at the head table in the reception hall.

"Are you all right, dear?"

She looked up to see her aunt Mildred, whose wrinkled face was the picture of concern.

"I…" Chloe struggled for words. "Yes. I'm doing all right," she said. It wasn't exactly a lie. She wasn't feeling badly—wasn't feeling anything but numb, so she assumed that meant she was functional. As long as she could function, she was all right.

"Have you gotten a hold of the groom yet?"

Chloe shook her head.

"His family?"

Chloe winced. "His mother told me he's unavailable for discussion," she said, unconsciously mimicking the woman's crisp, overly enunciated way of speaking.

Mildred made a snorting sound. "Convenient. He stands you up on your wedding day, with a *note,* and now he's 'unavailable for discussion'! That's rich!"

Although she felt the same way, Chloe had had this conversation already with at least a dozen members of her family. All her family, in fact, had stayed to try to eat some of the reception food, since it was paid for. Gerald—Chloe's vanished fiancé and groom—had not bothered to let anybody other than his immediate family know about his plan, so everyone from his guest list had shown up to the church and then beaten a hasty retreat once Chloe made the announcement that the wedding wasn't proceeding.

"Didn't you buy a house with this man not too long ago?"

"Yes," Chloe admitted, suppressing a sigh. "I did."

"You were supposed to move in after the honeymoon, weren't you? What's going to happen now?"

"I don't know, Aunt Mildred," Chloe replied, feeling weary.

"That's not the sort of detail you want to leave hanging," Mildred said with a disapproving cluck.

"Now, now," Chloe's mother Beverly interrupted, to Chloe's intense relief. "My daughter has a lot of details that she's going to have to address in light of…this unpleasantness. We're not going to handle all this in one afternoon."

"Of course, of course," Aunt Mildred responded, sounding contrite. "You call me if you need anything, Chloe, dear."

Chloe nodded and waved weakly as her aunt headed for the dessert table. "Thanks, Mom," she breathed. "If I have to answer any more questions about Gerald—"

"I know, I know. It's terrible," her mother said, and there was a vicious edge to her voice that Chloe rarely heard. Her mother was usually optimistic to the point of unflappability. "Your father has been raving like a lunatic. I finally got your Uncle Carl to calm him down."

"Dad?" The thought of her sedate father raving over anything but new tax tables was something of a shock.

"Yes," her mother answered. "He's been spouting off about buying a shotgun and going by Gerald's house. He's not serious, though the thought of doing physical harm to that…" Her mother let the sentence peter out with a menacing overtone.

"*Mom,*" Chloe said, now truly shocked.

"He left you a *note,* Chloe. He didn't even have the courage to face you," she countered. "And, after making all these plans, telling you that he's involved with someone else? That is *unforgivable.*"

Chloe felt her throat constrict and hastily looked away. Every time she thought of that particular sentence—*Chloe, I think I found someone more compatible and I've gotten more involved than I intended*—she felt a cold stab of disbelief. It had taken her months to get intimate with Gerald once they'd started dating. They had a mutual, supportive relationship—or at least that's what she'd thought. For pity's sake, they'd split everything, including the house and the wedding bills, right down the middle even though Gerald made much more money as an architect than Chloe did as a personal assistant. How much more "compatible" could this new woman be?

"And don't even get me started on that devil woman," her mother added.

Chloe sighed. "That devil woman" not being the "compatible" object of Gerald's infidelity but, rather, his domineering mother. "Well, at least she's not here," Chloe said, teary.

"After insisting on all this froufrou," her mother hissed, pointing to the bunting, the flowers, the ice sculptures of King Arthur and Guinevere at the main buffet table. "Now her son has the *nerve…*"

"Mom, I love you for being so angry for me," Chloe said, and she meant every word. "But it's not helping. Not right now."

Her mother took a deep, cleansing breath, then nodded. "Certainly. Just like your father always says—focus on the elements you can control, because there's no sense focusing on the things you can't. So…"

Chloe watched as her mother pulled a pen and a small organizer from her purse.

"What do you need to take care of?" Her mother looked like a court reporter, expectant, at the ready to take down notes.

"Do I need to write up the list now?" Chloe said, feeling pained.

"Well, your aunt Mildred was right," her mother said mildly. "There are an awful lot of details. I don't think you need to *solve* them immediately, but you'll feel better when you have an action list in place. I'm sure it all seems overwhelming, so think of how relieved you'll be when you can visualize the extent of your problems in black-and-white. So to speak."

Chloe looked away—looked at the ice sculpture that was slowly melting into the flower arrangements. She loved her family and knew that her mother was doing what she thought would be most helpful in this grave situation. It was a family characteristic, like the wavy brown hair they almost all shared or the slight almond-shaped tilt to their eyes. Being organized and efficient was downright genetic. But for once Chloe wished that she didn't have to be quite such a swift problem-solver.

I wish I could get away from all of this.

Her mother was still waiting, so Chloe straightened in her chair. "Well, there's the house," Chloe began.

"Got it," her mother said, jotting that down. "What else?"

Chloe closed her eyes, trying to will the scorching pain away. "I will need to speak with Gerald."

"That goes without saying."

"I need to figure out where to live."

Her mother clucked, sounding like Mildred. "You can live with us for as long as you need to, sweetie."

Chloe thought about the night she'd spent, last night, in her old childhood room replete with four-poster bed and ruffled lace canopy. She shuddered. "Um, I will need to find a job," Chloe continued, shifting her thoughts quickly.

Now her mother frowned. "Honestly, I still don't understand why you quit. It wasn't as if marriage was going to affect your work."

"Well, no, but there was enough gossiping when Gerald was simply dating me, his personal assistant," Chloe said. "When planning the wedding got crazy, he said he'd take care of my bills if I focused on this…."

She felt tears again and quickly swiped at her eyes before they could fall.

"Oh…" her mother said, instantly comforting.

"Anyway, even if I had kept the job, there's no way I could keep working with Gerald, knowing…what I know now, what he's done," Chloe explained sniffling, then berating herself for it. "So I need to find a new job."

Her mother dutifully added that to the list. "Anything else?"

Chloe blinked at her. *Isn't that enough?*

"Just three things. Take care of the house, find a new place to live, find a job…oh, and talk to Gerald, which I'm putting in the first category of house issues. There, that's not so bad, is it?"

Chloe didn't respond. The list was short, but it was ghastly.

Her mother glanced around. "So we'll put you up at our house tonight. And there's the rest of this wedding monstrosity to take care of."

Chloe's father approached them, looking like a stocky, balding James Bond in his tux. His eyes were still slightly wild, she noticed, and she instantly felt comforted.

"How's my little girl?" he said gruffly.

She stood up and hugged him. "I'm hanging in there," she said, rubbing her cheek against his shoulder.

"Well, of course you are. You're a Winton," he said stolidly. "What are you two doing?"

"Just did a quick list of what she's going to need to take care of," her mother said smoothly.

"That's my girl," he said, patting her shoulder. "Just because the world's going to hell in a handbasket doesn't mean you need to give in to the chaos, I've always said."

He sounded so sure of the statement that Chloe smiled even though she felt like a collapsed building inside. "Right, Dad," she said instead, trying for her bravest smile.

"You might not be able to choose your circumstances, but you can always choose your response to it."

"Yup," Chloe agreed.

"The trick to handling any problem is dealing with the worst aspect first. Then it's all downhill from there."

All downhill from there. Truer words were never spoken.

"When life gives you lemons—"

"Dad," Chloe interrupted. "I get it."

"Hmm? Oh." Her father reddened a bit. "Well, I'm just trying to help you feel better."

"I know. And I love you guys for it." Chloe sat down, looking at her mother's list. Decide what to do about the house…get a job…find a new place to live.

Talk to Gerald.

She knew she ought to. Some part of her wondered if maybe she shouldn't storm over to the new house they'd bought and bang on the door until he showed his cowardly face. She certainly wanted to—she was that angry. But what if he were with his new lover? The thought was like acid on an open wound. What would she do? What *could* she do? Was she even ready to face him? Or worse, face *them?*

Maybe it was cowardly of her, but the thought of facing

Gerald, knowing that he'd cheated on her and walked out on her, made her physically nauseous.

Instead, Chloe picked up her mother's pen and took the list in hand. "All right," she said, breathing deep and pushing all thoughts of Gerald out of her mind. "I'll deal with the wedding first. There's no way everybody can eat all the food we've ordered—we only have half as many guests as planned. So I'll see if the caterer can arrange to take leftovers to a homeless shelter or food bank." She jotted the note: *caterer— food donation.* "The flowers, too. They can go to a hospital, probably. I'm going to need to pay everyone…." She wrote a list of people who would be expecting checks at the end of the night—caterer, hotel, DJ. "And the gifts. We're going to need to return the gifts and send out an explanatory note." Another item added to the list.

By the time she was finished, she had a neatly printed column of details to handle and she had to admit her mother was right—she *did* feel a bit better. Organizing was calming for Wintons, she knew.

Dodging the Gerald issue is calming, as well, she privately admitted.

"Let us know when you want to go home," her father said, giving her another pat on the shoulder.

"We can type these lists up," her mother added helpfully.

"Oh, and your cousins wanted to stop by, to see if there was anything they could do to help," her father said.

"Which reminds me—you'll probably be getting a lot of phone calls." Her mother shrugged. "Everyone feels so badly and they all want to see if you need anything."

Chloe thought about it. She could handle this. Sure, she was staying in a twin-size bed that was hard as granite with age, surrounded by posters of bands and movie stars she'd liked in high school. Sure, her parents got up at five o'clock in the morning, and would no doubt continue to "help" her with the full focus of their relatively open schedule as retirees. And sure, she'd be deluged with offers of assistance from her well-meaning and equally organized family members....

She quickly grabbed the list again. "The honeymoon," she said.

Her father blinked at her. "Sorry?"

"I'm supposed to be going on a cruise," she said, adding one more item to the list. "The boat will be expecting us. I need to call them and cancel. I should do that right now."

Right now I should do anything but think about what I'm going to be faced with in the next week.

"All right, dear," her father said. "You do that and then we'll go."

Chloe headed to a quiet hallway to make the call on her cell phone. She appreciated the distraction. She knew she couldn't avoid her troubles forever. Then again, she also knew that, one way or another, everything would be all right.

She just wasn't sure how.

"I AM ALREADY HAVING a bad day, Kenneth," Captain Jack McCullough said ominously into his cell phone. "Please tell me you're running late or something simple like that."

There was a pause on the line, and Jack knew immediately that Kenneth was not running late and the "or something" was going to be bad. Call it sailor's instincts, call it gut reaction, even call it Murphy's law, but this was apparently one of those days when absolutely nothing was as it should be.

"I'm not working this cruise, Jack." Kenneth swallowed audibly. "In fact, I'm not going to be able to work for you anymore."

"It's not the raise thing again, is it?" Jack said. "Because you know I've been in a bind, financially speaking. I swear I'm doing the best I can. And if these private honeymoon cruises take off the way I think they will, I might be able to swing something in a few months. But I've promised gourmet food on this yacht, which will be damned awkward if you don't show up, Kenneth!"

"I know," Kenneth replied, and his voice did sound miserable. "But my hands are tied."

"You're leaving? Just like that? With no notice?" Jack clamped down on the spurt of anger that shot through his system. "Well, what is it? Something medical? You in some kind of trouble?"

"You could say that," Kenneth said. "I've found out my girlfriend's pregnant."

"Oh," Jack said, temporarily deflated. That had to be a bit of a shock—Jack didn't even realize Kenneth *had* a girlfriend, much less one he was serious enough about to have a kid with. "Well, that doesn't mean you should quit your job. If anything, I'd think you'd want to continue as chef in the meantime—"

"I have a new job lined up," Kenneth said. "In a restaurant."

Now Jack was more surprised than angry. *"On land?"*

"Listen, I'm not thrilled with it, either," Kenneth answered defensively. "But I'm crazy about her, and she needs me. So I'm staying."

There was a note of staunch loyalty in his voice, and Jack sighed. "Damn it. Well…congratulations," he said belatedly. "But you are leaving me in a jam. I mean, she's not in labor this second or anything." He felt petty bringing it up, so he stopped himself from elaborating further. "We'll make do. Besides, honeymooning couples won't care about the food anyway, right? That's not what they're here for." At least he hoped that was true. The last thing he could afford at the moment was an unhappy customer demanding a refund.

"Um, there is one more thing."

Now Jack's back prickled with prescience. "Oh, man, what else?"

"I hope they don't want massages, either," Kenneth said, and if possible, his voice sounded even more apologetic.

It took Jack a second to figure out what Kenneth was saying. The honeymoon cruises did offer massages, which was why he'd hired a woman who was willing to be maid and masseuse. Hmm...

"Helen?" Jack said, flabbergasted. "Your girlfriend is my masseuse?"

"The morning sickness is killing her, man," Kenneth said. "There's no way she can work on a boat now when just looking at a glass of milk makes her want to hurl."

"You have *got* to be kidding me!" Jack shouted. "My gourmet chef and my personal masseuse are both ditching me right before a weeklong, four-star, private cruise. At this rate, we're going to be demoted to one star. We're going to be the floating equivalent of the No-Tell Motel!"

"We didn't mean for this to happen," Kenneth protested.

Jack bit back a swear. "I know, I know," he said. "And I am happy for you guys, as long as you're happy. I...right now is not a good time for us to have customers refusing final payments or demanding deposit refunds, if you know what I mean."

"I'll put feelers out," Kenneth said, contrite. "I'll find you another chef by the time you get back from this cruise. And I'll have Helen look for another masseuse."

"That'd be a help," Jack said, although considering the meagerness of his current financial state, he knew that finding people of quality willing to work for peanuts was going to be tough. He was lucky because Kenneth and Helen both loved the ocean—or at least they had before all of this.

There was a buzzing on his phone, and he saw another call was waiting. "I've got to go," he said to Kenneth and switched over in the middle of yet another Kenneth apology. "McCullough Charters. How can I help you?"

"My name is Chloe Winton," a woman's voice said in a tone that would've been businesslike if it weren't for a note of something else, possibly something sad. "My…fiancé and I were scheduled to take a cruise this week."

There it was again—the tickle down his spine that signaled rough waters ahead. "Yes, Mrs. Winton," he said, putting on his very best customer-service voice. "We're looking forward to seeing you. We're scheduled to depart at six-thirty, but since it's a private charter we can leave whenever you prefer. Is there anything special you wanted?"

"I'm afraid I'm going to have to cancel."

Cancel. Crap. That would mean repaying the deposit, and no more money forthcoming. And he had bills that were already written against the deposit check. "May I ask why?" he said, racking his brain for a way to salvage the deal. "Perhaps there's something I can help you with?"

There was a pause on the line. "It's no longer a honeymoon, for one thing. The groom sent a note to me at the chapel saying he couldn't go through with it."

"Ouch," Jack said before he could stop himself.

"Yeah, something like that," she responded, and the business tone dropped for a minute, leaving her sounding rueful and very vulnerable. "So I don't think it's anything you can help with. I've got plenty of relatives giving me plenty of advice," she added with a laugh that sounded less than happy.

He could picture it now—this poor lady, stranded at the

altar, surrounded by a bunch of family busybodies. And what kind of guy would leave a woman on her wedding day? If he knew it wasn't going to work, then he knew it months ago. Why put her through the wringer in front of all her friends and family?

"Well, he's the one who paid the deposit," Jack mused, remembering vaguely. "He's paying for the whole thing—I've got a postdated check."

"That's right," she said, sounding puzzled. "I was paying for some wedding stuff in exchange."

"It's not your fault the wedding was canceled. You showed up," Jack said with certainty. "So why should you cancel the cruise? Why miss out on it because he's being a butt head?"

That got a startled laugh out of her. "I don't know that I'm in a honeymoon state of mind," she said.

"Ever been out on the open ocean at night?" Jack said, getting into the swing of it—and not only to save the sale. "It's the most peaceful thing in the world. The lapping of the waves, the breeze, the way everything looks and smells. It's pure freedom."

"Sounds like heaven," she admitted.

"And," he said, "it's miles from everyone who has any sort of advice to give. You don't even get cell phone reception most of the time."

"Really?" Now he heard it—the hint of a smile in her voice.

"I'll admit it. I don't want to lose the fare," Jack said candidly. "But I also think you've had a rotten day and you're probably going to be in for it for a while. If you stay in town, odds are good you'll bump into a bunch of well-meaning people who have no idea what to say to you, and the awkwardness is going to make it worse."

"Not to mention at some point I'll run into the butt head," she muttered, and now Jack laughed.

"Exactly. Who needs that? Come on the cruise. Leave all your stress on shore. Take the week off."

A long pause, and Jack wondered absently if he was being cruel—if he were making things worse. He'd never met this woman, but she sounded like a nice person, and he probably would've told her to do the same thing even if she were booked with a different charter ship. Still, he knew that his take on what should be done and most land-bound people's view on how to act tended to be radically different.

"Wouldn't I just be running away?" she finally asked. Her voice sounded sad but hopeful. As if she were begging him to come up with a reason for her to go along with his plan.

"Generals do it all the time. So do top executives. You're not running away. You know what you're doing? Repeat after me—you're *regrouping*."

"I'm regrouping," she echoed dutifully.

"You've been through a lot. You deserve a week away from all the pressure. To heal and get your head on right," Jack said, and in that moment he meant it sincerely. Even if he didn't see a dime, this kid needed all the help she could get.

"I'm regrouping," she said again and let out a surprised giggle. "Nobody's going to understand."

"So who needs to?" Jack scoffed. "Honey, you have only one person to answer to and that's you."

"That is true," she said. "Could you give me directions to your boat?"

"Sure," he replied enthusiastically and proceeded to tell her how to get to the Corona Bay docks, giving her the code and location for his boat's slip. "Drive careful now and let me know if you have any problems."

"Thanks," she said, then laughed. "I'm sorry...who am I talking to?"

Jack smacked his forehead with his palm. "Duh, sorry. I'm the owner and operator of the yacht you'll be sailing on tonight. I'm Jack McCullough."

"Captain Jack?" she asked with the suggestion of another giggle.

"Okay, in light of all you've been through, I'll let you get away with that one," he said with mock severity, "but no Captain Jack jokes, jibes or references. You have no idea how much flak I've caught since *Pirates of the Caribbean*."

"Then what should I call you?"

"Just Jack," he said. "Wait. No *Will & Grace* jokes, either. You can call me whatever you want as long as it's not 'Captain Jack' or 'Just Jack.' Call me 'hey, you' if you feel like it."

"Well, thanks, 'hey, you,'" she said softly. "I guess I'll see you this evening."

"You got it," he replied, and they both hung up.

Jack sighed, putting his cell phone away. He glanced around the deck of his yacht—the *Rascal*. It wasn't new and it wasn't superfancy, but the wood gleamed, and it was sturdier and faster than it looked. It was his dream—his life. He'd sacrificed a lot to get it and was sacrificing a lot more to keep it.

Which made him wonder, obliquely, about what he'd just done.

Did I, moments ago, convince a heartbroken, jilted bride to come out on a cruise with me?

Yes. Yes, he had.

Did I do it for the money?

He paced a little at that one. He *did* want to help her. But yeah, he'd done it for the money. Now the reality of what he'd pulled off hit him.

Besides making you sort of slimy, it also means you're going to have a weepy, emotional basket case on your hands for the next six days and seven nights.

Jack closed his eyes. It had seemed like the perfect solution at the time. She was in trouble, he was offering her a breather. It would also get him some cash—and he had no problem taking money from the schmuck who had stood her up in the first place. And she'd sounded sweet, if sad. He doubted she'd become completely unglued once they set out.

But if she did, what then? What if she decided she hated all men and made his life a living hell for the next week? Or what if she cried all over him?

Too late now, he counseled himself, still feeling troubled.

Then it hit him. She was going to be leaving the comfort, albeit nosy comfort, of her family. Instead choosing to enjoy the four-star luxuries of her private cruise. Except for the fact that they'd lost their private chef, their masseuse and their maid.

So what exactly was she going to be enjoying, besides enduring her troubles alone?

"Oh, hell," Jack muttered to himself. *Rough waters ahead,* his gut had told him. He would *have* to find out a way to navigate them because he'd gone too far to turn back now.

CHLOE STOOD IN FRONT of the yacht, her rolling bag handle gripped tightly in her right hand. It had been awkward walking over the planked decking in the low heels she'd worn with her soft-pink traveling suit. If she'd been with Gerald, he'd have pulled the luggage for her.

Don't think about Gerald.

She closed her eyes for a second. Not thinking about Gerald was impossible, especially in light of the fact that she was now on the brink of what should've been their honey-moon. And the fact that she was doing this alone seemed impossible, as well as everything else in the foreseeable future.

"Hi, there," she heard a voice say and she opened her eyes.

For a second, the man in front of her almost didn't register. She'd been with Gerald for four and a half years, and while she appreciated other men, she had never been hit by the looks of one the way she was right now. For the past six months, unless the man was either a caterer, floral arranger or hotel manager, she had not even noted his existence.

That was all changing.

The man had dark, walnut-colored hair, worn long enough to be unkempt, curling at the collar of his T-shirt. His eyes were a beautiful golden-green, lit almost ethereally by the setting sun. He had a broad, easy smile, and his whole demeanor was friendly and laid-back.

"Hey, you," she ventured, thinking of the captain's joke: *Call me "hey, you" if you want to.*

He chuckled, and she could see the muscles bunch and release beneath his shirt. To her surprise, her mouth went temporarily dry.

You haven't had sex in six months, she excused herself. *And you've just been through an emotional trauma. This is just chemical, a way to self-medicate and feel better.*

Except she didn't feel better—although she was feeling and that was a nice change from numbness.

"You must be Chloe Winton," he said. "Can I take your bag?"

"Thanks," she said, relinquishing it to him. He gestured to her to walk up the thin walkway that connected the yacht to the dock, and she realized if she took the step, then she was deliberately leaving behind all that had happened today. She should be yelling at Gerald right now, she told herself. She should be calling a lawyer about the house, as one of her uncles had recommended. She should…

She shook her head, then lifted her chin. "I'm regrouping," she said softly, so softly she doubted Jack heard her. She'd been murmuring the two words like a mantra since she'd gotten off the phone with him. With that, she took a step on the unsteady plank. And promptly bobbled.

"Whoa," he said, and he was behind her, one hand on her waist, steadying her. "You all right?"

"Fine," she said, taking a few more steps gingerly. His hand, she noticed, did not move from her waist until she was on the deck itself.

"Not used to boats, huh?" he said, stepping easily off the walkway and onto the deck as if it were rock-solid concrete instead of the shifting surface of a water-bound vessel.

"No," she admitted. "But I've always loved the ocean, which is why Gerald…"

Just the name caused a pang.

"Now, now, enough of that," he said, and he rubbed her shoulder absently, which made her feel both embarrassed and thankful. "Why don't I show you to your cabin?"

"That'd be great," she said. She followed him cautiously, still getting used to that swaying motion beneath her feet. As soon as she made it to her cabin, she was taking these dumb shoes off. She sent Jack an apologetic smile when he realized she was lagging, and he slowed down to accommodate her.

The ship itself was pretty, she noticed as she walked. She was no expert, but the wood looked like something expensive—teak maybe. They used teak on boats, didn't they? And the lines were clean. There were all kinds of nautical doodads that seemed well-worn but not unsafe. She went down the steps carefully, going along the claustrophobic hallway.

"The galley's over here," he said, pointing to a door, "and the crew's cabins are here…and here we are, your cabin."

He opened a door and she peeked in.

It was smaller than she'd expected. And it was mostly bed.

"There's the bathroom." He pointed to a closet-sized room. "There's a shower and everything else you'll need. It's pretty straightforward."

She nodded absently, although she couldn't take her eyes off the bed. It was huge, considering the room. Two people would probably have to be close to be comfortable. Which was probably the whole idea, she clued in, with a growing sense of sadness. There was what looked like a down comforter and some luxurious sheets. Satin maybe? Whatever they were, it was cream-colored and decadent. She'd likely be swimming in the things, slipping and sliding as the ship continued to sway.

"There are drawers here," he said, opening some hidden compartments. "And you can put your bag under your bed, here."

"Right," she murmured, barely paying attention. The lights were on a dimmer switch—they were low and romantic. There was a CD player, no doubt anchored to the headboard. She saw a collection of CDs in a built-in cabinet, all slow love songs or soulful ballads. She bit her lip, fighting tears.

"And if you'll look carefully," Jack continued, "right here, by the portal, is a button that operates our time machine. You don't want to hit that accidentally."

"You got it," she said, then she shook her head, startled. "I'm sorry. What was that?"

"Just seeing if you were still with me," he said, leaning toward her to look into her eyes. "You doin' okay?"

"Yes. Sure. I mean…" She made a vague gesture with her hands. In the context of what she'd been through the last few hours, she was okay. But for any other day of her life?

"No," she admitted. "I'm not doing okay."

He sighed heavily, the big inhalation making his chest seem huge in the close quarters. She found herself sitting on the bed, which put her almost eye level with his belt buckle. She craned her head upward to stare at him. To her surprise, he sat down next to her. At least it wasn't a water bed, she thought inanely, although the idea of a water bed on a boat struck her as redundantly funny. She smiled weakly at her own joke.

"I know I kind of talked you into this," he said slowly. "You don't have to come out on the boat if you don't want to. I mean, if you've got family you'd rather be with or something…I know this has got to be a rough patch." He winced. "Let me rephrase that. *Rough patch* doesn't even cover it. Hell, I don't even know how to say it."

"Neither do I," she said, realizing that fact. "I feel more numb than anything, though."

"Now I'm really feeling scummy," he muttered, surprising her. "Are you going to be okay here? I mean…well, you know what I mean."

"Am I going to be okay all alone in the honeymoon suite of a romantic cruise, dealing with the emotional aftershocks of being left at the altar by my supposed future husband?" she summarized, feeling each word like a lash on her skin.

"Well," he said, clearing his throat, "that's one way of putting it."

She thought about it. Thought about what she'd left behind. Her parents had argued vociferously against her going on the cruise, using the exact same logic. But the idea of being back home, surrounded by her well-intentioned family and friends, was far more claustrophobic than any small ship cabin could be. And while the ship was romantic, it wasn't as though Gerald and she had been feeling intimate lately, anyway. If they'd actually gotten married, all this ambience would've been wasted on them after they arrived, since they'd both probably just tumble in and simply sleep. She hadn't even had the full wedding and she felt like crashing into bed and staying unconscious for the full seven days. And with the size of the bed, she would probably be more comfortable alone, if she was honest about it.

As her father said, *When life gives you lemons...*

"I'm going to be okay," she announced clearly. "It'll take time, but...yeah, I'll be okay."

Then she turned her full attention to Jack. He looked concerned. Actually, he looked a little unnerved. Men didn't normally deal well with emotional women, she told herself, torn between amusement and irritation. Gerald had always found some excuse to vanish when she was in "one of her fits" as he called them, her rare outbursts of temper or upset. She'd learned not to expose him to them. When she felt like crying, she called her friends; when she felt like hollering, she drove somewhere isolated and screamed in her car with the windows rolled up. Afterward, she could calmly deal with whatever was bothering her. Generally by that point, Gerald didn't even have to become involved.

She frowned. That might have been part of the problem, too.

"One last thing," he said, sounding hesitant. "There's a minifridge over here. It's got, er, champagne and chocolate-covered strawberries. It's also got some beer, if you want it."

"Thanks," she said. "And don't feel guilty, okay? You didn't talk me into anything."

"Sure I didn't," he said, and his recriminating tone spoke volumes.

"No, really," she argued. "I decided to take some time to develop an action plan. I really am regrouping."

The look he sent her was almost one of pity, but he let it go. "All right. Since I've got you settled in, I'll cast off and we'll be on our way. We'll be cruising up toward Catalina, but we won't go all the way there tonight. If you need anything, just hit the intercom button here." He gestured to a panel by the door. "Whatever you want, ask, and I'll jump to."

"That sounds nice," she said. "Thanks very much…Jack."

He smiled, revealing two dimples that probably broke hearts in every port he'd ever sailed into. Too bad her heart had already been broken.

"No problem…Chloe."

She smiled back when he shut the door. The smile didn't last long, though, as she leaned back against the bed.

All right. You're here. Now what?

She could feel the motions of the boat—the whirr of the engine as it roared to life, the slow, steady sway as it moved out of its slip and carefully navigated its way to the Coronado Channel. She could see out the small window. The sun had almost entirely set, the sky bleeding from crimson to purple to navy, left to right. It was beautiful, so beautiful it made her heart hurt.

In the twilight, later, she decided to go about settling in. She'd be here for a week, after all. She unpacked her luggage neatly into the small drawers and stowed the bag under the bed. Then she grabbed a book—the romance that she'd purchased to while away the hours in the sun while Gerald fished or whatever. She realized within ten pages that she didn't want to read someone else's love story. A murder mystery might've been more the thing.

Restless, she wanted to pace, but there wasn't enough room, and she wasn't sure enough of her "sea legs" to brave the deck. She didn't feel queasy, which was good. But she did feel tense. No, *tense* was too mild a word. She felt *compressed,* as if she'd been vacuum-sealed into a body two sizes too small for her.

By the CDs, there was a brochure, just like the one Gerald had shown her when he'd described the cruise to her. She opened it, reading the copy:

"Welcome to the *Rascal.* Our honeymoon cruises are created with the happy couple in mind."

Not this time, she thought bitterly.

"While on board, feel free to make our ship your home. Wander the decks, ask questions of the crew. Our private chef prepares your meals. Our onboard masseuse is happy to provide for your relaxation. And our maid service will ensure that you have nothing to do during this time except focus on your enjoyment and each other."

She frowned. It wasn't very well written. She'd have done it differently, she thought. And for something advertised as four-star, the brochure itself could use jazzing up.

She bit her lip. She was morphing into "business mode" as Gerald called it, although he usually said it admiringly. He loved her practicality. At least, he'd said he did.

The tension increased a little. If this kept up, she'd be a foot shorter by morning and probably as dense as lead. She needed to relax.

Tentatively she hit the intercom button.

"Captain here, Chloe. What can I do for you?"

She swallowed hard. "I know it's a bit late—"

"Nonsense. It's only—what—almost eight o'clock. Are you, er, hungry?"

"No, no," she said. After eating out of guilt at the reception, she doubted she'd be hungry again for hours, possibly days. "But I am really stressed."

"A walk on deck maybe?" he suggested. "Nothing like moonlight and the sea to soothe a troubled mind."

"It's my body that's causing more of the problem right now," she said, rubbing at her neck, which felt as if it were trapped in a vise. "I was wondering, do you think you could send the masseuse to my room?"

There was a pause. "Er…"

"I don't mean to be a bother," she said, "but in the brochure…"

"No, no, of course," he said. "I'll, er, have the masseuse there in a minute."

"Thank you," she said and released the intercom button.

There, she thought. She was on an adventure. She was coping. She was *regrouping*.

2

IT FIGURED. THE first thing she'd ask for would be one of the four-star amenities that he could no longer provide. Jack grimaced as he rummaged through what was once Helen's cabin, the tiny berth that was next to where Kenneth used to stay—and no doubt part of the reason they got together, Jack realized. The yacht really wasn't that big. He found some almond massage oil and two clean towels.

He'd promised Chloe a good time, a relaxing time. And he was going to do exactly that—even if it wasn't quite what she was expecting.

He took a deep breath, armed with his massage accoutrements, and knocked on her cabin door.

"Come on in," she called.

He opened the door and then stood in the doorway, stunned.

She was lying on the bed facedown, wearing nothing but a sheet.

"Uh," he said slowly, feeling most of the blood drain out of every part of his body—except one part, and frankly that part did *not* need to be part of the massage-giving experience. "I guess you've had massages before," he finally added inanely.

Her eyes went wide and her face went pale. She started to sit up, revealing a lot of her breasts before she realized that she was naked and propping herself up that way wasn't helping matters. She collapsed back onto the bed with a squeak.

"I…I didn't realize that you were the masseur," she said in a low voice. "I thought—I guess it's dumb, but I thought it would be a woman. Or somebody else. You know."

Jack felt that same sensation of guilt burn through his chest. "A common misunderstanding," he said, hating his glibness. "If it's too distracting, I can go away."

She bit her lip—a cute gesture, he thought, which made her look innocent and young and at complete odds with her provocative nudity beneath the sheet, a detail that simply would not be ignored. "I…hmm."

She wanted to de-stress, and this had seemed like a good idea, he thought. Now she was probably even *more* tense.

Way to go, Jack.

"If you don't mind my staying," he said slowly, "I promise to be completely professional. And you have had sort of a trying day. If anybody could use a bit of relaxation, it'd be you."

Then it struck him. *Why are you convincing her to go through with it? What's wrong with you?*

She chuckled at the understatement. "True enough," she said. "I, er, guess it'd be okay."

He breathed out a silent sigh of relief, then realized: he was committed. He'd given plenty of back rubs in his day, but they'd hardly been anything someone would call "therapeutic." They were generally designed to gain entry to a woman's bedroom and, somewhat later, into her bed. They were seduction tools, not tools for relaxation.

His anatomy started to shift into that mode until he sternly counseled himself to knock it off. This was business, not pleasure.

He cleared his throat. "Do you like champagne?"

"Sorry?" she asked, looking startled.

"Champagne," he repeated, getting the bottle from the minifridge. She hadn't touched any of the alcohol, he noticed. "We offer it to the customers to celebrate, sure, but also to help them relax and unwind." And maybe if she had a little alcohol, she wouldn't be quite so critical of the amateur quality of her massage.

"I don't drink much," she said.

He raised an eyebrow at her. "I think today is a good day for an exception," he said wryly.

She chuckled at that, too, and he noticed her shoulders move almost imperceptibly lower—a good sign.

He popped the cork and grabbed one of the champagne flutes from the fridge, as well, pouring the light amber liquid in and stopping before the bubbles frothed over the top. "Here you go," he said, handing the glass to her.

She propped herself up on her side, tucking the blanket around her torso—but not before he'd gotten another glimpse of her breasts. She was definitely a feast for the eyes, he had to admit. Maybe five foot five, with long cinnamon-brown hair that tumbled in waves past her shoulders and creamy white skin that suggested maybe Irish or British heritage. The faintest natural hint of roses in her cheeks supported that. She was on the thin side, making the curves of her breasts and hips that much more accented.

She sipped at the champagne carefully, then she obviously understood he was waiting for her. He watched as she finished the glass and handed the empty flute back to him. "Thanks," she said.

"There. It'll take a few minutes for that to kick in," he said, "and I don't want to do anything too strenuous and ruin it. Nothing too deep-tissue," he clarified. He remembered when he'd hired Helen and she'd offered to give him a massage as a sort of interview. She'd done a "deep tissue" massage, and he'd thought he was on a medieval torture rack. The fact that he'd felt better the next day didn't help the fact that the massage itself had been way too rough.

Chloe sank down into the bed, shrugging slightly and groaning. "Whatever you think is best," she demurred, turning her face away from him.

He looked at the massage oil, opting to only use a small amount or else the satin sheets would be ruined. Maybe he shouldn't use *any*.

Did he really want to take the sheets away?

"Is everything okay?" Chloe asked after he'd rubbed his hands together for several minutes, trying to decide how to start.

"Sure. Yeah. Just...relax," he said hastily and reached for her shoulders, which weren't covered by the sheet. Her hair got in the way, but before he could say anything, she was reaching up with those long arms of hers, pushing the tumbled mass up, sighing a little in the process.

He had to admit, seeing her all pale blanched-almond skin and cinnamon-brown hair against butter-cream-colored sheets was a beautiful picture. One might even say delicious.

If one were, you know, somebody else.

What is wrong with her fiancé that he'd walk away from this?

He went to work on her shoulders. They felt like steel bands, corded with tension. She winced and groaned as he tried to gently work out the knots, sitting on the bed next to her.

"Holy crow," he said finally. "How long have you been like this?"

"Almost a year," she said, her voice muffled against the bed. "I've been planning the wedding for that long."

"You should get massages more often," he said, easing a knot out, feeling gratified at her low moan of appreciation.

"I kept meaning to," she admitted. "But when I was working, as well as planning the wedding, there was no time. And when I quit working, there was no money, you know?"

No money. Yeah, he knew that one well. Otherwise he wouldn't be playing Jack the Masseur for his chartered client.

"Why'd you quit your job?" he asked instead, inching the sheet down to her lower back. She had a great back, he thought. The slopes of her sides tapered into her hips, and she had a sprinkling of freckles, looking like a constellation over her shoulders. He felt his heart rate accelerate for no good reason and he focused on her words.

"Gerald—he's my fiancé—thought it'd be better if I stopped working."

"Wow," Jack said, smoothing his hands from her shoulder blades down to her lower back in long strokes. She was making happy noises now, and he kept doing what he was doing, using gentle pressure from his fingertips. "Real forward-thinking guy."

He immediately felt her tense beneath his fingers and cursed himself. If he were trying to make her relax, maybe reminding her of the guy who'd run out on her wasn't the best way to go about it.

"I worked for him, and people weren't thrilled with us dating. Getting married did not help matters," she explained, and Jack felt her muscles bunching up defensively.

"Okay, okay. Don't think about it," he insisted, rubbing at the tension until she was closer to the calm state he'd had before he brought up Gerald the Wonder Twit. "I just figured you'd be someone who liked her job."

"I did. Sort of," she said. "Well, maybe not the job specifically. But I like being busy and helpful." She laughed ruefully. "And, you know, getting paid."

"I hear you on that one," he said, giving her shoulders a sympathetic squeeze. He'd done most of her back and her arms. For a second, his glance shot to her perfect teardrop-shaped backside.

Well, she's probably tense everywhere…

He chickened out—or rather, he came to his senses before he could inch the sheet lower. Instead he simply placed it over her torso and moved another section of sheet so he could reach her legs. He massaged each leg individually, enjoying her groans of gratitude. She had great legs, long and shapely. She even had pretty feet.

Where exactly are you going with these observations?

He blinked, his hands pausing on her right calf. She was a customer and a recently abandoned bride. In other words, she was trouble with a capital *T,* and he needed to get a grip and quick.

"How are you feeling?" he asked.

"Mmm," she murmured in response. "Not bad at all."

He worked on her feet, eliciting sounds from her that were almost sexual in their pure pleasure. He had to force himself to concentrate and ignore the semierection that was threatening to go full-mast on him. "Liking your first experience on the ocean?" he said quickly, hoping for some distraction.

"It's much more soothing than I imagined," she said, her voice a dreamy whisper. "I wish I'd tried it before all of this."

He smoothed his thumbs over the arches of the bottoms of her feet, and she sighed ecstatically. Her toenails were painted a brilliant plum color, he noticed, smiling. "Well, you're trying it now," he replied, keeping his voice soft and soothing, as well. He let go of her feet. "And if there's anything I can do to make your stay more relaxing, please let me know."

"I certainly will. This is wonderful," she said.

He got up to make his way to the door. Only to be surprised when she turned over, the sheet sliding seductively.

He blinked. She was used to massages, apparently, and she was expecting him to do a full and complete job.

By this point, his body throbbed almost painfully. It wasn't as if he was hard up for female companionship. He knew plenty of women who didn't mind having a good, no-strings-attached time with him when he was in port in San Diego. But he'd been so busy keeping his boat afloat, literally and figuratively, that he simply hadn't had time.

And there was something about this woman.

She had her eyes closed and was breathing deeply, evenly. She was waiting.

He rubbed at her neck, beneath her jawline, very lightly. She smiled in encouragement. He rubbed her earlobes. He had to move closer to get the right position and he could smell her perfume, something vanilla, blending with the hazelnut of the small amount of massage oil he'd used in the beginning.

She smells good enough to eat.

The thought, impromptu as it was, shot forth a vision of her naked, lying there with her back arched as he shifted the sheet away from her, pressing kisses down that creamy stomach of hers, gradually moving lower...

He quickly took his hands away as if burned.

"Everything all right?" she said almost in a slur.

"Fine. Fine." He quickly worked on her arms, focusing especially on her hands. He figured he couldn't get into that much trouble with hands. He ignored her chest completely and then did another cursory rubdown of her legs.

When he'd finished, she was sleeping. Her breath was coming out in little rhythmic whooshes. With her hair spread out like a fan on the bed she looked beautiful and, best of all, relaxed.

He, on the other hand, fled the cabin with towels and oil in hand. He was sweating, he realized, even though it was not that hot a night.

He'd done the job—he'd stepped in for his missing masseuse and he'd satisfied the customer, completely relaxing her.

Now he needed a beer, he thought frantically, before his body started wondering what it would take to get *him* relaxed and satisfied.

CHLOE WOKE UP completely disoriented. She was in darkness, and the room didn't feel familiar at all. For one thing, it was swaying, and while she could taste the last vestiges of alcohol in her mouth, she doubted the rocking sensation was due to drunkenness. For another thing, she was naked, and the sheets felt cool and slippery around her skin. It was an unusual feeling, albeit a pleasant one. Also, she didn't have a pillow beneath her head, which should have been uncomfortable except for the fact that she felt strangely relaxed.

She'd had a massage, she suddenly remembered.

Right after having some champagne.

Both of which, incidentally, were given to her by Jack.

She sat bolt upright, feeling her heart trip-hammer in her chest. Remembering Jack and the reason she was on his ship to begin with quickly brought all her other memories crashing down. The wedding that didn't happen. The fiancé that never showed up. The mountain of details she was going to have to deal with…

The fact that she'd gotten on the ship in the first place to have the time, space and quiet to figure out what those details were and what her next step was.

She took a deep, cleansing breath. Now that she'd gotten her bearings, she felt more resolute and somewhat less despairing than she had hours ago at her ruined noncelebratory reception. Her stomach growled, to her surprise. There wasn't a clock, so she turned on a light and glanced at her watch. Eleven o'clock. She was starving.

She got up, rummaging in the drawers for some clothes. Unfortunately she'd packed for a honeymoon. Sexy lingerie wasn't going to help here, and she felt silly pulling on her "cruise wear" simply to wander toward the galley and see if she could grab a snack. She pulled open one of the drawers she hadn't packed, out of curiosity, and found two robes—obviously for the honeymooning couple. She pulled on some underwear and one of the robes and slipped on her canvas tennis shoes.

Cautiously she opened her door. It was quiet and dark in the hallway. She knew there was a crew of some sort, but she had no idea what their hours were. She didn't even know if Jack was sleeping or what and she felt stupid waking him up with the intercom to ask him if it was okay if she raided the kitchen. At the same time, she doubted that she could just wander into a hotel's kitchen at eleven o'clock at night—and the boat was basically a floating hotel, right?

She stood in the doll-size hallway, torn by uncertainty, when she heard low voices coming from behind a closed door. Jack had mentioned that was the galley, so she knocked softly. When they didn't seem to hear her, she repeated the knock a little louder.

The voices stopped abruptly and the door swung toward her, revealing Jack's face. "Oh, you're up," he said, sounding surprised. "Is everything okay? Do you need anything?"

"I'm fine," she said immediately and then was promptly embarrassed by the loud yowl her stomach emitted.

"You're hungry," he replied, grinning. "Come on in."

He opened the door wider, and she walked past him into a small room. There were two men already at the table, and they automatically stood up when they saw her. She smiled at the gentlemanly action, feeling hideously underdressed.

"This is my crew. Jose works the night shift—keeps us running if we're not anchored, checks on the yacht." He gestured to a shorter, Hispanic-looking man, who smiled and bowed slightly. "Ace, over in the corner, is our onboard mechanic and my day shift crew." The man in the corner, a blonde, surfer-looking guy, smiled broadly and winked at her. "Guys, this is Chloe Winton, our charter passenger."

"Pleased to meet you," Chloe said, nodding to both of them and smiling in return.

"So…er, what can I get you?" Jack said, turning to the fridge.

Chloe shrugged. "Anything would be fine," she said. "I don't want you to have to wake the chef up or anything. Although I don't suppose that there's anything left from the dinner menu? I'm more hungry than I thought."

"The dinner menu?" Jack said blankly, and to Chloe's surprise, Jose burst out in a fit of coughing.

"We'll leave you guys to it," Ace said, pounding Jose on the back before ushering the man out. "Good night, Chloe."

"Good night," she replied, mystified as they quickly disappeared, broad grins on their faces.

"Well, no. Nothing was prepared for dinner," Jack said, his gold-green eyes looking troubled. After a second, he sighed, stuffing his hands in his pockets. "Chloe, I have to come clean with you on something."

She blinked at him. She'd already had enough nasty, surprising revelations for one day. She almost cringed, waiting for it.

He opened the fridge. It was filled to overflowing with lots of savory-looking ingredients, although nothing prepared except pastries. "My chef, Kenneth, is an absolute dynamo. He's four-star all the way. If I showed you the menu he had planned for this week, you'd weep."

She waited for the punch line.

"And, much to my surprise and horror, he quit today. Just before you called me, actually."

She stared at him, seeing the embarrassment practically scrawled across his handsome face. And then she burst out laughing.

He grinned, rubbing a hand over the back of his neck. "Glad you can see the humor in it," he said, his voice rueful.

"I'm sorry," she said. "It's just…wow. Guess there was something in the water today, huh?"

He looked puzzled for a moment, then slowly grinned. "You mean, to cause people to bail without warning? I hadn't really thought of it that way."

"Of course," she said, sobering, "you can always get a replacement pretty easily." She felt her chin drop a little and she stared reflectively at the floor.

To her surprise, Jack nudged her chin back up with one finger. "Trust me, sweetie, so can you."

She felt her skin heat under the intensity of his gaze. She looked away first, making a big show of being interested in the contents of the refrigerator. "You said he left a menu?" she asked and marveled at the breathless quality in her voice.

"Sure," Jack said, rummaging around in one of the drawers. "Here we go."

She glanced over the paper. Seared ahi tuna on a bed of field greens with a lime-cilantro dressing was supposed to have been the evening's meal, she saw, served with chilled gazpacho soup. She quickly scanned the rest of the proposed menu. Raspberry-chipotle marinated ribs. Cannelloni. The menu was eclectic and mouthwatering, and in her current hungry state, it was like waving a red flag in front of a bull.

"I can cook for you," Jack said. "Simpler stuff than what's on that menu."

She thought the offer was sweet and smiled at him gratefully. "There's no need. I would cook, unless you'd rather I not use your kitchen?"

"Galley," Jack corrected, the dimple back in full effect. She wondered if he realized how lethal those suckers were—and then realized abruptly that of course he knew. "And I'll help you with the stove, since you need to pump the gas first. But otherwise, if you feel like cooking, by all means. Feel free, make yourself at home."

"I was a short-order cook in college for a while at an Italian café and restaurant," she said, smiling at the memory of it. "Hard work but a lot of fun. I haven't thought of that in years."

She then instructed him to turn on the gas range and she gathered the makings of the salad and ahi tuna. She quickly seared the tuna, which smelled very fresh and heavenly, and then quickly pulled together the salad.

Suddenly she heard another stomach-growling noise, only this time it wasn't coming from her. She glanced at Jack in surprise.

"Sorry," he said sheepishly. "But that looks a hell of a lot better than my dinner."

"What did you have?"

"Bowl of cereal," he muttered, causing her to laugh again. "I got spoiled having Kenneth around. I'll admit it. The guy wasn't much of a sailor, but he loved being out on the ocean…and he could make meat loaf taste like a slice of heaven."

"You know, he planned the meals for at least two people," she said. "Why don't you join me?"

Jack shifted his weight from one foot to another, crossing his arms. "I'm supposed to be your host," he said. "I feel like a twerp, not only not having a gourmet chef for you but having you wait on me."

"I love cooking," she said as she quickly threw another tuna steak in the pan and seared it. "No problem whatsoever." She then shot a quick, wicked grin over her shoulder. "Besides, I owe you for the massage—you knocked me out before I could tip you."

She spread the salad greens, fixings and dressing over two white plates that she'd found and put the tuna steaks on top. She put the plates on the table.

"Wine?" Jack asked, reaching for glasses.

"I think I've had enough for tonight," she said, and he poured two glasses of water instead. She sat down at the table, across from Jack. On a whim, she picked up her glass. "A toast. To getting away from it all."

"Hear, hear," he said, clinking her glass with his own. Absurdly, she felt better.

She dug into the meal as if she hadn't eaten in days. After all that food at the reception, she wasn't quite sure why she was so hungry. Maybe because she hadn't really tasted the food then—she'd eaten mechanically, under duress.

"I take it you're not having any seasickness issues," Jack said. "Thank you, by the way. This is delicious."

"No problem," she replied. "And no seasickness. I think I've pretty much got my sea legs, too."

"You're a natural," he said, smiling at her kindly. "You'll have a great time this week. I know it."

She smiled back, a little more unsteadily. "Well, it's not *exactly* a vacation," she corrected.

His smile slid. "Of course not. I didn't mean that."

"I know," she said, feeling badly for even bringing it up. "It's just…you were right—I need a place to get my head together. So I'm going to take the time and the peace and quiet and figure out what I need to do next."

"That seems like a good idea," he said, and she got the strange feeling he was just humoring her.

"What would you do?" she asked, curious.

"If what happened to you happened to me, you mean?" he said, after finishing off his tuna and greens. "Well, I'd be sailing away for a hell of a lot longer than a week, that's for sure."

She smirked, shaking her head. "Not if you couldn't afford it."

He shrugged. "I think I'd probably be drinking myself incoherent for the full week, then. Time enough to sort out details on the mainland. I'd probably feel hideously sorry for myself most of the time and I'd probably…I don't know…do something stupid. Yell at the waves, scare the dolphins, stuff like that."

"Would that help?" she asked.

"Of course not," he scoffed. "But that's me. I'm not really what anyone would call levelheaded."

She laughed, and his responding grin was like sunlight. "I am levelheaded," she admitted.

"Yeah. I got that." He winked at her. "But I like you anyway."

"I like you, too," she said, then felt the heat of embarrassment flush her cheeks. *You were going to be married today! What the hell are you doing? Are you flirting with this guy?*

"You're very kind," she explained.

He winced. "Kind. Well. That's…nice."

She obviously wasn't going to win this one, no matter what she said. She quickly got up and started clearing the table—and froze when his hand closed around her wrist.

"I'm kidding," he said, and his voice was soft and, she had to admit, kind. "You're easy to be kind to, and with everything you've gone through…I think you're amazing."

She held her breath, inexplicably.

"Amazing enough that I'm not going to have you cook for me *and* do the dishes," he said, taking the plates she was holding. "My mama raised me better than that."

He surprised yet another laugh out of her.

"Why don't you go on back to your cabin?" he asked. "I've got it from here, and I'm sure you're tired."

She nodded, heading for the hallway. She paused in the doorway. "Thanks, Jack," she said.

He shrugged. "My pleasure."

When he turned back to the sink, starting to scrub, she smiled to herself. A nice guy and a getaway. This was just what she needed. Everything was going to be fine.

She made it back to her own cabin before she started to cry.

AT NINE O'CLOCK THE next morning, Jack prepped the breakfast tray and slowly made his way to Chloe's cabin. At least the pastries were already taken care of, he thought, again mentally wishing Kenneth hadn't chosen this particular charter voyage to quit. Still, it was easy, and he didn't want Chloe to whip up breakfast, as well as dinner.

She was turning into a really nice lady and a great charter

passenger. If he could only get over the niggling guilt—and his growing infatuation—this could be a pleasant cruise.

He knocked on the door, hoping that it wasn't too early. They'd had dinner at eleven o'clock at night, but he got the feeling she was a morning person. "Chloe?"

He didn't hear anything for a long minute and was about to turn around and head for the galley when he finally heard her respond, "Yes?" in a muffled voice.

"It's Jack," he said. "I brought continental breakfast, if you're interested."

Another long pause, and he was starting to feel more and more badly about this idea, when finally she opened her door. "Thanks," she said, reaching for the tray.

He noticed immediately that her eyes were red and slightly puffy. She'd been crying. "Oh, man," he said. "Are you all right?"

He followed her, watching as she set the tray down on the bed. "No. I'm not all right," she said, and tears crawled down her pale cheeks.

Okay, Einstein...how did you want to handle this one? You're the one that got her here.

"Want to talk about it?"

"No. Yes." She shook her head, then rubbed at her temples with her fingers. "I don't know."

He took the carafe of coffee and poured her a cup, which she took, sending him a smile of gratitude. She sighed as she took a nice long sip.

"There you go. That'll clear your head a bit," he said, rubbing at the back of his neck absently with one hand. He had problems of his own that he had enough trouble with—and he'd certainly never been in the kind of trouble she was facing. He'd only lived with one woman, and that had been a consummate disaster. He certainly hadn't gotten anywhere near the old ball-and-chain act.

"Thanks," she said.

She was wearing the robe, and he realized she looked as she had the night before—only more rumpled, her hair tumbled in sexy, crazy waves all over the place. She also wasn't wearing makeup, which made her look less guarded and far more vulnerable. It made him want to smooth the tears off her cheeks with his fingertips, maybe pull her onto his lap and hug her, assure her that everything would be all right.

She brought out the damnedest reactions in him. He had no doubt that she could handle anything that life threw at her…he knew that from that first phone call, when she'd sounded like a cross between a sexy receptionist and a no-nonsense bill collector. She could take care of herself. But seeing her looking so fragile despite her abilities made him wish that she didn't *have* to take care of herself. That, just for a minute, somebody could take her troubles away. He'd pay cash money to see her laugh and smile without a care in the world.

He didn't think that cash was the solution, though, and he didn't think he was that somebody to take her troubles away. He never had been for anyone. Why would he start now?

"I guess I'll leave you alone then," he said awkwardly, starting to move toward the door, only to be stopped by her voice.

"It's just that I'm not sure we ever really loved each other, you know?"

Oh, crikey. What can of worms had he opened up here?

"I was his secretary," she said, pausing only to have some more coffee. Jack slowly sat down at the foot of the bed, careful to keep as much distance between himself and Chloe as possible. "He was handsome and successful, and…I don't know…charming."

Jack nodded. He figured the guy had to be charming—Chloe had to have seen *something* in him, right?

"I didn't even think he noticed me at first," Chloe said. "But he was so disorganized, so crazed. So I did little things to make his life easier. He appreciated it."

Jack made a noncommittal noise, a sort of sympathetic grunt.

"Then, one night, we were working late. He had a project he had to turn in," she said. "He asked if I wanted to go to dinner. I thought he was just taking me out to thank me for working late. Then he asked me out to dinner a few nights later, after the project was over. That time, I thought he was thanking me because the project was a success." She laughed humorlessly. "He finally said he wasn't thanking me anymore when he asked me to go with him to Santa Barbara for a weekend."

"Yeah, that would've been a hell of a project," Jack quipped. He already didn't like the guy; this was really pissing him off.

"I didn't go, of course," Chloe said, and Jack instantly cheered up. "He courted me for months before we…well, before we became an actual couple," she said. "And we dated for a few years before he asked me to marry him. Then it took another year to plan the wedding. And here I am."

"Here you are," Jack repeated, at a loss.

"He loved that I handled things for him. He said his life was better with me in it," she said, wiping at the tears on her face with the back of her hand and putting her empty coffee cup down with the other. "I loved feeling needed. I loved what I was able to do for him. I thought I was being appreciated."

"He was using you," Jack muttered.

Her eyes widened, and he realized he hadn't actually meant to make that observation out loud. Then she nodded, biting her lip quickly. "I suppose you could say that," she said. "But it wasn't like he had a gun to my head, you know?"

He was your boss, Jack thought but this time managed to keep his trap shut.

"I'm no victim," she said staunchly, and Jack's admiration for her rose another notch. "On some level, I knew what I was doing. But by the time it got to actually planning the wedding…well, I stopped making his life better."

"I doubt that," Jack said sharply.

"No, I mean because then it was all about the wedding," she said. "When we were just dating, we kept it pretty quiet. Once we were engaged, people made snide comments. And then his mother got involved." She made a sour face. "I don't think she ever really liked me."

Jack snorted at that. If the woman was anything like her son, the ever-popular Gerald, then he didn't put a lot of stock in her opinion, either.

"Even if we were in love, those obstacles would've been tough," she said. "Now I'm starting to realize I was so into the idea of being in love—having the perfect life—that I kept my blinders on. Right up to the point when Gerald left me at the altar for another woman who didn't have all this baggage."

"Please," Jack said tightly, "*please* tell me you're not letting this guy off the hook that easily."

"Well, he could've handled it better," she admitted, "but he was probably as caught up as I was. In a few years, I guess I'll consider myself lucky that he broke it off instead of being married and having a few kids or something and then finding out."

Jack let out a low whistle. "You may be the most relentlessly optimistic person I've ever met, you know that?"

She huffed impatiently. "I'm trying to sort this out," she said.

"Did you love him?" Jack asked her straight out, moving

the tray onto the surface of the minifridge and scooting closer to her. "Be honest now."

She met his gaze, then her eyes filled with tears. "I...I thought I did," she said. "I wanted to."

That wasn't the same, Jack realized. And then realized he was relieved, which was dumb. "Did you think he loved you?"

Now the tears escaped, crawling fresh paths down her cheeks. She nodded instead of responding verbally.

"He made you a promise and he hurt you," Jack said. "Now, I'm no genius when it comes to this sort of thing, and you probably don't even need my advice. But I'm the captain around here, so I'll throw my oar in."

She smiled at that one, and he reached out and tugged her into a semihug next to him.

"I'm not a big planner. Things work out or not, and you do the best you can. You're probably right—you're better off that he broke it off now instead of later, but you'd be a hell of a lot better off if he'd left before your damned wedding day."

She nodded against his shoulder, and he could feel the hot tears soaking through the material of his T-shirt.

"And you can rationalize all you want if you think it makes you feel better," he said, "but I don't think it really does. I think you're just trying to slap it into a box, pretend it's all cool and move forward. But I don't think that's really healthy."

She pulled away from him to stare into his eyes, her whole face frowning fiercely. "What's the point in screaming and crying about it? That gets you nowhere. There's no point in getting aggravated over elements you can't control."

"Are you kidding?" Jack said, bewildered.

"No," she said. "I've got a million things to take care of. I thought I'd take this break, get a clear head. I'm figuring out what happened with Gerald so I can move on and not be bogged down."

"Honey, if you can make that very statement and be free and clear of the whole episode…" Jack shook his head. "You're in the wrong line of work. You could be making a bundle teaching people how to get over their problems in twenty-four hours."

"You're making fun of me," she said, some snap in her voice to match the amber spark in her eyes.

"No," he said, then shrugged. "Well, maybe a little. The thing is, you've still got those feelings, and they're not going to go away just because they don't fit into that neat plan of yours."

"So what exactly are *you* suggesting?"

"I'm not suggesting anything," he said, putting his hands up defensively against that steel-tipped stare of hers. "I'm just saying…"

"That I'm full of it?"

He had to admit he liked her better angry than sad. He had dealt with plenty of angry women. And it was a nice change—ordinarily, the women he dealt with were angry because he was the one who had screwed up royally. "No, that logic and reason are great—most of the time. But sometimes you've got to just feel things. Ride with it." He grinned. "Do something stupid and foolish that makes no sense, because it'll help you feel better."

"Like what? Get drunk to the point of alcohol poisoning? Run up my credit cards? *Shoot Gerald?*"

"Well, not completely stupid," he amended. "And preferably nothing destructive—to yourself or to other people. But small stupidities can go a long way. Don't poison yourself, but get good and ripped. Don't max out your cards, but buy something you've always wanted. Don't shoot anybody…." He thought about it. "But you could always put a dead fish in his hubcap. In fact, I could help you with that when we get back."

She stared at him, wide-eyed in disbelief.

Oh, crap. Now I've done it. He fully expected her to either smack him or insist that he turn the boat around and take her home. Maybe both. In that order.

Instead she slowly smiled, almost as if she weren't even aware of it. "My family," she said, "would not understand you at all."

"I get that a lot," he said. "Why don't you eat something?"

He started to reach for the tray but was stopped when she put a hand on his cheek, gently forcing him to look at her.

"I don't understand you, either," she said softly, and that lopsided smile of hers pierced him like a bullet. "All I know is you have this amazing gift of making me feel better. Thank you, Jack."

And with that, she pressed a tiny kiss on the low part of his cheek.

It was completely innocent and, in his experience, completely rare. Which might have been why it had such a brutally strong impact on him. He felt lust, pure and simple, flood through him. He suddenly wanted to take her, then and there, and *really* make her feel better. If she wanted to forget all about her present circumstances, he'd do things to her that would make her forget her *name*. For a *month*.

But before he could act, he got a look at her eyes. Still red-rimmed with tears and fragility and pain. She was staring at him as if he was a hero. That was completely rare, too, and more unsettling.

"Don't mention it," he said, managing to make his voice sound normal. "Come on. Have a croissant."

And don't look at me like that again.

3

THAT NIGHT, CHLOE WAS still thinking of what Jack had said, about doing something little and stupid to feel better.

After that morning's heart-to-heart, she'd finished the croissants, fruit and coffee, going up on deck carrying her last cup carefully with her. The sky had been the lovely clear blue that she'd gotten so used to living in San Diego that she rarely even noticed it anymore. An occasional plush white cloud had dotted the horizon. There had been other sailboats out on this Sunday, taking advantage of the beautiful weather, as well. She'd been able to see the San Diego skyline off in the distance and make out the Coronado island chain. They'd just been cruising, leisurely, in no rush.

When was the last time I wasn't in a rush?

She had seen Jose walk by, checking on something but being as unobtrusive as possible, grinning at her with welcome before disappearing into the cockpit or wherever it was he took care of steering the boat. She enjoyed watching the front of the boat cut into the waves in front of her and loved the feel of the ocean swelling beneath her.

She knew she probably ought to get down to it: write out a list of discussion points for her conversation with Gerald, as well as work on her résumé and compile a list of likely target Web sites to start her job hunt. But she couldn't quite get motivated. She wasn't miserable—at least, she didn't feel the same way she had that morning, armed to the teeth with grim determination to put everything behind her, wear a brave face and soldier on. She was sort of stuck but strangely okay with that fact.

I want to do something stupid and foolish to feel better.

She'd made lunch and dinner for the crew, over their objections, and had enjoyed the process enormously. She'd forgotten how much she loved cooking, as well, and the trip was reminding her of it. When she was chopping vegetables or sautéing meat, she didn't think of anything but what she was working on, and that was meditative and relaxing all by itself. The satisfied sounds coming from the men eating her food were their own reward, she realized. Especially Jack, who seemed to love food almost as much as he loved his ship and the ocean. And she'd never met anyone who adored anything as much as he seemed to love the ocean.

She wondered absently what it would be like, to be the focus of that kind of passion.

So here she was, in her cabin, wearing her nightgown. It was only nine o'clock, and she was restless. She didn't have anything to read, there was no TV and listening to music only seemed to add to her frustration.

She belted the robe over her nightgown and slipped on her flat shoes and wandered up to the deck. She had plenty of practice and she'd be careful, but she figured she could pace at least. Maybe the sea air would lull her to sleep.

She stepped out on deck, and the sight momentarily robbed her of breath. The moon looked enormous, as if it were mere feet from the water, throwing its reflection in a million little diamondlike shards on the black ocean surface. There was a breeze, chilly and scented with brine, that caused her to clutch the neck of her robe a bit tighter. The sounds of the waves lapping against the hull were hypnotic.

"What did I tell you?"

She turned, gasping momentarily, then smiling. Jack was there, watching her. She didn't know how long he'd been there, leaning against the wall, in the shadows. He stepped toward her, the moonlight throwing the planes of his face into sharp relief. His eyes looked shadowed, and his brown hair looked black, leached of color by the nightly illumination.

"It's beautiful," she said, forcing herself to look out on the oceanscape and not at the man who had just surprised her. "And calming. You were right."

"Are you cold?" he asked, his voice tinged with concern. "It's nippy tonight."

"I'm okay," she said. "I was just...restless."

"Oh." He sighed. "Anything I can do to help?"

She bit her lip, hard. "I don't know," she said, taking a deep breath. "There might be."

He stood silent, waiting.

She closed her eyes, focusing on the tranquility all around her, dredging up the courage for her next step. "Remember what you said this morning, about doing something just to feel better? For the short term?"

"Sure," he said.

She felt the blush heating her skin, momentarily eliminating the chill of the wind. "I think I know what would help me feel better. I'm just not sure if I should ask you."

That made him pause. "I get the feeling this isn't getting you drunk or helping you trash somebody's car," he said with a shaky laugh.

She suddenly felt embarrassed. "Are you...oh, God, how do I ask this?"

"Spit it out and we'll deal with it." His voice sounded a little rough.

"Are you involved with anyone?"

"Involved?"

"You know, seeing anyone on a regular basis. Do you have a girlfriend? Significant other?" She suddenly blanched. "Wife?"

"No!" His response was so quick and so horrified that she actually giggled little in relief. "I mean...I see people from time to time, but no. Nothing serious."

"I guess that's a weird question to ask just before a request," she said, her own voice turning breathless.

"I think I can guess what you want, though," he said softly.

She stood there almost wilting in her own humiliation. "This is ridiculous," she said suddenly and started to walk past him, hurrying toward her own cabin. He stopped her by putting an arm around her shoulders. She tried shrugging it off, but he held tight.

"I said a little stupid but not self-destructive," he said. "This may be a little more than you're looking for. That is, if you're asking what I think you're asking."

"If you think I'm asking if you would have sex with me," she said sharply, "then yeah, that's what I had in mind."

He sighed, and she felt utterly, hopelessly foolish. "You're not the type," he said.

Her back straightened. She thought about asking indignantly *How do you know?* but realized that it wasn't as if she was fooling anyone. If she bumped into someone like herself on the street, she would hardly think it of her.

"It's an unusual situation," she countered instead. "I wasn't the type, that's for damned sure. But now..." She sighed, turning toward him instinctively, his restraining arm now turning into more of a half hug. "I'll level with you. I haven't had sex in six months, and before then we weren't exactly… we never…"

"You don't have to tell me," he said, but she bulled forward.

"I like sex, but with him it was never about sex," she said quickly. "He never wanted me for that—I mean, he never really was all that passionate about me—and I dealt with it. I never cheated on him and I never lied to him, but there were times when I just wanted…someone else. A fantasy. Does that make sense?"

He sighed heavily, but he didn't move his arm away. "Sort of," he finally admitted.

"Now I find out he cheated on me. All that comfort and planning that I thought I wanted—that I thought *he* wanted," she corrected, "wasn't it at all. And now I'm realizing I cheated myself, too."

She turned, looking into his eyes, which were mesmerizing in the moonlight.

"This isn't fair," she said, pushing her body against his. "I know that. It's using you, after you've been so wonderful to me, listening to me, being a friend to me. I don't want a replacement husband and I'm not looking to start a new relationship. But I don't drink and I don't want to wreck somebody's car. I just want to have sex. I want to remember what good sex feels like. I want to do it until I'm exhausted and I fall asleep smiling."

She could feel him still as a stone against her. She had never seduced anyone before—not that this could be considered a seduction, she realized. This was a proposition. She was propositioning him.

"You have to be sure," he finally said, his voice ragged. "You have to be *damned* sure."

She blinked, feeling her own hormones surge in response.

She realized on some level that she'd been steeling herself for rejection—that she had fully expected him to turn her down. "I'm sure."

"Because I'm not going to be your husband," he said, taking her shoulders in both hands and giving her a tiny shake. "You're a great woman, from what I've seen, and you've had some really crappy things happen to you. That makes me feel badly. But I'm not going to hook up with someone out of pity and I don't want to hurt you even worse just because you think that sleeping with me is going to be some kind of answer. I don't want you making me out to be something I'm not." His voice was downright fierce now, nothing like the laid-back seafarer she'd met only the day before. "I want you. But it's just going to be physical, and if that seems wrong, then you're going to be dealing with me for the rest of the trip. Now think about this very, very carefully. *Can you really handle this or not?*"

She swallowed hard. Her mind was racing, throwing disastrous possibilities at her. She'd feel terrible. She'd lose respect for herself. She'd lose respect for *him*. She'd be faced with a long journey with that knowledge. She'd only slept with three men in her life, and all of those were from long relationships. Could she handle this?

He was so close she could feel the heat coming off him. And her body suddenly made the decision for her.

She stood up on her toes and kissed him. Gently at first, tentatively tasting his mouth, feeling the muscles of his chest bunch under her fingertips. Trying to get closer to him, her breasts dragged up the length of him, and he groaned beneath her lips.

He suddenly took charge, surprising her even more. His hands, which had been clutching her shoulders, moved down to her hips, molding her to him, and she squeaked momentarily in surprise. He wasn't harsh, though, and the rough movement felt like heaven as she felt his hardness press against her stomach. She sighed, parting her lips, and his tongue traced the soft inner flesh of her mouth. She responded in kind, feeling her heart start to beat painfully quickly in response.

"Jack," she murmured when he pulled away. *"Jack."*

He pulled her head against his chest, cradling her hair with one hand. She could hear his heartbeat, a fast, steady thumping beneath her ear.

"I can't promise more than tonight," he said. "Damn it, don't make me the bad guy tomorrow."

"I won't blame you," she assured him, almost mindless with the rush of pleasure and need coursing through her. Now that she'd felt the rush, there was no way she was turning back. Her body wanted it too much. "I swear, Jack, I won't hold you to anything. Just be with me tonight."

She felt, as well as heard the tortured sigh come from him. Then she felt him lift her up as if she weighed nothing. With quick, careful steps, he took her back to her cabin and shut the door behind them.

She felt her heart racing in her chest, and her skin felt alive, almost oversensitive to his touch. He placed her on the bed delicately, slowly, as if giving her every chance to back out if she so desired. But she wasn't going to change her mind. Even as a tiny voice in the back of her head shouted that this was crazy, stupid, probably the most idiotic thing she'd ever done, she realized that she was going through with it—that there was no way she was backing out now.

He pulled away, staring at her as if she were the only woman on earth, and for a second it made her pause before tugging at the sash of her robe. Beneath, she wore a simple spaghetti-string silk nightie in a deep, almost rust-colored garnet-red, cut high on her thighs but otherwise devoid of any lace or frills. She wondered absently if maybe she shouldn't have chosen something sexier, but the expression he made when he saw it caused shivers to shoot up her spine. She rolled awkwardly, pushing the robe off the bed and onto the floor.

He was wearing a T-shirt and a pair of jeans—his usual attire—and he stripped the T-shirt over his head with one casual motion, revealing a body that made her body tighten in response. The guy had the most beautiful chest she'd ever seen—chiseled and muscular, no doubt from all the labor required to keep a ship like this running. His arms and shoulders were yoked, his abdomen flat and rippled into a six-pack. She wanted to smooth her palms over every square inch of him. She wanted to lick him.

She could not remember the last time she felt like this, if ever.

He put his hands on the buttons of his fly and then he paused, staring at her, the top button undone. She waited, breathless, to see what was revealed—only to see that he was again waiting for her to somehow reassure him that this was, indeed, what she wanted to do.

It would've been easier if he had taken the lead, she realized. She'd never really been a sexual aggressor, and to be honest, if he would just charge forward and make love to her, she could always assuage her conscience the next morning by saying things had gone too fast and he'd simply outmaneuvered her. But she wasn't a victim, as she'd told him that morning—this was going to be her decision, and she was going to live with it. So she sat up on the bed and, with hands only slightly trembling, took the denim in her own hands, nerves making her hands slow down as she undid each metal button. He groaned, leaning against the backs of her fingertips, and she could feel the cotton of boxers and the heat of his skin.

Suddenly nerves burned away in a flash pulse of pure

desire. She tugged at his waistband, and he helped her, shucking out of his jeans, socks and shoes and then shrugged out of his boxers, as well. His erection was magnificent, hard and long, jutting toward her. Shocked at her own boldness, she circled it with her fingers, smoothing her palm from the base to the tip with a steady confidence that elicited a surprised moan in response from him. She released him only long enough to tug the nightgown over her head, leaving only the matching garnet thong between them.

"I want you," she panted. *"Now."*

He slid next to her on the bed, reaching for her, kissing her ravenously. And his kisses—good God, the man was an artist. What he could do with his lips alone was mind-blowing. She clung to him, molding her body to his as his mouth plundered hers. She could feel her breasts crushing against that rock-hard chest of his, and the smooth, fevered flesh of his cock pressed against her thighs, causing her to go damp in a second. His fingers dug into the skin at her hips, pulling her even closer. She tore her mouth away to get a breath, to somehow get her bearings, but he chose to inch lower instead, kissing her throat, then lapping at each nipple until she was moaning, almost crying with need.

This was what I wanted, was her last coherent thought. *This was what I needed!*

His fingers moved down to her thong, pushing the scrap of silk out of the way before penetrating her wet curls. She closed her eyes, biting her lip against the overwhelming sensation of him pressing slowly into her, first one finger, then two, in a slow, sensual rhythm as mesmerizing as the sea itself. She gasped, her hips bucking of their own accord.

"I want you," he breathed, his words ragged against her shoulder.

"Please," she murmured back, her hips increasing in speed. "Please…"

When his fingers withdrew, she whimpered in protest.

"Just a second," he said and he reached into a little cupboard built into the headboard. He produced a condom, and she could hear the package tear and the low noises of him rolling it on. She reached down, pulling off the panties. She didn't want anything in the way. She wanted to feel him completely.

She felt him cover her like a blanket, and the heat of him, the sheer size of him, were overwhelming. She spread her legs, feeling him nestle between them, propped up on his arms so he wouldn't crush her with his mass.

"You're sure?" he said one last time. She could feel the hard length of him brushing against her entrance, sandwiched between her thighs.

She couldn't even answer. She simply arched her hips, cuddling his hardness, trying her best to get him inside her.

With a groan of relief, he pressed into her. She gasped at the unfamiliar sensation. It didn't hurt, but it was so strange, so different. He remained still inside her for a moment, and she could feel the tension of all his muscles beneath her fingertips. "You're…so tight," he marveled.

He withdrew slowly, then eased back in, the friction of him making her breath catch. She hooked her legs over his hips, making the entrance wider, causing friction where she needed it and causing her to moan as her hips began to move of their own accord.

It was all the encouragement he needed. He moved with gradually increasing speed, pulling her hips flush against him, stroking his way deeper inside her until she was panting unevenly and clawing at his back with her fingertips. He was breathing just as hard against her neck as his bucking became frantic against her. She felt as though she were being pulverized, as if the boundaries where she stopped and he began were torn down by sheer sexual force.

She felt the beginning tingles of orgasm start and she felt conflicted—she wanted the delicious on-the-brink feeling to last, but she also wanted what would no doubt be the overwhelming force of it to slam through her and make her mind a glorious blank. But he was moving fast…too fast.

"Wait," she breathed, but she realized what was happening. They'd gotten too hot too quickly, and now he was already too far gone to accommodate.

"Chloe," he breathed, and his hips pistoned against her, again almost getting her there. Almost. He shuddered tiny aftershocks against her sweat-moistened skin.

She felt a kind of closeness she hadn't felt in a long time, which in itself was nice, but she also felt slightly bereft. And the tiny voice, the annoying little commentator, was already leaping to the fore.

This was a bad idea, it said in its smug way.

Jack collapsed next to her, breathing hard. "Damn it," he said.

"It's all right," she said absently and wondered if it really was. "It was nice…thank you."

"Oh, jeez, don't thank me," he said. "Just give me a few minutes and I'll make sure…"

"No, that's fine," she said, alarmed. She needed to process this. And what if it were guilt? Or something else? What if they did it again—and she still couldn't come?

"What's fine?"

"You don't have to stay," she said, trying not to offend him. "I know you said it was just for tonight—and believe me, I can't thank you enough for it."

"You shouldn't be thanking me for that," he said. "You didn't even hit it, did you?"

She bit her lip. "Well, no, but I don't think that was your fault."

"You let guys off too easily," he said, his jaw tight. "Just give me another damned chance…."

"I'm tired," she said bluntly. "Good night, Jack."

He stared at her for a moment with utter disbelief. Then he got up, grumbling, and grabbed his jeans, tugging them on. She watched him get his clothes back on with regret, knowing what she now knew the clothes were hiding.

"This isn't over," he growled and then stalked out of her cabin, slamming the door behind him.

She rolled over, burying her face in the pillow. Of course it wasn't over. And *this* was why she didn't do little stupid things.

THE NEXT MORNING, JACK was sandy-eyed and furious, pacing the confines of the captain's quarters. He hadn't slept at all the night before. He wasn't angry at Chloe. Well, okay, he was a *little* angry at Chloe because she hadn't given him a chance to make it up to her and because she'd gone from a hypnotic sea siren to a dismissive ice queen in about fifteen seconds. Of course, once he'd thought about it (around three o'clock in the morning, after several beers) he'd realized that he would probably be pretty peeved, too, if he'd gone all that way and not "reached completion." And why should she trust him to do better the next time? He'd botched it pretty good the first time. Which accounted for the rest of his angry state that morning. He was boiling with self-contempt at his performance…or rather, lack thereof.

Ordinarily, he prided himself on being a skilled, considerate lover. He enjoyed sex and, like any good hobby, he'd practiced it plenty over his lifetime. He didn't just enjoy it for his own selfish gratification, either. Other than the fact that he would not stay onshore, his lovers had never complained about him in any way. He'd made sure of that.

So what had happened last night to create such a consummate disaster?

For one thing, she had blindsided him, in more ways than one. He knew that she was in a fragile state and yet he still hadn't expected her to ask him for sex…not and be serious about it. She might be the type to fantasize, but he would've bet his boat that she wasn't the type to actually act on it. Yet with all his stupid pep talks, his "do one little stupid thing" advice, he'd all but brought it on himself.

Then, when she'd actually asked him to have sex with her, he realized that he should have said no, emphatically, and sent her back to bed alone. In his mind, he assured himself that if the event happened, that's exactly what he'd do. But he should've known better. In his entire life, he doubted he'd ever taken that "noble" and celibate road when it came to women. What had surprised him then was the effort he'd made to sabotage himself—trying to get her to see reason, trying to show her that they had no future. And she *hadn't cared*. She had only wanted him for one night, she'd said, and while he'd known she was probably lying, his body had conned him into believing her…because he'd wanted her from the minute she'd stepped on his dock, looking forlorn and heavenly in that pink suit of hers. From the minute he'd seen her, a luscious study in earth tones lying naked beneath her satin sheet, he'd known that one way or another he'd probably have her, given any opportunity.

The last shock was when he'd finally gotten her to bed. With all her delicate, almost haunting beauty, he'd expected it to be gentle. He'd thought to woo her, to coax her away from her shyness…to make sure that this was, indeed, what she wanted and give her plenty of room to turn back. He might not be noble, but he wasn't a complete bastard, either. But she hadn't needed coaxing. If anything, the moment that door had closed, she'd become someone else—someone just as enticing as the vulnerable little miss he'd become infatuated with. Hell, *more* enticing. He got the feeling she wouldn't have taken no for an answer, even if he'd been able to pony up the moral fortitude to try denying her. The way she'd reached for him, the way she'd pushed and insisted, the way she'd responded were all unbelievably erotic. It was that combined with the surprise of her and the fact that he'd been lusting after her for forty-eight hours that had finally pushed him over the edge. He couldn't have held back any longer if he'd had a gun to his head.

He rubbed at his eyes with the heels of his palms, feeling like beating his head against something for his own stupidity and lack of control. There was one last shock. The fact that she calmly switched gears and sent him packing without any seeming remorse other than possibly being seen as rude. When she'd said that she only wanted him for one night, apparently she'd meant it. And instead of a relief, he found it completely annoying.

There was a knock on his door, and he scowled at it. "Come in," he snapped, fully expecting it to be Jose or Ace and hoping that it wasn't something serious or costly.

The door opened. It wasn't Jose or Ace.

"Do you have a minute?"

He sighed. Chloe was wearing a pair of white capri pants and a chocolate-brown halter top, her hair up in a ponytail and her face looking freshly scrubbed. If anything, she looked like a guilty teenager, come to confess to sneaking in late or something.

He bit back on temper. She had nothing to feel guilty about.

It wasn't her fault—it was his. And she had enough going on this week, what with being abandoned at the altar and all. He really didn't need to make her life more unhappy, did he?

"Sure," he found himself saying, gesturing to the small chair by his desk. He leaned against the far wall, keeping as much distance between them as possible. "How are you feeling?"

"Fine," she said, then she shook her head. "Actually, I feel terrible." He winced, and she must've caught it because she quickly added, "Not because of last night!"

"Well, you have every right," he started, but she interrupted him.

"I mean, I don't feel terrible about what we did last night. I feel terrible that I just sort of…you know…kicked you out like that."

There was a blush riding high on her cheeks, and she was studying the top of his desk as if it were the Rosetta Stone. He sighed.

"You had every right to decide when we were done," he said slowly.

"I could have handled it better," she countered, shaking her head some more. "It was rude, and unconscionable, considering I was the one who had dragged you to my room and practically forced you…"

"Okay, *whoa,*" he said, crossing the room and kneeling in front of her so she'd have to look at him. "Beyond the fact that I carried you to your cabin, there's feeling bad about something, and then there's self-flagellation. You don't have to be a martyr about this."

She looked up, her eyes snapping at the term *martyr.* "I'm not! I'm just…"

"I know. You're just not being a victim," he said, letting some of his frustration seep out. "Just like you did with what's-his-name, that idiot. You're letting men off the hook and taking the blame for something that's in no way your fault so you can feel like you have control over it. Well, last night wasn't your fault. I didn't do the job right, and you had every right to want time alone. You didn't force me to do anything, you weren't rude, you weren't *anything*. So stop letting me off the hook!"

She blinked at him, and he could tell anger was warring with guilt. "I did kick you out," she said.

"Yes, you did. So what?"

Her mouth dropped open.

"You're allowed," he said.

"I *used* you, Jack!"

Now he grinned. She sounded so scandalized by it, as if she'd committed a murder or something. "Well, *duh*."

Her eyes bulged in response. "And…you're okay with that?"

There it was again—that combination of innocence and wickedness that the woman seemed to project like a beacon. "Honey, I knew exactly what I was getting into," he said, although even as he mouthed the words, he wondered if he really knew what he was getting into *now*. "Call it rebound sex, call it a therapeutic lay…whatever. You didn't want permanent, you just wanted comfort." He shook his head with remorse. "And you were so amazing, so damned *hot*, that you knocked me for a loop. I haven't lost control like that since I was a teenager. And that's why I was upset. You didn't get any comfort—no matter how you tried to say it was fine. You got robbed, and I feel badly about that."

She was staring at him now with a look of dazed disbelief. "I was so hot you lost control?"

He nodded, embarrassed. "I'm sure that sounds like a cop-out, and you probably think it's an excuse because I'm not very good…."

She snorted. "Now who's being a martyr?"

He chuckled. "I gotta admit—I haven't had a lot of complaints. Which makes last night that much worse."

She bit her lip, which made him want to bite her lip. He looked away from her, trying to distract himself, only to find himself looking at his bed, which was still rumpled from his sleepless night.

I could make it up to her.

He sighed. "So are we okay?" he said, more sharply than he'd intended.

She was silent for a long second. Then she sighed in response to his. "You know, one night only would be smart," she mused.

He turned his attention back to her. "What do you mean?"

"I mean, I don't want a relationship and neither do you." It sounded as though she was trying to puzzle something out. "So if we did it again…wouldn't that complicate things?"

His body didn't hear past *if we did it again.* "I don't think so," he said, even as his mind—which did hear the whole statement—complained mightily. *Of course it would complicate things, you idiot! She's a client! She's no booty call…she's a keeper! And she's just lost a marriage! Do not proceed!*

"Listen," he said and he found himself stroking her cheek, enjoying the way she curved her face into his palm. "You're only here for another few days. I'm on the ocean all the time. We've got completely separate lives. We both know what we want and what we don't want." He wasn't sure if he was convincing her or himself or both of them, but he kept talking. "I want to make it up to you. I want you to feel better. If you don't want to do anything after that, I completely respect that and I'll keep it strictly professional afterward."

She stood and so did he. She was close to him. They were both close to the bed.

"And if I do want to do things…after today?" she said.

"You've got a full cruise," he heard himself say. "I can guarantee you'll have the most relaxing time of your life."

Her laugh was short and surprised, as well as husky, edged in arousal.

"I suppose it's only fair to let you try," she said and reached around his neck, lifting herself up for a kiss.

From the moment her lips touched his it was all over, he knew that. It could be complicated—it could be downright disastrous—but there was no way he'd stop touching her now.

He tugged at her clothes, feeling a little clumsy. He prayed that being tired would not affect his performance. After last night's poor showing, he felt he owed it to her. Hell, he probably didn't even deserve an orgasm today. Although, honestly, he doubted he'd be quite that noble.

She was kissing him as she reached back and untied her halter, letting the scraps of material fall to her waist, revealing those perfect creamy breasts of hers. He cupped them for a second, marveling at how well they fit his palms. Then he reached for the button of her pants, unzipping the fly slowly and smoothing the fabric off the gentle curves of her hips. She was wearing a pair of bikini panties, and he eased those off, as well. She kicked the whole ensemble off, removing the halter last. She was now gloriously naked and staring at him with those temptress eyes that she'd revealed the night before.

Don't mess this up!

He didn't even take off his clothes, unwilling to court disaster again. When he nudged her onto his bed, he could see her surprise. He kissed her thoroughly, feasting on her supple mouth, until he felt her hands roaming restlessly over him, tugging at his T-shirt. He removed it, but when she reached for his pants, he inched back.

"What's wrong?" she asked, her voice full of concern.

"This is for you, remember?" he said and then kissed her throat, moving lower, between her breasts. He pressed kisses against each inside curve, relishing her small gasps.

"You don't have to…."

"Hush," he whispered against her stomach, enjoying the tremors that his breath produced. He'd wanted her like this when he'd massaged her, he remembered, his body going rigid at the simple memory.

"Jack…" Her voice was uncertain, but her fingers curled into his hair.

"It's okay," he reassured her, tickling a trail past her belly button with the tip of his tongue and then pressing small, heated kisses against her inner thighs. "Trust me," he said, taking one last look at her and winking at her.

He dipped between her legs, tasting her, reveling in her. She hadn't done this before, he could tell. Her gasps and jerky, reflexive movements revealed that much. However, she also enjoyed it. She was breathing in short, uneven gasps, and her hips began to move beneath him, pressing up to meet him before withdrawing. He focused on her clit while he inched a finger inside her, pressing up on her secret spot.

She cried out, a noise of pure pleasure, and he smiled against her, continuing. She was panting now, murmuring incoherent words of encouragement until finally she exploded, letting out a rippling shriek of happiness.

He leaned back, smiling, sure that it looked smug but not meaning to be. She looked overwhelmed, shocked by what had just happened.

Now you know how I felt, lady. He was so happy he was almost giddy with it—and he wasn't the type to be giddy over anything.

"Oh, my God," she said after breathing hard for several minutes. "I never…that was…"

"You're welcome," he said. Now *that* was smug. He stretched out next to her, propping his head up with one arm.

"But you didn't…" she said belatedly, pointing to his pants, which he was still wearing. There was a noticeable tent-pole effect, thanks to his body's hardness.

"No, I didn't," he said.

"But…that's not fair."

"Now you know how I felt last night," he said, pushing a strand of hair away from her face.

She nodded. "It's better if it's both of us," she said. And her eyes were warm.

He smiled. A woman after his own heart. This time when she reached for his belt, he let her, helping her by easing off his pants and boxers. He got another condom, rolling it on hastily. She reached for him, welcoming as the ocean, and he slid into her. She was already wet and ready, but she still moaned appreciatively. He could feel her snug passage closing around him, and it was all he could do to breathe.

Slow, go slow, he counseled himself, easing back and then pressing in, trembling at the sheer sensual overload of the feel of her, the smell of her. She angled her hips, taking more of him in, wrapping her legs around his waist. She did this little twist with her hips, driving him crazy, making him speed up. *Go slow!*

"Oh, Jack," she breathed into his ear, and her hands clutched at his shoulders. Her hips were moving in the same rhythm as they had been earlier. "Jack, I think I'm going to…"

He felt her tighten around him, and it was suddenly impossible to go slow. He let his body take control, moving faster and harder into her, her hips meeting his every thrust, her breathing matching his.

"*Jack!*" she cried out, and he lost it. He felt the release hit him like a freight train and he shuddered against her helplessly, his body pumping furiously as she clung to him.

Now he collapsed, rolling to one side but not releasing her from his arms.

After long moments he looked at her.

She was fast asleep, her arms hooked around him, a smile on her face.

He felt…actually, he couldn't describe how he felt. But he did know two things.

One, that he'd just had one of the best sexual experiences of his life.

And two, that he was probably in for a world of trouble.

CHLOE STOOD ON THE deck, watching as they navigated the channel that led back to the Coronado harbor. She felt like a completely different person than she'd been when the *Rascal* had pulled away from its slip, only seven days before. Then, she had felt devastated—that is, what little she could feel in her state of numbness was devastation. Back then, she'd thought her life was a complete shambles. But things were different now.

Now she *knew* her life was a complete shambles, she thought with a grin. On the plus side, she no longer seemed to care all that much. And that was an entirely new state of affairs.

She'd spent the past five days—and nights—doing nothing that had been on her original mission for her botched honeymoon cruise. Instead of brainstorming all the details she needed to cover when she got home, she'd cooked for the very appreciative crew, having a blast. Instead of writing out an action plan, she'd gone fishing with Jack and Jose, catching nothing, but having a lot of fun. And instead of crying into her pillow every night…

The smile on her face at that thought could probably be seen from space. Her pillow had been witness to a lot of astounding and sexually unbelievable things in the past five days, but crying certainly wasn't one of them.

"So," she heard Jack's voice emerge behind her. "Looks like this is the end of your cruise."

"Yup. I guess the honeymoon's over," she said, tongue in cheek, then realized with a pang that it really was, in several senses. She could also feel more than see Jack's tension at the comment. She knew he was by no means permanent and should've realized that anything even vaguely marriage-related wouldn't fly that well. "Sorry. Bad joke."

She'd known that she couldn't keep Jack, and while he was amazing in bed, she was in no state to tell what he'd be like out of it. Besides, she'd just gotten out of a relationship—jumping back into one would be the height of stupidity. All Jack had guaranteed her was a vacation, and she'd had that and then some. But, like all vacations, this one had to end. She'd have to face reality at some point.

It looked as if that point was now.

"I hope you enjoyed your trip," he said.

She grinned at him. "I have to admit," she said, stretching in the sunlight, "it had its high points." She was gratified when he chuckled at her understatement. They stood that way for a few minutes in comfortable silence, not touching, merely savoring the day.

"I almost hate to ask this," Jack finally said, "but what are you going to do now?"

"I have no idea," she admitted in a rueful tone. "But I'll be fine." She paused, then shrugged. "Just in case you were worried," she added, not sure if that was why he asked the question.

"Actually, I wasn't." He reached out and put a hand on her shoulder, causing her to shiver in response. After one short week with him, she'd know his touch if she were blindfolded in a crowd twenty years from now.

"You wouldn't worry about me?" she asked, more to distract herself than anything.

"I don't need to," he responded, his thumb making a small circle near her collarbone. "You're one strong lady, Chloe Winton. And I know this sounds cliché, but...you're going to be all right."

"Thanks," she said softly.

He took his hand away, to her relief and regret. "You know, the guys are going to miss your cooking," he added, clearing his throat as if to eliminate the emotion caught there. "You're going to be a tough act to follow. You even gave Kenneth a run for his money, and I never thought I'd say that."

"Well, if that whole finding-another-job thing doesn't pan out, maybe I can use you as a reference," she joked, even as the joke brought home the fact that, yeah, she'd really need to look for a job.

"Reference, hell," he said. "I'd hire you myself."

She turned to face him finally, blinking at his statement. He looked a little stunned, too.

She thought about it. It had been idyllic, this past week on the ship. But that hadn't been working, per se. That had been playing with the occasional meal preparation. And how much of her relaxation was from working on the *Rascal*...versus how much had come from the hours she'd spent losing herself in sexual oblivion with its captain?

Either way, the idyll was illusory. No matter how much she dreamed, she knew that.

"Well, I appreciate the offer," she finally responded, forcing herself to keep her tone light. "Who knows, right? But as you said…I'm sure I'll be fine."

And just like that, she shut the door on any future ideas she might've had about the *Rascal* or its captain.

He nodded, and she could've sworn he looked relieved—and a bit irritated. Which made no sense. Still, what did these days?

Jose steered the boat through the narrow waterways, finally pulling into their slip. Chloe watched as Jack and Ace jumped out, securing the lines to the cleats on the dock. Then she went belowdecks to her cabin, where she'd already packed. She rolled her bag back to find the walkway set up. The three men stood there, smiling at her.

"Thanks for choosing us to cruise with," Jack said.

"And for feeding us," Ace added.

"Come back anytime," Jose offered, ignoring Jack's sarcastic rolling eyes.

"I appreciate it, guys," she said and then impulsively hugged all of them, saving Jack for last.

"Here, I'll take your luggage to your car," he said. "Least I can do."

She started to protest but finally let him after waving to the crew members. They walked in silence down the docks, heading back up to the parking lot where her car was waiting. She turned to Jack. "Thanks for everything," she said—and meant it.

"Don't mention it," he said, putting her luggage in her trunk. Then he stood by the driver's side, and she fumbled with her keys awkwardly, unsure of what to say. Or do.

"You take care of yourself, okay?" he finally said.

"You, too," she replied and reached to hug him again.

He didn't just hug her. He gave her a slow, lingering kiss that took her breath away and made her body ache.

After long moments he pulled away, breathing heavily. "I'm glad I met you, Chloe."

Before she could even think of what to say to that, he'd turned and was walking away.

I'm glad I met you, too, Jack, she threw back mentally. He was just what she'd needed, when she'd needed it. And he was a good man, besides.

A small part of her wanted to watch his broad-shouldered figured disappear down the walkway, back toward the ship, but she'd wasted enough time. She forced herself to get in her car, and with a small sigh she drove away.

4
___

"WHAT DO YOU MEAN I'm overdrawn?" Jack barked into his cell phone. With his other hand, he rubbed at his temples.

He had hoped to find a way to distract himself from his haunting thoughts of Chloe. Thoughts a commitment-phobic, seagoing guy like himself had no business entertaining. And apparently, fate had taken him up on his request. At the moment, romantic thoughts of Chloe were the furthest thing from his mind. He was too intent on saving the first love of his life, the *Rascal*. And from the annoyed messages from his bank and some other creditors, he got the feeling that he was in over his head.

"Mr. McCullough," the banker said in that well-cultured but irritated voice of his, "you've been overdrawn for the past week, and now your credit card is maxed out—which cancels out your overdraft protection. We have gotten several irate calls already from people expecting payment…."

"But how is this possible?" Jack said. "I deposited a check just the week before I left!"

There was a pause. "Would this be from a—" followed by a quick pause and the sound of rustling paper "—Gerald? Gerald Sutton?"

Gerald. Chloe's ex. "Yeah, actually, it was."

"There was a stop payment ordered," the banker said.

"*What?*"

"He called and refused payment on the check," the banker clarified, as if Jack didn't know what a stop-payment order meant. "He insisted that it be canceled."

"Son of a bitch." The dull ache Jack was feeling just behind his eyes was starting to escalate to minor migraine. "Did he give a reason *why?*"

"Something about services not received or rendered." And the snooty-sounding guy actually sounded accusatory toward Jack—Jack, who was his client, for God's sake.

"So I offer a service, and you're okay with the fact that I don't get paid for it? And my business account gets overdrawn because of it!"

"You'll have to take that up with him," the banker said and he did sound a little apologetic—to a very minor degree.

"Oh, believe me, I will," Jack spat out. Then, in his achy, fury-tinged brain, his logical side made an observation. "Wait a second. It was a local bank—it should've cleared almost immediately. When did he stop payment?"

More rustling of paper, and the banker gave him the date. "*Son of a bitch!*" Jack did the mental math. For Gerald to stop payment before the check cleared, he would've had to have canceled it almost as soon as Jack had deposited it…which meant he'd canceled it almost a week before Jack took Chloe out on the *Rascal.*

Which meant the butt head had known that he wasn't going on his own honeymoon cruise and that he could've given Chloe warning instead of standing her up at the altar.

"Really, Mr. McCullough," the banker said in a disgusted tone. "This sort of language isn't necessary. And this isn't my fault."

Jack bit back another oath and then sighed. "You're right. This isn't your fault. I'll get in contact with the client."

"Uh, Mr. McCullough, that still doesn't resolve the situation," the banker pointed out. "You're overdrawn. When were you planning on rectifying that issue?"

"Well, I was planning on rectifying that issue with another check from Gerald Sutton," Jack said with asperity, "but I guess we can count *that* out, huh?"

"Mr. McCullough, this is the sort of thing that ruins credit and certainly hurts your account status…."

"Tell me something I don't know," Jack snapped. "Listen, I have to go shake this guy down, so I can pay you guys and then pay a half million other guys thirsting for my blood, okay? I'll call back later."

"But Mr. McCul—"

Jack hung up on the banker, feeling his blood boil. Gerald frickin' Sutton. The name to his pain.

"Everything okay, boss?" Jose asked nervously.

"Yeah, fine," Jack said. "You can go ahead on home. We're not sailing out again until Thursday anyway. Another honeymoon couple." *And please, God, let their check clear.*

"Uh…all right. Later, Jack." With that, Jose left. Ace had already gone—something about a new girl or something. Ace wanted to show her a good time before they set sail again.

At this rate, setting sail again was looking pretty damned grim.

Jack retreated to the desk in his cabin, digging up the check that Gerald had given him. He called the phone number. "Hello?" a male voice asked—deep but sort of tentative.

"Is this Gerald Sutton?"

"Yes, it is," the bass voice responded. "Who is this?"

This is the guy you're trying to screw over, you piece of crap.

Jack took a deep breath. "This is Jack McCullough, captain of the *Rascal*."

A long pause. "I'm sorry?"

"That would be the ship you chartered for your honeymoon cruise," Jack clarified. "That would've been last week?"

"Oh," Gerald responded, then quickly sounded embarrassed as he put two and two together. *"Oh."*

"Know why I'm calling?" Jack asked, trying hard to keep his voice even.

"If this is about the check, I was well within my rights," Gerald said, his voice rising a couple of octaves. That must be his "mad" voice, Jack realized. "After all, I wasn't using your honeymoon cruise. I didn't even get married!"

"Yeah, I know about that," Jack said. "Left the girl at the altar. With a *note*," he added, unable to keep his disgust hidden. "In front of all her friends and family. *Nice.*"

"You don't know what happened, and how dare you judge me," Gerald squeaked. Yes, the man actually *squeaked*. "And how exactly are you the wronged party? Why should I pay you for a cruise nobody even took?"

"Oh, somebody took it all right," Jack said.

"I certainly did not!"

"No, you didn't," Jack agreed. "Chloe did."

Now another long pause. "Chloe went on the cruise?"

Jack let out a frustrated breath. "Didn't you wonder what the hell happened to her after you pulled your vanishing trick? Wonder why she didn't call you? Or why she didn't stop by your house?"

"Well…no," Gerald stammered. "I was away. In Santa Barbara."

Taking a little getaway of your own, huh? "She needed time to think, *get away* from her family and her troubles," Jack said between gritted teeth. "You stuck her with the wedding. The least you could do is pick up the tab on a vacation for her."

"Is that what she told you?" Gerald sounded peeved but also a guilty. *Scumbag.*

"No, that's what I put together," Jack said, feeling guilty himself. *Actually, that's what you convinced her to do.* "So are you going to be a punk or are you going to pay for the cruise and give the poor woman you abandoned a break?"

Gerald coughed nervously. "Well, but that's not fair," he tried.

"You canceled the check a week before the wedding, butt head," Jack said, his patience finally worn out. "You could've spared her the public humiliation, but you didn't. So how exactly is *that* fair?"

"Shut up!" Gerald snapped. "I don't owe her—or you—a damned thing. If you want to get paid so badly, go get the money from your passenger—Chloe! And don't bother me again!"

"I could sue you," Jack said, even though what he really wanted to say was *I could kick your ass from here to Madagascar, you useless rat.*

"Try it," Gerald said, laughing bitterly. "My family's loaded. Our lawyers would eat you alive."

"You son of a bitch." There really wasn't any other phrase for guys like Gerald, Jack realized.

Gerald hung up without an answer.

Jack stared at the cell phone for a second, contemplating throwing it at a wall, but it wasn't the phone's fault, and frankly he couldn't afford another one right now. He carefully put it down in a drawer, out of harm's way. Then he stared at the mountain of paperwork on his desk. Bills, with Past Due printed on them in red ink. His admittedly rough budget—and how much he would need to bring in to pay another chef and masseuse. At this rate, he had no idea how he was going to pay anybody, even if he could find replacements. And the passengers he was picking up on Thursday were expecting everything to be top-of-the-line…he remembered that the husband was a pain in the butt.

Just what I need—another problem.

Jack put his head down on the desk for a second, then straightened up and opened another drawer. This one contained the other Jack—his bottle of Jack Daniel's. He took a swig straight out of the bottle, feeling the warmth of the whiskey hit him like a cannonball in his stomach.

As he'd once counseled Chloe, he was about to do something little and stupid…because he couldn't think of anything else to do.

The thought instantly brought back Chloe's chosen "little and stupid" solution. His eyes went to his bed, remembering the last time he'd had her in it…and near it, against the wall. And on the floor, come to think of it.

What you really need is a little more of that kind of solution.

He shook his head. No, he had enough problems. The last thing he needed was a woman like Chloe Winton, who would probably be the best thing that ever happened to him—right up to the point where he broke her heart by leaving.

CHLOE DROVE BACK TO her parents' house feeling strangely calm. She already knew that they'd be greeting her with questions: where were her checklists, what was her action plan, things like that. And she wasn't quite sure how to tell them that after a week away, she still didn't have any clear idea of what she was going to do next. Ordinarily, that out-of-control sensation would be enough to cause her to break out in a cold sweat of anxiety, but not today. Today she just felt…loose.

She shook her head, smiling at the thought. *Loose* as in

flexible, she corrected, not as in the loose woman sort of way. Although technically she might qualify there, as well. Now that she was physically away from Jack, the whole thing seemed too unreal to be credible. It was as if she'd just had a weeklong daydream.

She was still smiling when she walked through the front door. "Mom! Dad! I'm home!" She left her roller bag in the entryway, at the foot of the stairs. She was somewhat surprised that they weren't waiting for her in the living room. She hunted around, finally finding them in the home office, by the garage.

"Hey, guys," she said, surprised by the somberness of their expressions. "Are you all right?"

"Oh, honey," her mother said, coming over and hugging her. Her voice sounded near tears.

Chloe instantly felt alarm shoot through her. "What is it? What's wrong?"

"We've had a terrible week," her mother answered, turning to her father. "You just wouldn't believe it. We certainly couldn't believe it."

"What happened?" Chloe insisted.

"The wedding," her father said, and his voice was deadly cold. "All the bills we paid on the understanding that the Suttons would be paying for half. All the deposits we paid. Everything." He let out a deep exhalation. "We got a call from Mrs. Sutton, Gerald's mother. She says that since the marriage was canceled, she can't see how Gerald should be financially responsible for any of it."

"What?"

"I know!" Her mother dabbed at her eyes. "We figured it was in good faith—we'd all agreed, and you made so many concessions for that evil woman, added so many expenses.

For her to say now that they're not going to be financially responsible!" Her tone was beyond incredulous. "And *he* was in the wrong, after all. He left you! He *stranded* you in front of all those people! He humiliated you!"

"Yeah, I know," Chloe said, the sting coming back twice as strong. "I can't believe this. I had no idea they'd stoop this low."

"I'm going to sue those bastards," her father said. "For every last cent. And I'll *win,* damn it. I don't care what kind of flesh-eating lawyers those Suttons have!"

Chloe winced. Actually, she did know the kind of lawyers the Suttons had. Even though it seemed clear that Chloe and her family were the wronged parties, by the time those pin-striped sharks were finished, they'd probably convince a judge that Chloe pay Gerald for mental cruelty or something. They were that good and that vicious.

"We're on a fixed income, Chloe," her mother pleaded. "We were so happy to be able to retire two years ago, and I was so sorry we couldn't help more with the wedding, but there's no way we can pay for this."

"I have some savings," Chloe said, mentally flashing through her bankbook. "And I can probably break into my retirement fund. I can pay for most of what I need to."

"But that will wipe you out completely!" her mother said, aghast.

"It's fine. I'll just live here until I can get back up on my feet," Chloe said staunchly. "It was what I was planning to do anyway. Besides, we're going to need to divide up the house now, as well. I might be able to wring some concessions out of him on that one."

"Good luck with that," her father commented. "If his mother has anything to say about it, you're not getting nearly the market value for that thing. Hell, she may try to get *you* to buy *him* out."

"She's a demon," her mother added. "I try not to talk badly about anyone, but I have never met anyone as evil as that woman!"

"You're right on that one," Chloe agreed. "Let me call Gerald, see what's going on. There has to be a solution to this."

"Oh, I hope you're right." Her mother sounded like a fluttering, wounded bird.

Chloe left the room and headed for her old bedroom, her heart pounding with nerves and frustration. It was one thing for Gerald to humiliate her, to decide that he didn't want her and leave her in the lurch. But for his family to screw over her parents, who had done absolutely *nothing* to them except give birth to an unsuitable wife for their golden son....

She pounded Gerald's phone number into her cell phone.

"Hello?" she heard him say.

"How could you?" she asked without preamble.

He took a second. "Chloe," he said with a low, rumbling sigh that clearly said he had been waiting for this to happen. She was surprised he had picked up the call at all, but then, he never checked his caller ID. She imagined he wouldn't make the same mistake next time. "Listen, things just...happen sometimes."

"No, things don't just happen," she countered. "You deciding to cheat on me doesn't just happen. You deciding to not come to our wedding doesn't just happen. And your rich family sticking my poor parents with the bill for that damned reception certainly doesn't *just happen,* Gerald!"

"That's my mother, not me," Gerald said, and at least there was the slightest note of apology.

"So *you* pay for it, then!"

"You know I don't have that kind of money," he said and then stopped at her snort of disbelief. "Not liquid, anyway. I can't get my hands on that kind of cash!"

"Yes, you can," she said. "I've seen your books, remember?"

"That's the architectural firm's money," he said dismissively. "And you were just a secretary."

Her blood boiled at that. "I might've been just a secretary," she said in a lethal voice, "but I know more about accounting than you ever did."

"Well, I don't have the money," Gerald said. "And I didn't get married…I didn't eat any of the food, I didn't use the hall, none of that. You and your family did!"

"We couldn't get the money back, you idiot!" She couldn't help it. "What, did you think I'd get a refund because my fiancé didn't show up?"

"Listen, all I know is you're doing plenty of things that I didn't do and you're expecting me to pay for it!" Gerald's voice grew irate. "Like your little honeymoon jaunt!"

That sentence hit Chloe like a bucket of ice water. "What was that?"

"I got a call from that ship captain saying you went ahead and took the cruise without me," Gerald said, his voice sharp and vaguely triumphant. "I could've gotten a refund on *that,* but no, you just went ahead and took it!"

Chloe felt her cheeks redden. Yes, she had gone ahead and used the cruise—among other things. "I suppose you're right there," she said.

"Damned right I'm right!"

"So I'll pay for the cruise," she said, "and you can pay me for the rest of the wedding stuff, and we'll call it a day."

"No, you'll pay for the cruise and then you can just call our lawyers," Gerald said. "There's nothing in writing that says the Sutton family is responsible for half of those bills. You don't even have a legal leg to stand on."

Chloe knew that Gerald had a mercenary side—she'd seen

it occasionally at the firm. But this wasn't him. This, she could tell, was his mother. He was all but channeling her words. And for that woman, it wasn't about the money. It was about punishing the classless little "secretary" who had believed she could social climb by marrying the precious Sutton son. No matter how much Chloe had tried to convince the woman she was marrying Gerald because she loved him, the mother had refused to let go. And now she was doing everything she could to crush Chloe and her family into the ground.

"How is it," Chloe mused, "that I never noticed what an unbelievable liar and cheat you could be?"

"Yeah, well…" Gerald spluttered, then stopped, obviously unable to come up with a reply.

"All right then," she said. "The house. We just bought a house together. What about that?"

"I don't feel like talking about all this right now, Chloe."

"Well, you're going to have to!"

"No, I won't," he said. "I've got a dinner date with Simone and I don't have time to talk."

He threw that in just to hurt her—to force her to hang up. *Simone.* Chloe remembered seeing her around the firm occasionally. She was the daughter of a family friend. She had to be maybe twenty-three years old, just out of college. She would have the right breeding. Hell, they had a house in the same neighborhood as the Suttons. She probably was handpicked by Gerald's mother.

"Besides, I think that's also being handled by our lawyers. I don't think we should talk again, Chloe," Gerald said, finishing off his one-two punch of cruelty. "This has all been way too upsetting."

Well, God forbid you get upset by all of this.

"This isn't the end of it," Chloe said.

"It is for me," he said. "Goodbye, Chloe."

And with that, he hung up.

Chloe sat there for a second, on the edge of her childhood bed, listening to the dial tone ringing in her ear before finally shutting off the phone.

Oh, my God. Oh, my God.

It was a good thing she didn't have an action plan, she thought inanely, because anything she could've planned would have been torpedoed after a conversation like that. She didn't know he was capable of that kind of meanness. She didn't know anyone was.

Chloe plowed through her archived boxes of paperwork. She hadn't moved the boxes to the new house, thankfully. With her retirement fund, her savings and selling a few things, she should be able to cover the wedding bills so her parents wouldn't have to. She'd even be able to cover a few months' worth of mortgage on the house. *Of course, with Gerald's logic, if I'm not living there I shouldn't have to pay a dime,* she thought, depressed. But she got the uneasy feeling that he'd let the place foreclose and ruin her credit out of spite, so she budgeted for that, too. Leaving her with…

Not very much. Actually, less than not very much.

I have got to get a job, she thought frantically. Something that paid as well as her last job, if not better. Oh, and there was another thing—what kind of reference was she going to get when her last employer was the same slimeball that had put her in this position? Not to mention the fact that the economy in town wasn't that great. She'd looked into temping, just a little, after she'd quit working for Gerald. Despite her skills, she didn't have the degree or the title necessary to command the top-dollar hourly rate. And it could be a while before she got another permanent job, with all these obstacles.

She could just cry.

She knew her parents were worried about her, but she also knew they were in no position to help her, and she wasn't going to ask. She didn't want to beg money from her relatives, either, even if they could help…the Wintons weren't really all that affluent a clan. There was a solution here, she thought as she took out a pad of paper amidst the piles strewed on her parents' kitchen table. She just had to find it.

Then, out of nowhere, one part of her conversation with Gerald hit her.

So I'll pay for the cruise….

Which meant that Gerald had stiffed Jack, as well. And she got the feeling Jack was in no position to lose a couple thousand dollars.

She felt immediately guilty, even though Jack had persuaded her to go ahead with the trip. Of course, Jack had a lot better chance of breaking even than she did. If he did some things differently…advertised differently, made a few changes, he would probably not only break even, but do very well financially.

And then, the smallest ribbon of hope started to curl through her. He *could* do well if he had the right partner. And she had an idea of just who that partner could be.

JACK WINCED, EVEN though the chef he was interviewing over the phone couldn't see it. "Wow. That much, huh?"

"I think you'll find my services well worth it," the applicant said haughtily.

For that damned much money, the guy had better be serving the food on gold platters, Jack thought. "Well, I'm afraid that's out of the price range I was hoping to offer."

The chef gave a considering sniff. "What range did you have in mind?"

Jack said it and then winced again when the guy laughed. "Hey, you get to cook on a private yacht," Jack added defensively. "A lot of people find that to be a perk."

"Well, I think I'll keep looking," the chef said dismissively, and then hung up.

Jack crossed the name off his list. Most of the calls he'd dealt with this week had been more polite, at least, even if the outcome had always been the same. He'd gotten lucky when he'd found Kenneth—a young guy fresh out of culinary school and a cooking genius. He would try the school again, but they were midsemester, and he needed a warm body ASAP to cook for his next charter clients. They were already being difficult, right up to writing specifically what menu they wanted and what sort of sheets. If he tried to pass off grilled cheese sandwiches on them, he got the feeling they would not only not pay him, they'd probably bring him to court for false advertising or something.

Why couldn't they all be like Chloe? he thought with a note of anxiety. She had been the perfect passenger, the perfect client…just great to have around.

Then the mere thought of her brought up a whole stew of emotions that he'd been trying to keep buried, so he quickly switched gears. At least he'd found a masseuse, also a recently graduated type who was willing to take a lower rate in exchange for "experience." He hadn't met her, but he hoped she'd work out. He'd been lucky with Helen, too. The new masseuse had made it quite clear that she didn't clean things—and since he wasn't quite sure how he was going to pay for the chef at this point, he figured he'd be cleaning cabins by himself until his financial situation improved.

Well, idiot, you're the one who wanted his own boat.

He sighed, ignoring his conscience's mental castigation.

Yes, he had dreamed of having his own private charter yacht. He loved his life…most of the time. But he had to admit the life of a sea captain was a lot less sexy and free than he'd originally thought back when he was a teenager in military school. Then, the thought of having his own ship and doing what he wanted when he wanted had seemed like heaven on earth.

Little did he know that heaven apparently required a lot of money and a butt load of paperwork.

Stay focused, he counseled himself. He could bitch and moan later. The important thing now was making sure this cruise went off without a hitch so he could get paid, so he could get the bank off his back and quiet some of his more wily creditors. The worst being the loan holder for the *Rascal.*

As much as he might complain about the problems and hassles of ownership, it would be even worse to lose his ship completely.

Two hours later, he had to admit he was starting to sink into despair. He had to find a chef and he was running out of time. He needed a miracle.

"Jack?"

He looked toward the voice calling out from the dock. And for a second his mind went completely blank. "Chloe?" he finally said, uncomprehending.

"Yup," she said shyly, shifting her weight from one foot to the other. She was wearing a pair of jeans and a T-shirt with a pair of canvas tennis shoes, looking bright and casual and nervous. "I bet you weren't expecting to see me back this soon."

He wasn't expecting to see her back ever, he thought. "It's a surprise," he finally commented.

"A bad one?"

He shook his head quickly. "No! No. Of course not." And

it wasn't—he felt better in the flash of a second than he had in the past three days. "Come on up."

She walked up the gangplank much more nimbly than she had the first time she came on board the *Rascal*. Good grief, had that only been ten days ago? It seemed like a lifetime.

"How are things going?" she said when she reached him. Her whiskey-colored eyes almost glowed in the setting sunlight.

He almost hugged her, but considering how he'd said goodbye to her, physical contact probably wasn't the brightest idea. "Things are going…" He thought about it, how he might put a good face on it. Then he sighed. "Things suck, actually. How 'bout you?"

She laughed, a short, harsh sound. "I'm right there with you, pal." Then her laughter cut off and she looked sorrowful. "I hear that Gerald wouldn't pay you."

That son of a bitch, Jack thought—but if anybody would know about Gerald's qualities firsthand, it'd be his ex-fiancée. "Yeah," he said.

"I went on the cruise, so I ought to be the one to pay you," she said.

For a second, Jack felt a ray of hope. Of course she'd be take-charge and pay for the cruise. He might have guessed that not only would Chloe be a cool passenger and an amazing woman, but his financial savior to boot!

Then he remembered—she wasn't working and she'd said she was too broke for massages. "I don't want you going under just because you feel you owe me," he said quickly.

Did I just say that? he thought. He didn't think he was a bad guy or anything, but practicalities and business generally came before emotions, women and especially emotional women.

So how did Chloe keep bringing out this foolish, noble side of him?

"I'll admit it, I don't have the money," she said, and his spirit sank a little.

"No problem," he said. "Don't worry about it. I'll figure out something. After all, I twisted your arm to get you to come—it's pretty much my fault."

"No, I intend to pay you," she insisted. "But I wanted to discuss something with you first."

He shrugged. He wondered if she wanted to talk about their week together. It had been amazing—and confusing. And he was in no state, honestly, to deal with it right now. Not with all the rest of his life crashing down around his ears.

"Gerald refused to pay for his half of the wedding, as well," she said instead.

Considering he'd steeled himself for an entirely different sort of conversation, her casual comment jolted him. "That bastard!"

"Yeah, that's pretty much what I said." She smiled that wry smile of hers. "Not only that, but he's sort of holding our house hostage. I'm going to need to wade through the whole mess with his family's lawyers, and believe me, those guys are no joke."

"So I've heard," Jack said, remembering Gerald's high-pitched threat.

"I had to raid my savings to pay for all the wedding stuff. Even wiped out my retirement," she said. She wasn't dramatic, she wasn't even near tears. She just sounded strong and determined. "So I'm going to need to make mortgage payments to keep my credit clear and I'm going to have to find a job—but that's going to be kind of tight for the short term. And I'm going to need to hire a lawyer."

"Wow," he murmured. "And I thought I was in a jam."

"The thing is, I need to make a mint in a relative hurry," she said.

Then she stared at him. He didn't mind—he was enjoying the view of her himself—but he wasn't tracking where she was going with this.

"I want to make you a proposition."

His body tightened at her words. The last time she'd propositioned him…the warmth hit him in a rush. "What kind of proposition?" he barely got out, suddenly forgetting all of his financial woes in the face of a wave of desire.

She cleared her throat. "A business proposition," she said.

He blinked. Why was he having so much trouble following her? Okay, so he wasn't thinking with his head, but still. "What sort of business proposition?"

"I think you could be making a lot more money on your cruises and booking a lot more," she said. "And I'll bet you could save a lot with your bookkeeping and consolidating your banking."

His eyes widened. "I'm listening."

"I may not be much of a sailor, but, well, I am a kick-butt manager," she said, blushing a little. "I think I could help you a lot. I think we might be able to help each other."

He sighed. "That sounds great, Chloe, but there's one problem. I'm broke, remember? I couldn't afford to hire you, much as I'd love to help."

"I'm not asking you to hire me," she corrected gently. "I'm asking you to let me help you in exchange for a share of the profits." She paused, then smiled shyly. "Sort of as a partner."

A partner. He took a physical step back, he was so surprised. The *Rascal* was his ship and his alone. He'd never in a million years considered sharing it with anybody else.

"We'd need to talk about it more," she said, her voice soothing and persuasive. "Obviously, we don't want to jump into anything. But at the same time, we both are in a crunch and we don't have a lot of time to waste. So...are you up for discussing it?"

He thought about it. She was cool, no question—but that was as a passenger. And what she was proposing was a long shot, at best. Even more confusing, they'd be working together, in close proximity more than likely. After the week they'd spent together, full of fun, sun and rebound sex, what would that do to their working relationship?

It had disaster written all over it.

"I don't..."

"I'll also act as your cook," she offered. "And I can do housekeeping, too."

He swallowed hard. "When can you start?"

5

UNTIL RECENTLY, CHLOE had never propositioned a man in her life. Now she'd done it twice, to the same man, in a two-week time span. And, amazingly enough, he'd said yes. Both times.

She had no idea if she was making the biggest mistake of her life or what, but whatever she was doing, she was doing it quickly.

She looked again at the menu plan the charter passengers had ordered. Jack should have charged them extra, considering the ingredients they were requiring. He was charging too low as it was, considering the amenities he was offering. At the same time, she wasn't sure that he was offering the right amenities. She was shocked to find out he didn't have a business plan. She might've been "just a secretary" with Gerald, but she'd learned all about business from the architectural firm. She'd apparently picked up more than she'd thought. She'd certainly picked up enough to know that Jack could be doing a lot better. With any luck, they would be making more money in less time, and she'd make enough to not only cover her share of the mortgage until she could sell the dumb thing but pay a lawyer to get the rest of what she was owed from Gerald. It was a tall order, but she would persevere.

Of course, there were a few other problems to tackle along with her new partnership.

Jack walked into the galley, looking harried. "How's lunch coming?"

"Don't tell me—they're asking for it," Chloe joked.

"Demanding, actually," Jack said. "Man, if I didn't need the money..."

"We're all doing stuff we wouldn't ordinarily be doing," she said, finishing the last decorative touches on the lunch plates. "Don't worry, they're taken care of."

"Thanks," he said. "They're all set up on the bow deck—that's up front. I'll carry it out if you could just clean up afterward."

"No problem," she agreed easily. "And let them know I'll be cleaning their cabin while they're enjoying lunch. That ought to chill them out."

Jack smiled, the first really relaxed smile she'd seen him wear all day. "How did I get lucky enough to find you?" he said, giving her a teasing tug on her ponytail.

She turned and winked at him, enjoying the relaxed, joking atmosphere. It reminded her of her own week on the *Rascal*.

He reached for the plates in front of her, accidentally brushing a forearm against her breasts and causing a bolt of heat to disperse from the pit of her stomach. She drew in a breath in surprise—and, she hated to admit, pleasure.

He paused, his hands on the plates, staring at her, his gold-green eyes practically luminescent in the dim fluorescent lights of the galley. For a second, it was as if the guests—hell, the whole boat—disappeared.

She remembered that sensation, too. In fact, she remembered it all too well.

She forced herself to clear her throat. "They're probably complaining about how late lunch is," she said, her voice a touch too husky.

It seemed to take him a second to register what she said. He gave her a wobbly smile. "Right. Right. I'll just get these out to them, then."

He took the tray, balancing the heft of it with ease, and then headed out into the hallway.

When the door closed behind him, Chloe let out a deep breath, feeling more heat flush through her. That was a close one.

She hadn't brought up their previous arrangement, and neither had he. She hadn't done anything remotely physical with him—not even shaking his hand, she realized. It was as if they were knife fighters, circling each other warily in a pit somewhere. Not that they were adversarial. They were just…cautious. And considering how explosive their brief physical encounters had been, she didn't think they were going overboard. If anything, she wondered if maybe they could be more careful.

If I react this way when we're in the same room for a day, she thought, her heart rate starting to pick up in speed, *what am I going to do when we're out at sea for a week at a time, on one small ship?*

They were going to have to deal with it, she thought. She would probably have to say something. Put everything in black-and-white. Make everything crystal clear. She'd made too many assumptions and rushed blindly ahead when she'd been with Gerald, and look where that had gotten her.

The thought of Gerald was the dash of cold water she needed. She straightened her shoulders and headed for the door, ready to talk to Jack immediately.

She almost got knocked out by the door swinging in. It was Jack, without a tray.

"They seem happy," he said, sounding relieved. "Thank God you're a good cook."

"Yes. Well." *Okay, here's your shot,* she told herself. "You know, Jack…"

He sighed, nudging her chin to look at her. "You are amazing and you are wickedly competent."

She paused, thrown off course by his compliment. "Uh, thanks."

"And I get the feeling that if anybody could help bring the *Rascal* around, it'd be you."

She smiled, squirming a little on the inside. "Well, I'm certainly going to try."

"I have to admit, I was uneasy with the idea of a partnership, though," he said, moving past her and leaning against the galley's counter, crossing his arms. "And if I weren't in such a jam…hell, I like you, Chloe, but I never would've said yes."

She nodded, frowning slightly at the turn of the conversation. Of course, this would make her decision that they shouldn't have sex again somewhat easier to say.

"But as long as we're in this, I think we ought to have a few ground rules."

"I think so, too," she agreed.

"Let me finish," he countered, putting up a hand. "We both need this too much to get…distracted. And after, well, the last time we were together…"

He let the sentence peter out.

She swallowed hard. "You know, I was about to say we should probably agree not to sleep together again."

Now he looked more than relieved—he looked as if he'd gotten a stay of execution. "Exactly."

She couldn't help but feel a little insulted at the depth of his tone. Sure, she'd been about to propose the same thing— but did he have to sound so happy about it? She knew she was probably being unreasonable, but the past few weeks had been hell on her ego as it was. She had to scrape together what dignity she could find.

"Not that our time together wasn't great," he hastily amended. "It was. You know it was. I mean, it was…great," he finished lamely.

"Don't help," she murmured.

He sighed heavily, frowning in return. "I can't afford to screw this up," he said in his brusque business voice. "And neither can you."

She nodded. He definitely had a point there.

"So no matter what else, this has got to be the most important thing between us. Agreed?" He put a hand out.

She nodded. "Agreed."

She took his hand. It was broad, calloused, strong…hot. She instantly flashed to the feel of his hand on her shoulder. On her breast.

As if she'd touched a hot stove, she jerked her hand away.

"Okay, then," he said. Was it her imagination or did his voice sound strained? "Just business."

"Just business," she echoed weakly.

They stared at each other for a long minute. Then the door swung open again.

"Morning."

It was Inga, the new masseuse that Jack had hired for this cruise. She was young, about twenty-four years old. She had long blond hair that Chloe suspected wasn't really blond. Chloe also suspected the girl hadn't been born with the name Inga. She was tall, closer to Jack's height than Chloe's, and she had the impossibly perfect body of a model, thin and willowy. The only counterpoint to that was her larger-than-life-chest. Again, not a factory original. Chloe knew she was probably being unkind, but the woman somehow rubbed her the wrong way.

"What's for breakfast?"

"It's noon," Chloe pointed out.

"Oh." Inga yawned, stretching her arms overhead and causing her chest to stick out even more. "So what's for lunch, then?"

Chloe looked at Jack, who shrugged apologetically. "There are sandwiches in the fridge," she said. "Help yourself."

"Is that all?"

Chloe gritted her teeth. "They're good. Try one," she said. "I have to clean out the Whitneys' cabin."

As Chloe headed to the door, she saw Inga walk up to Jack. "Maybe I could make us something," she said, her tone deliberately provocative.

Chloe felt a jolt of jealousy sting through her and she let the door close.

Of course, Chloe's relationship with Jack was strictly business. That didn't mean he had to keep *all* his work relationships that way, she realized.

Ignoring the angry burn in her chest, she went to clean the cabin and think of other ways of ignoring Jack, Inga and the whole situation.

How COOL IS IT THAT we got Chloe?" Ace asked Jack two weeks after she'd joined the crew.

Jack made a noncommittal grunt, keeping his attention riveted on his desk. "She's booked three more cruises for us," he said, marveling at the fact that she'd managed to get even more money for them. He wasn't sure about the brochure redesign she wanted—that would cost money, and he didn't see the point in fixing what he had—but some of the other stuff she'd wanted to institute seemed smart.

"She's a godsend," Ace said in reverent tones.

"Yeah, well, that godsend just took away your free

weekend," Jack countered mildly. "We've got another cruise tomorrow, so get your R & R tonight."

"Oh," Ace said, a little less enthused. "Well, that's okay. I don't want this girl I'm seeing to get too committed too quickly anyway."

Ace walked out, leaving Jack to ponder that statement. He used to feel that way, he remembered with some fondness. Back when he actually, you know, had time to have a fun social life. The kind that involved sex with hot women that had no future entanglements.

Now he had a hot woman, no sex and all the perils of potential future entanglements. True, he also had the beginnings of what looked like a beautiful business relationship.

He wasn't sure how he felt about the trade-off.

Chloe walked into his cabin, her hair tumbling around her shoulders. She was wearing her reading glasses, something he found cute in a librarian-sexy way. If only she was wearing a plaid skirt and some saddle shoes.

He shook his head, dismissing the prurient picture his mind conjured. "What's up?"

"Sorry. I just wanted to see if you'd gone over the brochure stuff," she said. She was biting her lip. "And I know I booked those three cruises kind of close together, but, well, you know."

"I know. We need the money," he said, sighing. "Well, I didn't have a life anyway."

"Yeah, me neither," she chimed in with a little sigh.

He instantly felt badly. It had been two weeks since their agreement and a full month since her disastrous near-wedding. That meant it had been *three* weeks since the last time he'd seen her naked.

Not that he was counting.

"So, anyway, the brochure," he said, forcing himself to focus. "I still don't know why we can't use the ones we've got."

He was sitting at his desk and he didn't have another chair—space was at a premium in the ship, and he didn't really have palatial quarters. Chloe sat at the edge of his bed, pulling out the notebook she always seemed to have on her. She put the end of the pen between her lips, nibbling thoughtfully.

It wasn't supposed to be erotic, he knew that. Still, Chloe, in his bed, with something in her mouth.

Man, you have got to get laid or something. You're losing it.

"Jack, you're offering a four-star service, but these brochures look…well, two-star at best," she said.

He winced. "Please, don't spare my feelings. Just tell me what's really on your mind."

"I'm sorry, I know you worked hard on them," she said. "But if I learned anything at the architectural firm, it's appearances matter. Especially with big-money clients. That's why the food I serve has all those 'frilly touches' you think are so girlie. It's all about presentation," she finished, her tone firm.

He sighed. "Yeah, well, that's going to cost me some money, Chloe. And we sort of need the money right now, remember?"

She smiled. "I've got a friend from when I worked at the firm. She's a designer, and she's going to give us a discount. And if I can sweet-talk the printer who did my wedding invitations…"

He grimaced. The invitations she'd spent tons of money on for the wedding that never happened. How that fiancé of hers could sleep at night baffled him. "You're probably right…hell, I trust your judgment more than my own most days. Why don't you get me some pricing, and we'll see how it goes," he prevaricated.

She smiled at him, and suddenly he felt warm. Not sexy warm, although he always had a low-grade fire burning whenever the woman was around. It was a different kind of warmth. A sort of glow. She looked at him as if he were a superhero. Which was stupid, considering he hadn' really done anything but say he'd think about it. Still, i wasn't as though he was going to ask her to stop looking at him that way.

She got up, then rubbed her lower back.

"You okay?" he asked, concerned.

"Just out of shape," she said, although from what he could see, her shape was fine. From what he *remembered,* her shape was more than fine. Hell, her stamina more than matched his "I'm not used to being on my feet this much, and between the cooking and the cleaning…"

Now guilt hit him hard. "And you're staying up all hours working on this stuff," he said. "Damn, Chloe. Ace is right We are too lucky to have found you."

She grinned with delight at this. He got up, stood next to her. Against his better judgment, he reached out and rubbed against her back. She made a low noise.

He stopped immediately. "I didn't hurt you, did I?"

"No-o," she stammered, then he could've sworn she was blushing. "It felt good, actually."

"You're probably overdue for some body work," he said

He didn't mean for it to be suggestive—honestly, he really didn't. But he immediately realized how close they were standing when he said that. And, to his horror and fascination, she leaned ever so slightly closer to him. He could smell that vanilla-laced scent of hers, and his body reacted as i always did when he got too close to her. *Full steam ahead.*

Her eyes were huge and golden-brown, staring into his

Her breathing was shallow. "You're probably right," she murmured. "I could probably use…something."

Oh, man, did he have a few suggestions on what that *something* could be.

A knock on the door interrupted them, and to his relief, she took a step back. Actually, she jumped away, which caused her to trip and tumble onto his bed. "Yes?" he said in a strangled voice as he quickly sat at his desk.

It was Inga, his new hire. She took in the scene—Chloe was sitting on the bed by this point, and he was at the desk, so everything looked proper, he assumed. Still, Inga's eyes narrowed with suspicion.

"Something you needed?" he asked, glad that his voice was even and that his at-attention lower body was hidden by the heavy wood desk.

"Just wanted to see if it was okay if I stayed on board until tomorrow," Inga drawled, her blue eyes going low-lidded. She was just a kid, in her early twenties, and from what he could see, she was a classic good-time girl…that is, always looking for a good time, and never being disappointed. She'd said a few things that suggested she was angling for a good time with him specifically. He hadn't encouraged her, but then, he hadn't done anything to discourage her, either, he supposed. At any other point, he might've considered it. But now, especially with Chloe on board, and after their week together…

He shook his head. No, getting involved with someone he worked with was out of the question.

He threw a quick glance at Chloe, the way her eyes widened.

Well, getting involved with someone I work with is discouraged…not completely out of the question.

He shook his head again. He was completely losing it.

"It's not all right?" Inga said, puzzled by his expression.

"Huh? Uh...I guess it's okay." He shrugged. Jose had stayed on board on occasion, and Kenneth used to stay on board all the time when he was "between housing," as he put it, meaning temporarily homeless. Jack wondered what the deal was with Inga. "Most people would rather spend their shore time with friends, though."

"I could use the break," Inga said breezily, shooting a quick look at Chloe. "Are you staying overnight?"

He assumed Inga asked because she and Chloe were sharing a cabin at the moment. Both being new to the ship and women, it made sense for them to bunk together and it meant fewer cleaning duties for Chloe. Besides, he didn't want another repeat of what had happened with Kenneth and Helen, and Ace occasionally had a wandering eye—better not to leave the women in their own cabins just yet.

Suddenly he remembered Ace's admiration of Chloe, and his chest tightened uncomfortably.

It was definitely better that the women not have their own cabins.

Chloe shook her head, looking stern. "I'm staying onshore," she said, and there was an edginess in her voice. "I've got a lot of work still to do."

Jack felt badly about that, but Inga looked pleased for no good reason. At least none that he could discern. Maybe she liked staying up late and Chloe didn't or vice versa.

"But I'll be back tomorrow, bright and early, ready for our charter," Chloe added, taking Inga's pleased expression down a notch.

"And you stay here, right, Jack?" Inga asked.

He shrugged. "Well, yeah. I live here."

"That's so cool," she said, her drawl making it sound more like *kew-el*. "Well...I guess it'll just be you and me, then."

He tilted his head, putting the pieces together. Okay, he was pretty dense, but even *he* knew a come-on when he heard it laid out that blatantly.

"If you could just sign off on my hours—I like to keep track with my own time card. Oops!" Inga said brightly. He hadn't noticed that she was holding a pen, but she dropped it. And then turned and very slowly and deliberately picked it up, facing away from him. Her butt was just *there,* perfectly rounded in her low-riding shorts. He couldn't help it. His eyes bugged out slightly.

He turned to look at Chloe, who was also staring, her eyes wide.

"Sorry about that," Inga said as she slowly straightened and looked over her shoulder. Then she sashayed to his desk, leaning over and giving him full view of her cleavage as he hastily scribbled a signature on her time card, which only had two patrons on it. "Okay, I'm going to just grab some stuff at the grocery store to put in the fridge. But then I'll see you tonight," she said, loads of promise dripping in her voice. With that, she walked out.

He sat frozen. *Like my life was not complicated enough.* This little girl had him in her sights like a sniper—and he wasn't sure that a pure good time was the only thing on her agenda anymore. Anyone that determined made him uneasy.

Well…except Chloe.

He turned to Chloe, at a loss for words at Inga's behavior. Not that he owed her anything, but, well, he had slept with Chloe. Just because they weren't doing it now didn't mean that he wouldn't feel something if some guy started hitting on her right in front of him.

To his surprise, Chloe burst out into giggles. "Man, now there was an example of presentation!"

He chuckled, too, although he felt a bubble of irritation. "You're not honestly going to leave me alone with this woman all night," he said. "You've got to have mercy."

"I don't know," Chloe mused. "She's young, she's pretty...."

He wondered if she was fishing for something, some inkling of his intentions—or if she was just making fun of him. "She's a barracuda," he said. "If she got me into her clutches, you wouldn't even find my shoes in the morning. Couldn't identify me with dental records."

Chloe's laughter rose. "What, does that little girl scare you?"

He grinned. "Right down to my socks. Come on, you can't just ditch me here with little miss Daisy Dukes," he pleaded.

She sighed. "If you're that frightened, I can just hit an Internet café and come back."

He leaned back with a huge sigh of relief, which, he realized, he was only half joking with. "Thank you."

"Hey, it's only because I need you hale and hearty to make this business work," she said, standing up. "Otherwise, I'd let you fend for yourself."

"You're a hard woman," he said.

She paused at the doorway, her joking smile melting into something more hesitant. "Jack?"

He was already thinking about the charter and still in a jovial mood. "Yeah?"

"You know, if you decided you wanted to...be alone on the boat...with anyone," she said slowly, "you could just tell me. That'd be all right."

At first, he wasn't sure what she was talking about. Then, abruptly, he did realize what she was saying.

If you want to sleep with Inga, I'd be all right with it.

He supposed she thought he'd appreciate it. For no good reason whatsoever, it made him mad.

"If I decide to," he said, his voice cold, "I'll be sure to let you know."

She didn't flinch, but he still got that impression—and felt like even more of a jerk.

"You do that," she said and fled.

He sighed, putting his head down on his desk with an audible thump.

"Smooth move," he chided himself. But, damn it, he knew he had the right to have sex with other people if he wanted. They weren't involved. They hadn't had a relationship. It was just business.

But the bottom line was he didn't want to have sex with anyone else. He still wanted to have sex with Chloe.

And, damn it, whether they could or not, he wanted her to feel the same way. If that wasn't stupid, he didn't know what was.

CHLOE SAT AT THE Internet café, not too far from the Coronado docks, checking her e-mail. She'd already told her parents she'd be staying on the *Rascal* that evening instead of staying with them. She felt relieved, actually. She'd much rather stay on board, even if she was sharing a room with Inga, than go back to her parents' house. Her parents had not been as pleased when she'd called.

"When will you be able to stop with all this?" her mother had asked plaintively. "It just seems so…well, so frivolous."

"I'm not getting any responses to my résumé," Chloe had answered. "And even if I did, the admin jobs that are coming up wouldn't be enough to cover my mortgage. This is somewhat crazy, but you know the adage—desperate times call for desperate measures."

"Your father and I could take out a loan...."

"No, Mom," Chloe had said sharply. And that had been the end of that. Still, Chloe had done the calculations. She was earning a percentage from Jack, and it was pretax. She was going to have a hell of a time when taxes finally came due, but for now she was preserving her credit rating. Gerald was still avoiding her calls and insisting that she only converse through his family lawyers. Well, she now had their phone numbers and was trading e-mails with them on a regular basis.

As she typed in her password and waited for her mail to come up, the scene she'd just been through with Jack and Inga played through her mind inexplicably. She'd never really been the jealous type. Of course, with Gerald cheating on her, maybe she should have been, she admitted to herself with some bitterness. But it had never occurred to her that she ought to be jealous. If Gerald or any of her other boyfriends had felt the need to be with someone else, then she wasn't going to stop them. She was understanding, if nothing else. Some of her girlfriends had mentioned that she was too accommodating.

When Inga had made such a flagrant flirt of herself, it was all Chloe could do not to stand up and plant a foot right on that ostentatious denim-covered derriere of hers. The nerve! To just...just *throw* herself at Jack when Chloe was sitting right there!

It was tacky was what it was.

And Jack had reacted like a typical male, his eyes almost popping out of their sockets.

Although, what made all of this worse was Chloe had absolutely no right to be angry with Jack over his reaction. It wasn't as if they were in a relationship. For that matter, it wasn't as if they were in a fling. He'd insisted on no sex, and

if he hadn't, she would have. So they were business asso-
ciates, all the more reason why Inga wouldn't necessarily
assume they were anything more personal. And Inga was
twenty-four, a young twenty-four at that, and obviously used
to getting her way with sexual wiles. So if she wanted to pull
some ploys on her captain and boss, why was Chloe taking
it so personally?

Because he's mine.

Chloe sighed. The thought was completely irrational and
stupid besides. She'd been engaged, been on the very doorstep
of being married a month ago. Maybe she hadn't loved Gerald
as much as she could have, but she'd been loyal and committed, and in a way, she was still heartbroken—if not for him,
then for the dream of a loyal and committed relationship. One
that she knew she'd never have with someone like Jack. So
what was she doing? Mooning over him? Was the sex so incredible that now she was fantasizing about a white picket
fence and forever with this man?

She closed her eyes. Admittedly, the sex *was* incredible.
But that wasn't the point of all this.

She glanced over her e-mail. Several "thanks, but no
thanks" responses to her applications for executive secretary
positions and office manager positions, employers who felt
she wasn't qualified enough or that she lacked references.
Thanks, Gerald. Then an e-mail from Gerald's family lawyers.

Miss Winton, the e-mail said, regarding the sale of the
house. We are in the process of selling it, but current
offers are not up to what we feel the house is worth. Mr.
Sutton feels quite sure that a more significant profit could
be made. We remind you that you are still responsible for
your half of the mortgage, since you are in fifty-fifty ownership of the deed. If you fail to pay, then we will have no

choice but to give full remuneration to Mr. Sutton once the house finally sells.

Chloe reread the e-mail twice just to be sure she understood what they were saying. Then she was so angry that her hands shook.

Gerald knew that she didn't have a job. It had been his idea, hadn't it? The thought was bitter. And now Gerald and his mother and his lawyers all thought that if they waited her out, she'd be so financially desperate that she'd agree to signing away her portion of the down payment and any money that might be made on the resale of the house, just so she wouldn't drown under the mortgage payments. They were making sure that not only was she financially destitute, she wouldn't be getting out of the hole they presumed she was digging for herself anytime soon.

The worst part about it was, it wasn't that Gerald even needed the money. His family certainly didn't need the money. No, this was some kind of punishment although what *she'd* done to deserve vengeance was beyond comprehension. Hadn't *he* been the one to abandon *her* at the altar here?

Had she been stupid? Or crazy? Had he always been this way? And if so, how did she miss all the signs?

How could I possibly have considered marrying someone this cruel?

She took a long, slow sip of her decaf coffee, the warm liquid thawing out the frozen numbness in her chest. No, he hadn't always been like this. In fact, she was willing to bet he wasn't really like this now. He wasn't cruel—deep down, he was very easygoing and amiable, hardly the gung ho, take-no-prisoners business type his own family wanted him to be. No, he was the way he had always been.

He was weak.

She looked out the window at the busy street beyond, almost meditative. She had been stupid, she privately admitted. She'd known he was weak, but she'd thought it made him endearing somehow. All her family were people who enjoyed running in and saving people, giving suggestions, taking charge. She'd ignored his weakness or worked around it or catered to it. When he'd wanted to dodge one of the crankier older partners in the firm, she'd come up with excuses. When something had gone wrong with a project, she'd helped him fix it or often figured out a way to shift the blame. She'd protected him and supported him. In short, she'd done what she'd done her whole life, and he'd seen how her strength could compensate for his weakness. She'd thought that made them a perfect team and so had he. The only real sticking point had been his family—his mother. That was the one woman Gerald simply could not stand up to. Chloe had done everything she could to work around Gerald's weakness there. She'd tried to win the woman over, which is why their wedding expenses had spiraled out of control in the first place. She'd thought that if she watched her step and jumped through whatever insane hoops the woman set out that she and Gerald would make it. It had caused enough of a strain that she should have seen—not only was Gerald (or any man) not worth it, but if that was the way their marriage was going to run, it wasn't going to make it anyway. But she hadn't.

Chloe got down to the last bitter drop of her coffee and realized that she had put herself into this mess as much as Gerald had.

She picked up her cell phone, grimacing with pain. Still, because she'd been stupid in the past didn't mean that she had to lie there and take it now. One of her father's other favorite sayings popped into her mind.

If you burn yourself on a stove twice, it ain't the stove's fault.

She wasn't surprised when Gerald didn't answer his phone; he hated confrontation, especially when he knew that, even if he didn't admit it, he was somehow at fault. She waited for the message prompt, then said in a clear, quiet voice; "Gerald, this is Chloe. I got word from your lawyers that you aren't satisfied with any of the offers on the house. I was also told that if I'm not able to keep up my end of the mortgage payments, you'll just take over—and take the down payment and any profit, as well. They act like it's some kind of magnanimous offer. Well, you and I both know that this is utter crap. I'm fairly certain this wasn't your idea, but I don't care. You're letting it happen, and *that is inexcusable.*"

Her voice had risen a few decibels, so she took a deep breath as her eyes started to tear up. She paused, then continued.

"I'll make the payments, don't worry about that. But it's *my house,* too. I'm bringing in my own Realtor, and you're not authorized to take or refuse any offers without my input. And before you send your damned form letter saying I should handle all this through your lawyers, don't worry, they'll hear this, too. But I want you to know this, Gerald—you're the one that walked out on me. You probably thought I'd been too much of a doormat the whole time we were together to fight you, no matter what you did. And you were almost right. One way or another, I want the house sold in one month. I repeat— *one month.* And I'll tell you right now—if you or your fancy lawyers try to make things difficult for me again, I'm going to make sure you're sorry you tried."

She clicked the phone off and then noticed that several of the surrounding patrons were staring at her over the edges of their laptops. She ignored them, packing up her belongings and throwing out her paper coffee cup. She headed for the door.

This is what happened when she didn't have a plan written out, she thought with grim determination as she headed back to her car. She was making enough to pay back Jack and make her mortgage payments, but her Mom was right—it was pretty frivolous when she had a war front with Gerald that she needed to be fighting. Jack and the ship were fun, but she couldn't focus on fun. She needed to unload the house, get some money, then get back into the real world.

Jack, as much as she liked him—and as weird as their "business relationship" was—wasn't real.

6

"WE HAD A WONDERFUL time," the new Mrs. Spencer said to Jack and Chloe, shaking their hands as they left the deck of the *Rascal*. Her young face was beaming.

"We might even come back for our anniversary!" Mr. Spencer said, also shaking Jack's hand. "Especially if you add fishing…"

"Oh, you and fishing," his bride said, taking his arm and winking at him.

"We're glad you had a good time," Chloe said. They waved to the couple as they watched them walk away. Then Chloe sighed. "Okay. I'm off to clean their cabin and do a quick pass in the galley. Our next charter couple comes in this afternoon. I feel so stupid—I didn't mean to book them that close."

Jack took a deep breath. Since their little conversation after Inga's display, he'd felt that things were tense, and what was worse, he got the feeling that he wasn't the main reason Chloe was unhappy. That was a good thing, of course—the last thing he needed was Chloe unhappy with him, considering their partnership. But the bad thing was, at least when he was the cause of unhappiness, he had a pretty good grip on what the problem was and what, if anything, he could do to fix it.

He hadn't really felt like fixing a woman's problems until he met Chloe. Probably because the woman looked as if she'd been carrying a boulder most of her life and trying to look cheerful while she was doing it, to boot.

"You're too hard on yourself," he said, wishing he could reach out and give her a hug. "Besides, after this next charter, I'll be able to cut you a check. The Spencers were generous with a tip in addition to their fare, so we're looking pretty good right now."

"That's good." She sounded relieved.

"You know," he ventured, following her to the honeymoon cabin and leaning against the door frame as she stripped the sheets, "you've been pretty quiet lately."

She threw the dirty laundry on the floor and got a new set out from a cupboard, making the bed quickly and efficiently. "Well, it's not like I've had a lot of free time to stand around gabbing," she said, and it was a little snappish for her.

"True enough." This was not going well at all. "I just was wondering…oh, hell. What's wrong? You've been upset since you hit that Internet café."

And since Inga made such an ass of herself with that pen-dropping trick. But he wasn't going to add that out loud—not even with a gun to his head. He wanted Chloe to be as attracted to him as he was to her, but that didn't mean he wanted her to be upset with him for the rest of her life, either. That would make working together hell, and he was starting to realize that being in business with Chloe was probably the best thing that had ever happened to him, and the *Rascal*.

She ignored the question until she'd plumped up the pillows and put the multicolored comforter back on the bed. Then she turned to him. "I've been having problems with Gerald."

Jack gritted his teeth. "I should've guessed."

"We're selling the house we bought together. It's been a headache trying to get enough cell phone reception to talk to his lawyers. But I think it can get done," she said. Then her cute heart-shaped face scrunched with determination. "No. It's *getting* done."

She sounded like a cross between a fairy princess and a drill sergeant, and he smirked. "That's my girl."

She looked at him, startled.

He wasn't sure what had prompted him to say that, so he cleared his throat. "So with the house sold, you'll be free and clear of the guy, right? That'll all be over?"

"Yeah," she said slowly. "Well, I could fight him for the wedding money he owes me. But I probably...I don't know. This has been hard enough."

"Is it that important?" Jack said, hating to see her so wracked. "Why don't you let him have the damned thing if it means that much to him? Just let it go?"

Her eyes widened, and he realized she was shocked at the question. "He's trying to screw me out of what's rightfully mine," she said. "He used me all the time, and I let him. He's trying to weasel out of this now just so he doesn't have to deal with his mother's anger. And I'm tired of letting him!"

Her cheeks turned pink with emotion, and her eyes flashed. Jack suddenly wanted to drive out and beat the crap out of Gerald, just on general principle. "You're right," he said. "I just...I don't want you to be upset, that's all."

After a few deep breaths, she shrugged. "That's real life for you," she said with a humorless laugh. "Upsetting."

It doesn't have to be.

Now Jack did go with his impulse. Before she could grab the dirty breakfast tray, he stepped in the room, the door shutting behind him, and he took her in a bear hug. It wasn't sexual. It was meant to comfort and reassure.

She tensed against him like a board for a minute, then she melted against his chest.

"It's going to be all right," Jack said, rubbing her back with small circles. "You're going to kick his ass."

She chuckled against him and he smiled. "I know," she said, pulling away, and he could see tears rimming her eyes. She brushed them away quickly, but not so quickly that he missed them. "I'm going to be fine. I just need to cover the mortgage until I get the thing sold and then I'll be able to start over." She grinned at him. "And then you'll finally be free of your workaholic semipartner."

He stared at her. He knew that this was temporary. Hell, he'd been nervous enough at first to insist that it be temporary. But he hadn't realized how well Chloe was going to mesh with his team or, for that matter, with him. He had known that he wanted her and liked her.

He was starting to suspect that he could grow to need her, and as disconcerting as that thought was, it was nothing compared to the thought of her just walking away.

"You know, you've been doing really well here," he said. "You like it here on the *Rascal,* don't you?"

She laughed. "I get to see the ocean every day and cook and hang out on deck in the sun when I'm not working," she said. "What's not to like?"

"I know we've been working hard, but it wouldn't have to be forever," he said. "I've been doing a lot of thinking and…this may sound nuts, but have you considered, you know…"

He trailed off as she stared at him, looking puzzled. "Have I considered what?" she finally prompted.

"Staying."

She blinked. Then she shook her head. "I enjoy the cooking, but the cleaning can be pretty wearing," she said.

"But you're good at everything else, too. The marketing and admin stuff," he said. "I was thinking maybe you could stay on as something more permanent. That we could continue this working relationship. Like, you know... partners."

There. He'd said it.

His stomach dropped as if he was on a roller coaster. *Whew.* Now he knew what guys who proposed felt like.

Funny that he should make that connection.

He didn't have time to think of the ramifications because he was too intent on Chloe's response. She looked dreamy for maybe a split second. Then she looked wary. "I don't...I hadn't really thought about it," she said slowly.

"Well, maybe you should," Jack said, sitting on the bed and nudging her to sit next to him. "You love it out here. I can tell. And you're really getting the hang of stuff."

"Yeah, but it's like...I don't know...a *vacation*," she said with a small laugh. "This isn't a real business."

"I beg your pardon," he said, offended.

"Well, I mean, it's a business for you," she said.

"And it's making your mortgage payments."

She digested that for a minute. Then she sighed. "I know. And it *has* been fun," she said as if she were only just realizing it. "But...there are all sorts of issues to think through. I'd need to make a list."

He barked out a laugh, then looked at her contritely when she glared at him. "Sorry. That's just so *you*. Why can't you just say, 'sure, why not?' Why not just roll with it?"

"Would you be okay with my being fifty-fifty partners?" she countered. "And would it be partnership in the business... or would I be able to partially own the ship?"

He jolted. He hadn't thought about it in terms of numbers and money and whatnot. And the *Rascal* was his. Chloe might be hell on wheels as far as getting organized and booking business, but this was his home and his boat!

She smirked. "Your expression of horror is one good reason why I'm not just rolling with it."

"Okay. I'll give you that one," Jack said, shaken. "But we could probably work out something. What other objections do you have?"

She looked at him...and suddenly there was a gleam in her eyes that he remembered. She leaned forward slowly, her face stopping just a few inches from his.

"There is one other complication."

He swallowed hard. His hands gripped the edge of the bed, forcing him not to just lean in response and close the distance between them. "Yeah?" he croaked instead.

"We'd want to keep it strictly business," she said. "And basically we'd be living together on the same ship. Close proximity..." she murmured, and there was one less inch separating them. "Constant contact."

She brushed a hand over his. He could feel her breath tickling his chin, and his body went hard immediately.

"We've managed this long," she said. "I don't know about you, but sometimes it's been challenging."

Challenging. If that wasn't the understatement of the year.

"I'm not trying to tease you here," she said, pulling back. "I'm trying to point out a fact. I got involved with a man I was working with before. I got burned...badly."

Lust warred with protectiveness as he took in her woebegone expression and the fact that her slight flush—and the way her breasts jutted out against her thin T-shirt—belied the fact that she was more than making a point. She was truly turned on.

He probably should have stopped himself, but by that point he didn't care.

"You won't get burned by me," he said and reached out, kissing her neck and swimming in her shivers. "I'm not like him. I'm not like anybody you've ever been with, Chloe."

She moaned and she gripped his arms, moving her head so her lips met his.

He kissed her, long and hard, his hands bunching at her waist until he pulled her into his lap. He couldn't believe how incredible she felt. She twisted until she was straddling him, her breasts crushed against his chest, his erection nestled at the juncture of her thighs. He cursed the denim between them, especially when her hips rolled slowly, grinding against him.

He knew it was nuts. They had passengers coming in a few hours. He had a million details to think of, and so did Chloe. But in that moment the only thing that mattered was the fact that he'd been on fire for her for the better part of a month and a half. It was like trying to deny a starving man food. He wanted—no, he *needed*—Chloe, and now that the floodgates were open, there was no way he could stop it.

Her fingers twisted in his hair, and her tongue tangled with his as both their breathing sped up. He pulled away long enough to press hot kisses across her chest.

"Jack," she breathed, her thighs clenching around his. "We shouldn't…."

"I know," he said, nipping at her neck. "But, Chloe, I've wanted to…."

"So have I…" she said, and he felt pleasure rip through him like a tornado. "But…but…"

He kissed away any further objections. She could be the most rational woman in the world right now. Hell, the ship could be sinking. He didn't care. All that mattered was being with Chloe, *now*.

He was reaching for the hem of her T-shirt when the door swung open.

"Hey, Chloe, did you borrow my—" The words stopped abruptly.

Chloe twisted to see who was speaking, and Jack groaned as the motion brought even more friction against his hard-on. He glanced around her torso.

Inga stood in the doorway, looking shocked, her red mouth dropping open. "What the hell?" There was more surprise than anger in her voice.

"We're a little busy right now," Jack said, his voice sounding rough, but before he could stop her, Chloe clambered off of him, leaving him hard and wanting.

"I'm sorry, what did you need?" Chloe said quickly, her voice too breathy and high to be professional.

Inga dismissed Chloe's inquiry with a look of scorn. She stalked back down the hallway, letting the door shut.

Chloe sighed, then looked at Jack. "See? These are the kind of problems that would come up."

Jack sighed. She was right. He knew she was right.

He just didn't care right now.

There has to be some way she can stay and we can get around that damned no-sex clause.

"Just think about it," he said. "And maybe we can talk about it a little more tonight."

"I don't know...."

Ace knocked before opening the door. "The passengers have called," he said. "They're coming an hour early. Will we be okay?"

Jack could tell Chloe's mind was back to business. "I've got to take care of these," she said, swiping up the dishes and retreating to the galley.

Ace looked at Chloe's retreating form, then looked at Jack. "Everything okay?"

"Not quite," Jack said. "But it will be."

Chloe wasn't the only person who could plan things. And tonight he'd make her an offer she couldn't say no to.

JUST THINK ABOUT IT.

Ha, Chloe thought. As if she'd done much of anything else since they'd cast off and headed for the ocean.

Well, she had thought about the charter passengers, the Newcombes. Unlike their last clients—the lovely Spencer couple—the Newcombes were slightly older and a lot less likable. For one thing, Mr. Newcombe was a flirt. Actually, more than a flirt—the man was a lech. He was very good-looking, and obviously that gave him the impression that he could do whatever he wanted with impunity. He'd winked at her and kept making comments when she'd served them lunch, and by dinner he'd already gone through a good chunk of their mini fridge, judging from the alcohol on his breath. She'd set up dinner on the front deck, to enjoy the sunset. But he didn't seem to notice the sky at all, staring at her instead.

"So…you're the cook, huh?"

She'd nodded pleasantly, trying her best to ignore him.

"Nothing hotter than a woman who cooks," he said, leering at her, even though her crewneck T-shirt was nothing to leer at. Then he turned to his wife. "You should learn how to cook."

The wife merely took a long sip of her iced tea, looking out on the waves. Chloe felt sorry for her, wondering how the woman could've hitched herself to this loser. "How is your seasickness doing?" Chloe commented, trying to be friendly and include her in the conversation.

"Much better," Mrs. Newcombe replied in clipped tones. "I've got some pills later that really do the trick."

Mr. Newcombe wasn't pleased at that. "Isn't that the stuff that knocks you out?" Chloe heard him say as she retreated toward the galley. "How the hell am I supposed to have a honeymoon with you passed out?"

"Maybe you should've thought of that before you started hitting on the cook!" Mrs. Newcombe snapped back. "You're lucky if you get any sex at all on this trip, you jerk! It wasn't my idea to go on a cruise!"

Chloe fled. She didn't know what they had, but whatever it was, it wasn't love.

Chloe had been busy prepping for the week's meals, and now it was ten o'clock at night. She was bone-tired. If Inga would assist with some of the cleaning, that would help enormously. Jose and Ace each gave a hand when they could, and so did Jack for that matter, but Inga seemed to be a walking cyclone, creating mess and clutter wherever she went. She also had made it quite clear that she wasn't hired to be "menial labor." She was going to mean problems, but Chloe hadn't said anything to Jack because she didn't want him thinking she was jealous of the girl. Although, after what Inga had witnessed between Chloe and Jack in the honeymoon cabin, Inga was furious and had done a million passive-aggressive things all day to show Chloe how ticked off she was. Chloe wasn't going to be able to put up with that for another month, no way. Maybe tonight she'd talk to Jack about it.

The memory of her and Jack twined together on the honeymoon bed that morning seared through her. The taste of him, the feel of him hard beneath her.

She stopped herself. No, she wasn't going to talk to him tonight.

She went back to her cabin, intent on getting a full night's sleep before dealing with the evil Newcombes the next day—she felt sure after their dinner argument they would be grouchy and unpleasant tomorrow. To her surprise, the door was locked when she got there. "Inga," she said in a low voice, trying not to disturb the honeymoon cabin, "open up."

She wondered absently if Inga was trying to get back at her for stealing away Jack. She also wondered if Inga was going to pull any other tricks to prevent Chloe from getting any rest…like putting something nasty in her bed, or whatnot.

After a few minutes, Inga opened the door a crack. "Can't you see the scarf on the door?" she said, her voice cross.

Chloe hadn't noticed, but there was indeed a filmy scarf tied around the small doorknob. "So?"

"That means I've got company," Inga snapped. "Get lost."

"But I need to get sleep!" Chloe protested.

"So go sleep with *Jack*," Inga replied. "You two being so close and all."

With that, she shut the door with a click of the latch, leaving Chloe in the hallway, stunned and furious. She stood there for several minutes, as if expecting Inga to say the whole thing was a joke, so that she could get some rest. But after a few long moments, Chloe heard the distinct and telltale sounds of bed creaking and moaning, with Inga sounding a little more vocal than was probably necessary, saying things like "Come on, big boy" and "Ooh, yeah, right there." Chloe felt quite sure it was for her benefit—just one more way to both get even and to get her to go away.

Chloe blushed. Then she stormed down to Jack's cabin, knocking carefully.

"Come on in."

She walked in, letting the door shut behind her. "She's kicked me out of my…"

Before she continued her angry tirade, she glanced around. If she thought she'd been stunned before, it was nothing compared to now.

He'd cleaned his cabin, which normally looked like a disaster area. The bed had fresh sheets and was neatly made up. The desk was organized, the way Chloe liked it—she'd worked there enough recently to know it never stayed neat for more than an hour after she left it. There was the omnipresent scent of the ocean, but more than that, there was a scent of clean woods, cedar and pine. The final touch: there were little lights everywhere, small Lucite blocks that glowed in turquoise and midnight-blue and sea-foam-green, making the whole room seem soft and ethereal, like an aquatic paradise.

"I wanted to run these by you," he said, his voice business-like and completely at odds with the romantic tableau he'd obviously created. "So many couples ask about candles, and I just don't want the fire risk, so I found these little guys. They're battery-powered and they sort of add to the mood. What do you think?"

"They're wonderful," Chloe said. Then she shook her head. "Listen, Jack…"

"Shhh," he said. He'd showered, she realized, his almost-black hair still damp and curling slightly against the collar of his shirt. "I thought we could talk tonight."

The way he said it…she knew he didn't mean talk. Her body started to respond automatically, and she closed her eyes.

"This isn't a good idea, Jack," she said, even as she felt his arms close around her.

"You're the one that always tells me there's a solution for everything," he murmured against the skin below her right earlobe. "I'm sure if we think about it hárd enough, we can come up with something."

She forced herself to focus. "Inga kicked me out of our cabin," she said, hoping that would jar him off course. "She's having *sex*."

To her surprise, he shrugged. "Probably with Ace. That guy has a penchant for high-drama blondes. I'll talk to them both tomorrow." He took her hands, gently tugging her toward the bed. "But let's not waste time talking about them tonight."

"I've got nowhere to sleep!"

He nudged her until she sat, his comforter plush beneath her. "Sure you do," he said with a smile, sitting next to her.

She sighed, a mixture of irritation and—she hated to admit it—anticipation. "You know, sex doesn't fix things."

"'Course it doesn't," he admitted readily. "But it does make waiting for the solution a hell of a lot more fun."

She giggled, knowing he was conning her. "Okay, let's talk," she said.

He sighed this time. "You're right. I should've known you wouldn't simply fall into bed, no matter how charming I·tried to be."

"I give you points for trying," she said. "The whole thing's really lovely. But it doesn't really change our situation."

"I know. I want you," he said. "And I want you to work with me. With us."

"And that, in a nutshell, is our problem," she said, leaning back. The bed felt blessedly comfortable against her muscles. She propped herself up on one elbow, looking at him, her tone serious. "If we have sex, then we're just having sex. If we have a relationship, I don't think we should be involved with business. And if we're in business…" She let the sentence trail off. "We've had that discussion. You seemed all in favor of keeping work and sex separate."

"I'm not stupid," he said, lying on his back, putting his hands behind his head. "I know this is all fast. And you're coming off a serious relationship. I know the facts, Chloe."

Traitorously, the sight of him stretched out made her body tingle. She inched ever so slightly closer, staring at the strong planes of his face as he stared at the ceiling.

"So…" He turned to her, his green eyes more intense in the low light. "How do we fix this?"

Her mouth went dry. "I don't know."

"But…would you *want* to fix it?"

She closed her eyes. The thought of working on the *Rascal,* the thought of being out on the ocean, of having a part of her own business…

The thought of having Jack in her bed, making mind-blowing love to her every night.

"Yes," she heard herself whisper. "I want to fix it."

"Then that's a start," he said and he rolled toward her, his hand reaching out and stroking a lock of hair from her face. "Why don't we take it slow and see how it goes? We don't have to sleep together," he said softly. "Not right away. We can see if the business side would actually work out. We already know how hot we are together," he said, and she felt a shiver rock through her. "We can see if it lasts when we add business stuff to it."

"What if it doesn't?" she said, as his fingers threaded into her hair, stroking her scalp. It felt right.

"Everything's a risk, Chloe," he murmured. "I think we're worth it, don't you?"

How could she say no to that?

He leaned toward her for a kiss, and she was just about to when they heard a screech in the hallway.

"What was *that?*" Chloe said, sitting up immediately, her heart racing with fear. More yelling. Jack was out in the hallway in a flash, Chloe right behind him.

Mrs. Newcombe was standing in the hallway in a robe and a nightgown, screaming at her husband, who was standing, naked except for boxers, looking sweaty. And, to Chloe's surprise, there was one more participant in the fracas.

Inga, naked except for the sheet wrapped around her.

"Slut!" Mrs. Newcombe shrieked, flying at Inga, slapping at her.

Jack dived in, separating the women. Jose and Ace quickly arrived, drawn by the noise. "What the hell is going on here?" Jack demanded, holding Mrs. Newcombe.

"That bitch," Mrs. Newcombe said, obviously meaning Inga, "was *screwing* my husband!"

Chloe looked at Inga, who barely even blushed. Chloe rolled her eyes. *Oh, for Pete's sake...*

"You were passed out!" Mr. Newcombe retorted. "On my damned honeymoon! What did you expect?"

Now Chloe was truly shocked. Was this guy for real?

"We're *married*," Mrs. Newcombe shouted back. "You're my *husband!*"

"You knew what this was!" Mr. Newcombe's eyes bulged unattractively, and Chloe could smell the gin on his breath. "It's a goddamned *business arrangement,* Felicia, and you knew that when you made me sign the prenup! Let's not pretend this is something other than what it is! You wanted a business partner and a good time, arm candy that you could show off to your rich friends. And I wanted money. So what the hell are you complaining about?"

Mrs. Newcombe went ghost-pale. "You're going to be sorry for this," she promised, the venom in her voice tangible.

"I'm already sorry," he slurred.

Mrs. Newcombe turned her attention to Jack. "Let go of me," she ordered. He did. "And I want you to turn this boat around. We're leaving."

"All right," Jack said, obviously relieved.

She went back to the honeymoon cabin, slamming it shut. Mr. Newcombe looked as though he was going to pursue the argument, banging on the door. "You can't lock me out!"

Jack grabbed his fist before he could pound again. "Take it easy tonight," he said. "Sleep it off."

Mr. Newcombe lifted his chin pugnaciously. "Why don't you mind your own damned business?"

"While you're on my boat," Jack said, his voice lowering dangerously, "you *are* my damned business. And before you think about taking me on, I've got two crew members. You'll want to think again."

Mr. Newcombe glanced at Ace and Jose, who both looked grim…and ready for action.

"Fine," he said. "But where the hell am I going to sleep tonight?"

Inga made a little snort. "Well, it's not going to be with me," she said. "These cots are way too tiny."

"Should've thought of that before you screwed him," Jack said, his voice cold as a glacier. She made a face, ready to protest, but he held up a hand. "I'm dealing with you tomorrow. Mr. Newcombe, you can stay in one of the cabins. Ace, if you could set him up on one of the spare cots…"

Ace nodded, leading Mr. Newcombe to the room he stayed in. "I'll bunk in Jose's room on his spare cot," he said, obviously not wanting to spend much time with their troublesome charter.

"Fine. Jose, you're on night shift—change course and

bring us back to Coronado," he said. "Everybody else, get some rest. We'll clear this up in the morning."

He took Chloe's hand and led her back to the cabin. Chloe's stomach felt sick at what she'd just witnessed.

"Jesus. If it's not one thing it's another," Jack said, closing the door behind them. "I'm firing Inga tomorrow, that's for sure."

"That was just ugly," Chloe said. Understatement of the year.

"I'm sorry," he said. "Ruined the mood, huh?"

"I just want to sleep," she said, her muscles all of a sudden aching.

Jack sighed, then nodded. "Don't worry, I won't try anything."

Still, he crawled into bed next to her after putting out all the lights, and she could just...*feel* him, his presence, his heat. She still wanted him. But after seeing what she'd seen...

You knew what this was... Just a business arrangement...

No, she thought. She'd have to think this through. No matter what good intentions she had, how logical she thought she could be about all this, it had disaster written all over it. As much as she wanted to find a solution, maybe there just *wasn't* one.

THE NEXT MORNING, Jack felt exhausted. He hadn't slept with Chloe, or anything—he'd be feeling a lot better if he had. He remembered that from their week together, that even when he'd only managed an hour of sleep he'd still wound up feeling unbelievably energized. Instead, last night he'd slept *next* to Chloe, and let's face it, that wasn't remotely close to the same thing. He'd breathed in the perfumed scent of her, felt every twitch and turn of her body. And he hadn't *touched* her.

He had never met anyone who was able to tie him in knots quite the way Chloe could, that was for sure.

He sat in his now-empty cabin. Chloe was fixing breakfast for the feuding newlyweds—or at least trying, since Mrs. Newcombe still hadn't emerged from the honeymoon cabin and Mr. Newcombe was still sleeping it off in Ace's cabin. They were close to Coronado, and with the cruise cut short, they'd have the rest of the week off. He wondered if Chloe was going to go onshore or stay on the boat with him. He wondered if there was any way to convince her to stay so they could talk it out together. He got the feeling that she was more the type that needed to be alone to think. The only problem was, the more she was alone, the worse he felt his odds were.

If he was going to cobble any sort of future with this woman, business or personal, then he needed a fighting chance, and that meant face-to-face or nothing.

There was a small rap on his door. "Come in," he said.

The door opened, and it was Mrs. Newcombe, fully dressed in a linen pantsuit and silk tank top, looking like an upper-crust socialite…except for the puffiness of her eyes, still red-rimmed from crying, that even the most expensive cosmetics couldn't quite conceal. "Mr. McCullough, if I might have a word?"

"Of course," he said, then realized he really needed to get another chair in here if people were going to keep discussing business. He gestured to the bed. "Sorry, it's the only other seat in the house."

She nodded and sat on the very edge, her hands clenched together. "I wanted to apologize for the scene last night," she said, her words so sharp they could've cut glass.

"I'm just sorry the whole thing happened in the first place," he said sincerely.

"That...*woman*..." She clenched her hands tighter together, if possible.

"Will no longer be in our crew," Jack assured her. "She's an independent contractor anyway, but she should have known better. Frankly, the whole thing was a mess."

Mrs. Newcombe took that with a tight-lipped nod. "I just couldn't believe he'd do something like that," she said instead. "I mean...yes, I could believe it. But on our *honeymoon* cruise. It's beyond me. Who could be so vicious? Who could just ignore how important a wedding is?"

Jack sighed. "I know. One of our earliest fares was a woman who got stood up at the altar by her groom. She just came by herself."

"I wish I had done that," Mrs. Newcombe said wistfully. "I should never have gotten married in the first place."

This was getting into personal territory. "I'm so sorry," Jack repeated.

She shrugged and dabbed at her eyes with her fingers, even though he couldn't see any tears forming. Not quite yet, anyway. "It's over and done with. However, there is the matter of the cruise being cut short."

Jack sighed. Of course, money would come into play now. As if his morning didn't suck enough. "Yes, but...well, it's regrettable, but you're canceling the cruise of your own accord. It's not our fault."

"Technically, it was your masseuse's fault," she said.

"Technically, she's an independent contractor," Jack replied. "You could always refuse to pay her for any, er, services rendered." He winced. That had come out badly. "But we acted in good faith and we would've continued with the cruise. It's not being cut short by bad weather or mechanical failure or anything in our control."

"So you're expecting me to pay for the whole thing?" Her voice cracked. "Just…just because my husband is a slime?"

Jack closed his eyes. God, he felt like a slime himself. "We ordered supplies—food, gas, stuff like that—in good faith, for a full cruise, Mrs. Newcombe."

"I see." She sighed.

He opened his eyes and looked at her. She looked…wilted, squashed, like a cabbage someone had sat down on.

"It's just so damned unfair," she said.

He blinked. He was trying to be reasonable.

"I didn't even want to go on this cruise. He did. Said it'd be romantic. Said it'd be nice for us to get away." Her tone was mocking, laced in acidic bitterness. "I don't know what he was thinking, but I was used to doing things that, you know, made him happy. I thought we were both getting something out of the marriage."

"Uh, Mrs. Newcombe…"

"But it was all what I could do for him," she said fiercely. "Did he ever once think about how I might be feeling? How he could do something to help me, for a change? No! He didn't! *Not once!*"

Uh-oh. She was mercurial, and man, did this lady have a temper. Jack stood up. "Okay, you're getting all worked up again. We'll be back onshore soon, and then you can divorce him or kick the crap out of him or both. But for right now, you're still on my ship," he said, making full use of his authoritative-captain voice. "And while I feel badly about your situation, I didn't cause it. You did."

Her eyes flared. "How dare you!"

"Nobody held a gun to your head to marry that yahoo," he said. "And you ordered the cruise. So it turned out badly. It happens. Now you can make the best of it or not, but I'm not going to refuse to get paid just because you married a jerk-off."

Her mouth opened and shut a couple of times in shock, making her look like a fish wriggling on deck. Jack suddenly felt like a complete and utter bastard.

"I am sorry…."

"No, no," she said, standing up. "I should've known better. It's just *business* to you men." And with that, she left his cabin.

Jack sighed, rubbing his hands over his face. He was just stepping in it left and right these days.

He decided to go to the galley to get a cup of coffee. Ace was steering, and Jose was sitting there, talking to Chloe. Inga was still in her room, not surprisingly, and that was good— he wasn't up for dealing with one more emotional basket case without caffeine.

"Morning," he grunted, reaching for a mug and the coffee-pot. "I'd say *good* morning, but it hasn't been."

"Already?" Jose said. Chloe, Jack noticed, was making scrambled eggs with ham and peppers and was assiduously avoiding looking at him. "What else happened? Did the lady and Inga get into a knife fight or something?"

"No, no," Jack said, sitting down. "But Mrs. Newcombe doesn't want to pay for the full cruise. I had to tell her it wasn't our fault that…well, you know."

Now Chloe did turn around. "So you're going to charge her the full fare?"

He nodded, wary at her tone of voice. "It wasn't our fault," he repeated.

"Well, no," she said. "But there were some contributing factors."

"Don't bring up Inga," Jack groaned. "She's out of here as soon as we dock, I swear to God. I think we're going to take massages out of the package altogether, anyway. It's not worth the aggravation."

"Still, it's not like they're taking the full cruise."

He watched as she filled three plates with the egg concoction, putting out some for Jose, him and then herself. She sat down next to the two of them, eating daintily. "I thought you were the one that didn't want to get screwed over," he pointed out. "She can afford it, and besides, she knew what she was getting into."

He noticed that when he said that last bit, she grimaced, wincing as if he'd cursed. "This isn't about being screwed over," she said after a long pause. "This is about...being compassionate."

He sighed. "She signed a contract, she agreed to pay."

"I signed contract, too," she said quietly. "I agreed to pay for the wedding. I didn't have anything in writing with the guy who was supposed to be my husband. And now here I am."

He might've guessed this would circle back to Gerald the Butt head.

"Well, his loss is our gain," Jose said, both gallant and philosophical.

She smiled at Jose wanly. "Thanks, Jose. But my point is, sometimes you've got to stick to your guns. But sometimes you've got to be compassionate. She's not trying to screw you—or I should say, screw *us*. She's just trying to get even with him and get some of her dignity back."

Jack looked at Jose, who kept his face inscrutable. No help there.

"Well, I hate to be the one to say it," Jack finally commented, "but I thought you needed the money. You know—mortgage payments?"

She pushed her eggs around her plate. "You don't have to

refund all the money. I mean, we did order food and supplies and things."

He nodded.

"But...you could give her a refund." She looked at him and he suddenly felt two inches tall for being so insistent about the money side of things. "A partial refund. You could give her a break. That would help."

"And how will you manage?" Jack asked.

"Our next charter ought to put me over the top," she said. "Otherwise, I could just walk out today. I've got almost enough for the last payment."

Jack felt his stomach clench, and it had nothing to do with the delicious eggs Chloe had prepared. "You mean, leave?"

"I'm not saying I will," Chloe assured him, although her eyes looked troubled as she said it. "I'm just saying...I could."

He sighed again, feeling his insides twist. He didn't think Chloe was manipulating him. It wasn't her style. But he did know that, while a part of him felt like a mustache-twirling villain for holding Mrs. Newcombe's feet to the fire over the full cost of the cruise, he probably could've gone through with it. He needed the cash way more than the put-upon Mrs. N.

However, the thought of disappointing Chloe—and worse *losing* Chloe—just didn't make it worthwhile.

"I'll talk to her," he said. "I'm sure I can work something out."

Chloe smiled gratefully, and he got that superhero feeling again, coupled with a sense of foolishness. He prayed he wasn't being conned here.

"So you're on for one more cruise, huh?" he said before he could help himself.

"I told you I needed time to think," she reminded him, then seemed to remember that Jose was in the room and blushed

Jose simply smiled at the two of them. "It'd be great if you could stay, Chloe."

She grinned, then shifted the conversation to small talk. Jack just ate the rest of his breakfast in silence.

She was still thinking. So he was still in the running. And he had one more cruise to really figure out how to keep her there. More important, he would figure out *why* he wanted her to stay so badly. Because right now she was starting to wind him around her little finger, and he didn't like that at all.

7

CHLOE FELT WEIRD BEING on land. After they'd successfully unloaded the Newcombes and Jack had evicted Inga, Chloe told him that she'd be going onshore. It had been too long since she'd seen her parents and she desperately needed to think.

What do you think about being partners?

The question both thrilled and unnerved her. Gerald had always treated her like…well, a secretary, but that was what she was. On paper, anyway. He'd appreciated everything that she'd done, without question. But equal partners? Even with every thing she'd dealt with in the wedding and the research she'd done when they'd bought the house, he'd acted as if that was part of her job. As if marrying him itself was part of her job.

So how is that going to be different with Jack?

She pulled into her parents' driveway feeling weary, both physically and mentally. The difference with Jack, she told herself, was that Jack wasn't interested in marrying her. He was interested in having a business partner—and he was interested in having sex with her.

They were both intriguing offers, but together, she got the feeling they'd be disastrous.

She let herself in the front door and was instantly assailed with the scents of her old home—her mom was making a po roast, which meant mashed potatoes and corn and carrot glazed in honey. She could hear the strains of Count Basie coming from upstairs somewhere, meaning her father was home, no doubt puttering away on the Internet. She smiled. It wasn't exciting, but it was sort of nice to have a place to decompress.

"There you are!" Her mother bustled forward, giving her a big hug. "I thought we'd lost you to the sea! Honey, Chloe's home!"

After a few minutes, her father came lumbering down the stairs. "There's my girl," he said, giving her a hug to match her mother's.

"It's good to be here," Chloe said, feeling surprisingly emotional. She wasn't crying, but she did feel choked up.

"Oh, you poor dear," her mother said, instantly putting an arm around her shoulders and ushering her toward the kitchen. "Sit down. Can I make you some coffee? It's all right, you're home now."

Chloe accepted a mug of decaf, sipping at it. This was home, of sorts, but she had to admit it wasn't her home anymore.

"So what's going on on that boat of yours?" her father said, sitting next to her at the kitchen table while her mother put finishing touches on the dinner.

"It's been busy, but we're doing a brisk business," she said, filling him in on the charters she'd booked. "I've worked off my debt and then some, that's for sure." She set her jaw, feeling grim. "And I gave Gerald an ultimatum—the house needs to be sold in a month. I don't care if it's at a loss. I want out from under these payments and I want him to stop threatening me. We got a great deal on it, and from what I understand, the offers would be higher than what we paid for it. So there's no reason for him to keep dragging his feet."

Her mother snorted. "That man…"

"Now, now, dear," her father interrupted. "The important part is, once the house is sold, you'll be able to breathe easy for a little while."

Chloe frowned. "I guess," she said, trying to remember what "breathing easy" felt like. "There's still a lot I'll have to do...."

"But you won't have to worry about money anymore for a while is what I mean."

She laughed. "Well, I'll need to eventually. I like eating."

"Your mother and I can give you a roof over your head and three meals a day—and the occasional snack," he said drily, winking at her. "The important part being, you'll be able to quit this whole boat business."

Chloe felt a pang. "Well, I suppose so."

His eyes widened, his bushy eyebrows almost jumping to his receding hairline. "You suppose so? Good grief, sweetie, you look like a walking corpse!"

Chloe laughed. "Thanks, Dad."

"You know what I mean," he said gruffly, as her mother joined them at the table. "You've been working too hard."

"I've been pushing it a little," Chloe admitted. "Still, it's not all bad. There are a lot of pluses."

"Name one," her mother challenged.

"I get to be out on the water," Chloe said, feeling the hint of a smile dance around her lips. "It's tough work sometimes, but the sensation of the open sea is really great. And I get to cook, which is more fun than I remembered."

"You're also cleaning," her mother said. "You can't tell me you find that fun."

Chloe thought of her aching back. "No, you've got me there. But we might be able to hire a new maid."

"I thought you said this guy was strapped for cash!" Her father sounded irate, as if Jack were somehow cheating her.

"Well, we fired the masseuse," Chloe said, grimacing. Inga's last few hours on board were not pleasant. Chloe had made sure that Inga didn't do something retaliatory, like trashing all Chloe's belongings before leaving. Inga hadn't, though, although she'd had some loud and choice parting comments for the entire *Rascal* crew. It had been ugly. "Anyway, we'll be better off with a cleaning person— massages weren't going well as far as offering more value to the cruise. Fortunately, we haven't changed the brochure yet. We'll take them out."

"We?" Her mother shook her head. "You're identifying too much with this business. You used to do that with Gerald, too, remember?"

Chloe slumped. "This is…well, this *could* be different."

Her father and mother exchanged worried glances. "Of course it could be," her mother said, but her voice was filled with doubt.

"In fact," Chloe said slowly, "he's asking me if I want to go into partnership with him."

Her parents fell silent in the face of this announcement.

"As in, you'd stay on the boat and work?" her father asked.

Chloe nodded. She hadn't meant to tell them, but it was too prevalent in her mind. It had slipped out almost of its own accord.

"Doing what you're doing now?" His eyebrows were practically knitting together, he was frowning so hard. "Working as hard as you're working now?"

"But being a part of the business," Chloe hastily assured them. "Which is more than I ever was with Gerald, really. Very different."

"You're not thinking of *investing* in this boat, are you?" her mother asked, aghast.

Chloe blinked. "Well, I don't really have the money to invest, exactly...."

"So how would you be considered a partner?"

She hadn't worked that detail out. And from the horrified looks on her parents' faces, she got the feeling they weren't going to be their usual problem-solving selves and help her find a way to cobble together a proposal for Jack. In fact, she got the feeling they'd already done their problem solving—to get her to come back home.

"I'm still ironing stuff out," Chloe said. "In fact, I figured I'd think about it the next two days, here, before I've to go back."

"Do you have to go back, though?" Her mother was gentle and yet relentless, like a mink-covered sledgehammer. "You've got the last mortgage payment, don't you? And the house will be sold soon?"

"I need one more charter to cover the last payment," Chloe said.

"So one more cruise and you'll be out," her father said.

"Unless I decide to become a partner."

"Chloe, darling, you're not thinking clearly," her mother said, sounding agitated. "Why in the world would you want to become a partner on a cruising yacht?"

Chloe sighed. "Why wouldn't I?"

"You'll never make any real money that way," her father said.

"I wasn't making real money as a secretary, either," Chloe said, feeling defensive. "This would be an opportunity to actually see the profits from a business I'm working so hard on."

He looked at her mother, who picked up the ball. "Well, there are other issues. You won't have benefits. You won't have retirement. It's all well and good to say this would be fun, but you've got to think about your future."

Chloe pressed her lips together. She knew that they meant well and that they were worried. She was worried herself. That was why she'd come home to think about it. But the more they pressed, the less she wanted to listen to them, as much as she loved them. She was tired of doing the "right" thing. She wanted to…

She flinched, sitting upright in her chair.

I want to do something stupid and foolish.

She closed her eyes. God. The last time she'd said that was when she'd gotten together with Jack.

That didn't turn out that badly.

Her parents didn't notice—or if they did, they decided to ignore her expressions in favor of hammering home their point. "There is one other issue," her mother said, clearing her throat. "Your love life."

Chloe's eyes flew wide-open. "I beg your pardon?"

"Your love life," her mother repeated.

"Seeing as I don't have one, I'm not all that worried about the repercussions of my business decisions," Chloe said, laughing a nervously. Of course, it was her love life—or at least sex life—that was causing the main obstacle to her leaping right into the business. But she certainly did *not* want to discuss that with her parents.

"And you're not going to have a love life if you're on some small yacht with the same couple of men day in and day out," her mother said, smiling as if she'd just aced a serve. "The only new men you're going to meet are going to be newly-weds, not people open for a relationship."

Chloe thought briefly of Mr. Newcombe and sighed. Well, there *were* newlyweds who were open to relationships of sorts, but God willing, the *Rascal* wouldn't be booking any more of those.

"I know you, Chloe." Her mother's expression was serious and caring and mirrored by her father's. "Gerald might have been the wrong choice, but I know how badly you want love, how much you want to be married. How much a solid relationship means to you," she finished. "Do you really think you can replace that with this little business scheme and still be happy?"

Chloe's mouth dropped open at her mother's insight.

There it was, the crux of the problem.

She was interested in the business, without question. She enjoyed the sex.

But she'd want more than that. And she wasn't sure Jack could or would give her what she needed.

They didn't need to have a discussion about the details of their partnership, she realized. Or, rather, they needed to discuss a different kind of partnership. The thought terrified her, but she knew she had no choice.

"So what will it be, Chloe?" her father said in his rumbling low voice.

Chloe sighed. "I'm going back for this last charter," she said. "And I need to discuss the details with Jack. If we can work something out, then I'll stay."

"And if not?" her mother pressed.

"If not," Chloe said, feeling her stomach go cold, "then I'll just walk away."

"Mr. and Mrs. Rorshan?" Jack said, greeting the couple as they walked up the gangway.

"Please," the husband said. "We're Tom and Lily."

Jack studied them warily. It had been two days since the Newcombe fiasco, as he was calling it, but it still stung. This young couple seemed normal, he thought. The guy looked to be in his late twenties, and from talking to him on the phone,

Jack gathered he was some kind of computer genius—and loaded. This was going to be their biggest cruise yet. Two and a half weeks, to be exact. And not to Catalina or Mexico. This time they were going to Hawaii. It had been a long time since Jack had gone out to the islands and across that expanse of ocean. He found he was looking forward to it.

"This boat is wonderful!" the bride enthused. She looked to be in her twenties, as well. Her hair was a shoulder-length mess of corkscrew copper curls, a contrast to her husband's short blond hair. They were both good-looking people, smiling and friendly. "It's perfect, Tom. You were right."

She leaned in to kiss her husband, and for a minute it was obvious that they thought they were the only two people on deck. His hands gripped her hips and her arms locked around her neck.

Well, at least we're not going to have a repeat of that "you knew what this was" kerfuffle, Jack thought with a grin.

After several long minutes—and seeing that Tom's hands were starting to edge under her shirt—Jack finally cleared his throat.

They broke apart, laughing a little self-consciously. "Sorry," Tom said, although from the sparkle in his eyes Jack guessed the only thing he was sorry about was the fact that he and his pretty new wife weren't someplace more private. "I guess we're impatient to get our honeymoon started."

Lily blushed, making her cream complexion look rosy and cute. Her eyes sparkled, too, as she laced her arm in her husband's.

"Well, then, let's not keep you waiting," Jack said, winking. "Honeymoon cabin's this way."

"Will we be leaving right away?" Lily asked.

Jack frowned. Ordinarily he'd be telling Ace or Jose to get

them going, since their passengers were on board. But now, they were waiting on his last crew member. He would've said he could set his watch by Chloe, but today she was late.

He got the feeling that things were afoot. She'd been alone for two days and she'd said that she needed "time to think." Who knows what trouble her mind had gotten him into in a mere forty-eight hours.

"We'll be going shortly," Jack said. "You'll have dinner at sunset, on the ocean—no worries there."

"Oh, we're not worried," Tom said. "I think she just wanted to know if we, you know, needed to be on deck for anything. For the next couple of hours."

Lily laughed again and blushed some more, and her eyes were brighter than a blowtorch.

"Uh, no," Jack said. "In fact, you can stay in your cabin the whole time if you want. Or have your run of the ship. There's just me, the cook and two crew members. We're at your disposal."

Lily's smile curved into something decidedly more naughty. "Well, we'll probably come out for dinner," she said. "If only to refuel."

Tom gave her a walking half hug, and they grinned at each other broadly.

Oh, yeah, Jack thought. These two weren't going to be any trouble at all. Hell, he could probably serve them vitamin E and graham crackers and they'd be fine. They were obviously here for one reason only. When he put their bags in their cabin and shut the door behind him, he heard them slide the bolt in the lock. He would've laid odds that the two of them were naked and/or getting busy within five minutes. Not that he was eager to prove his assumption. He headed for the deck, away from the cabins.

"We casting off, boss?" Jose asked from the top deck. "The engines are ready to go."

"We're still waiting on Chloe," Jack replied, curbing his impatience. Where the heck was she?

Ten minutes later, Chloe came running up, duffel bag slung over her shoulder. "I'm so sorry," she said between breaths.

"No problem," Jack said, giving Jose and Ace the go-ahead. "Everything okay?"

"Yeah," she said, sounding embarrassed. "I just…you're not going to believe this, but I overslept. Till close to noon. I haven't done that in longer than I can remember."

Jack grinned at the memory. "You slept in when…"

He stopped before he could say *when we were sleeping together.* He thought about those days—when he was lazy, too, because they'd averaged about two hours of sleep at night, if that. And were always ready for more.

"Uh, you must feel comfortable at your parents' place," he said instead. "You know, living like a teenager again."

"Actually, it was the opposite," she said. "I slept lousy there. I guess I've gotten used to feeling the waves, you know?"

He nodded. He knew that exactly. He always had trouble sleeping when he was onshore after all his years living on the *Rascal*.

"That," she said, "and I had a lot on my mind."

He winced. Just as he'd suspected.

"Which I'd like to talk to you about," she added.

He sighed. "Jose? You guys okay taking us out?"

Jose scoffed at the question, and Jack realized he couldn't dodge having the conversation with Chloe based on his captainly duties. "All right," he said to Chloe. "Come on. We'll talk in the cabin." He got the feeling he wouldn't want Ace or Jose listening in on this one.

Chloe followed him down the stairs to the hallway, passing the honeymoon cabin. As Jack had predicted, there were already sounds of marital bliss occurring.

"Those the guests?" Chloe asked in a whisper as they hurried to the captain's cabin.

"Yeah. Nice couple," Jack said. "I think it'll be smooth sailing with those two."

"That's good," Chloe said, her voice obviously relieved.

"Especially considering how far we're going," Jack agreed.

Chloe blinked, and he remembered—the Rorshans were actually guests he'd booked on his own. He was so used to Chloe handling the details he wasn't used to filling her in on things. "He's rich. We're going to Hawaii."

Chloe's eyes bulged. "Across the Pacific?"

Jack smiled, amused. "Unless you know another way."

"Oh. I...huh." Chloe looked unsettled and pale. He gestured to her to sit down on the bed, and she did without a word. "We've usually been pretty close to the coast, that's all."

"Don't worry," Jack said, realizing that she was scared. "I've done the San Diego-Hawaii run tons of times. It's perfectly safe. I know what I'm doing."

"Okay," Chloe said. After a moment, she smiled back at him, her expression full of trust.

What would I give to have somebody look at me that way every day?

Jack sighed, sitting at his desk. "So let's get this over with. What did you want to talk about?"

The smile slid off her face, much to Jack's disappointment. "Get this over with? That's a positive way of looking at it," she groused.

"You have that look about you," Jack replied. "Besides, you should know by now that whenever a woman tells a guy

'We need to talk', she's about to nail his butt to the nearest convenient wall."

. "That's sweet," she said, scowling.

He leaned back. "But not wrong."

"It's about the partnership thing."

"I figured." He braced himself. "So what are your terms?"

She scooted back on the bed until she was leaning against the cabin wall, and for a second he considered joining her. No matter how rough her decision was, he got the feeling that if he was in arms' reach, it would be a lot easier on him. Just touching her tended to make his worst days much, much better.

However, this was assuming that she wasn't about to say *We can have the business but not the sex.*

She breathed deeply. "I think we need to clear up a few expectations," she said carefully. "Before we decide to do anything more permanent."

He frowned. He wished women would get to the point. Chloe was great and more straightforward than most women he'd met, but times like now, she tacked around an issue as if it were the Bermuda Triangle. "Okay," he said. "Expectations about what?"

"What do you want out of life, for example?"

He blinked, wondering where the hell *that* came from. "You're looking at it," he answered. "I want the *Rascal* out on the water. I want to live my life my way." He smiled. "I want to make enough money to keep doing both of those things."

"Fair enough," she said. "Um…is that all?"

"Isn't that enough?"

Apparently, that was the wrong answer. It was her turn to frown.

"Well, what do *you* want out of life?" he asked, wondering how he could have muffed a question that arbitrary.

"I want to feel as if I'm a part of something," she said. "I think the *Rascal* could be that."

"That's good news," Jack said, feeling better.

"I want to be financially independent."

He thought about it. "We don't make millions around here, although we're doing a hell of a lot better since you joined the crew."

"I don't need to make millions," she responded, and he relaxed even more. "I just want to make sure I make enough to live well and retire at some point if I want to."

"Makes sense." He was only thirty-four, but he was starting to wonder about that whole retirement thing. She was logical enough to start thinking about it now. Of course, with somebody like Gerald as her husband, she would probably have had to watch her own backside or he'd have stolen her funds out from under her. "Anything else?"

She sighed. "This is where it gets sticky. You remember how we met, right?"

"Like I could forget!"

She was silent for a long moment. "I want to get married," she said.

He froze.

"Not to Gerald—that was a huge mistake," she said. "But I've been thinking about it. I want to matter to someone. I want to be in a relationship where I know that I'm working toward a future, and he is, too. I want to be in something loyal and committed." She took a deep breath. "I want to be head over heels in love."

He stared at her, not sure of how to respond. From the way she was staring back, he could tell she was expecting an answer of some sort.

"Oh," he said finally.

She looked away.

"I guess that's all the answer I needed," she said and got up off the bed.

"You just sort of sprang that on me," he argued, getting up, too.

"You like sleeping with me," she said, grabbing her bag, "and you like what I'm able to do with your business. But you don't want a wife or even a woman in your life, from what I've heard."

"That's not fair," he said, realizing his mistake too late.

"It's not unfair. It's fact. If you don't want it, I'm not going to insist and try to make something work that's flawed from the beginning," she said, her tone maddeningly reasonable, which only made things worse. "I've done that already and I'm not doing it again, thanks."

"Damn it," he said, grabbing her shoulder and turning her toward him, "I'm not like Gerald!"

She smiled and gently cupped his cheek with her hand. "I know that," she said, and her smile was like banked embers— soft and warm. "But you don't love me, either."

His mouth worked, but no words came out.

She moved her hand, his cheek still warm from her fingertips. "I'll go get dinner prepped," she said, and without another word she walked out.

Jack sat down heavily on his bed. He should've known it would come to this.

A COUPLE OF DAYS later, Chloe was on deck looking at the ocean. In fact, there was nothing to see but the grayish blue-green swells, large ones, surrounding the boat for as far as the eye could see. It was a bit unnerving, yet it was also exhilarating. She was careful not to linger too close to the rails, even though part of her wanted to—wanted to stand on the bow like that girl in *Titanic,* feeling as if she were flying. The sky was dotted with the occasional bird, and she'd seen dolphins swimming in packs or pods or whatever groups of dolphins were called.

The couple, Tom and Lily, were easy to cook for—and they'd taken a lot of meals in their rooms. They didn't even want her to clean the room or make the bed, because "We'll only mess it up again" as they'd said. This left her with a lot of free time. She hadn't packed any books in her hurry, and thanks to her conversation with Jack, she was not going to him to talk about anything—business or personal.

There wasn't any point. After this trip, she would be out. Once Tom and Lily's check cleared, she'd pay the last month of mortgage. She'd talked to the lawyers—they had a bid that they were accepting. She was going to make a small amount of money, even. Not enough to offset the wedding or recoup her savings but enough to start over.

And that's exactly what she had to do, she thought, as dark as the waves that crashed against the hull. She was going to have to start over.

Why did you ask him if he loved you?

She closed her eyes, the pain and humiliation of that conversation still marinating in her. She did want to be in love, but being logical, she knew that they'd only known each other for a little more than a month. They'd been physically intimate, but that didn't mean anything. At least to some men, that didn't mean anything, she corrected. She realized now that her week with Jack had meant something very profound to her. It had shown her a whole new way to live. That sounded melodramatic, but he'd shown her that she didn't have to have everything perfect. That sometimes it was good to just feel your feelings, and get past them. Granted, she probably couldn't live her *whole* life that way, but it had worked wonders. She'd processed her feelings for Gerald. And thanks to Jack, she'd come up with the idea of working with him, giving her a way to save herself financially. She'd gained a whole new appreciation of the ocean and was developing a real love of ships. Those were all good things.

She knew now that she wanted all of that: the freedom, the happiness. She really did love working on the *Rascal,* and a part of her was heartbroken at the thought of leaving it and Jack, she admitted.

Maybe you're being too hard-line about this.

It wasn't like the way it was with Gerald, she thought reflectively. Jack had made her no promises, hadn't said he was anything other than what he was. And he wasn't asking her to leave the business, as Gerald had. In fact, he wanted her to stay whether they had a relationship or not. Was she being shortsighted? Was she throwing away a fantastic opportunity because she couldn't separate her emotions from her livelihood?

She was leaning against the wall of the steering cabin when she heard Tom and Lily laughing at the back of the boat. Which meant that they were cutting off any way for her to get back to her cabin. She decided she'd stay where she was, out of respect for their privacy. She loved the boat, but that was the one thing it lacked: space to move around unnoticed. If you worked or lived on it, then you became part of a team, period. There was no room for loners. She'd liked that, too.

"Nobody'll see us," she heard Lily say in a stage whisper.

"Naughty," Tom said back. "You are one naughty girl." To which Lily let out a responding giggle.

Chloe was jolted out of her reverie. They were sunbathing out on the back deck, she presumed. Maybe Lily was talking about sunbathing topless—or rather nude, since she'd included Tom in her statement. It must be nice to be that in love, Chloe thought with an undercurrent of sadness. She thought she heard them kissing. It was sweet.

She was watching the clouds billowing in the sky when it occurred to her that the sounds she was hearing were definitely *not* kissing. What the heck were they doing out there in the open? She listened more intently. Then, against her better judgment, she crept closer, peeking from around the wall.

They were naked, which she'd sort of expected. But they were most assuredly not sunbathing.

Chloe's breath caught in her throat, and for a second she froze as her brain processed what her eyes were witnessing. Tom was lying on the deck, the towel beneath him as if he were sunbathing. Lily was straddling him, her back arched, her head thrown back. He held her hips and pulled her to him, his hips rising gently as she pushed down to meet him. She would wriggle slightly, and Chloe could see his face tighten with passion. They were both breathing hard—that was the sound Chloe had heard but could not believe—and making other tiny sounds of ecstasy.

Chloe felt a tug of longing, a tingling that shot through her whole body. She quickly averted her eyes as she realized what she was doing and fled for the bow of the deck. She sat at the pointed rail, as far away from the lovemaking couple as possible. She shouldn't have investigated. She felt embarrassed at what she'd seen...and envious.

Unbidden, thoughts of her week with Jack came flooding back as if they'd just happened.

We never made love out on deck.

But they'd done everything else, her memory reminded her. He had been the most extraordinary lover. The fact that they were now becoming platonic friends and business partners of sorts didn't diminish that one bit. And he'd wanted her—still wanted her.

As much as she wanted freedom and financial challenges, she couldn't get around that basic fact. She wanted him, too. It had not gone away. If anything, it had gotten stronger in the past few weeks. Every time he'd gotten close to her in the galley, every time she'd sat on his bed, she'd had to force herself to focus instead of reliving the past, the feel of him pushing into her, the heightened sensations of his touch and taste and scent, the pounding rush of release.

She was leaving, and leaving would mean she'd want one more night with him, she realized. That was probably terrible of her to even think; it was tantamount to using him, then walking away, and any man who proposed the same she'd probably slap. But if he wasn't going to be able to give her anything else, she doubted he'd mind.

And if her emotions hurt her as a result…well, she had no one to blame but herself.

In the back of the boat, Chloe heard Lily's growing cries of completion mixed with Tom's moan. They no longer cared if there was an audience or not. Chloe closed her eyes, miserable with desire and regret.

She knew Jack had been trying to explain his position. Now she'd let him explain, and then they'd realize they each had to go a separate way. In the long run, she wanted the whole enchilada: business *and* love.

In the meantime, they would finish business, part as friends…and have sex.

8

HERE HE WAS, IN THE middle of the Pacific, surrounded by dark water and even darker skies. The sea was getting temperamental, and he knew that the *Rascal* was in for one rough night. Still, with all of that, he found himself dwelling on one thing.

He knew it was way too fast and crazy, but he knew somehow that he had fallen hard for Chloe Winton. He hadn't been in love before—not like this, anyway. This was complicated, but more than that, it was strong enough to make him willing to face the complications. No woman had ever been worth putting up with drama before. Meanwhile, his entire relationship with Chloe seemed like nothing *but* drama. Still, he was going headfirst into it. He wasn't sure what that would entail, but for now he felt he'd do what it took to make her happy.

He acknowledged why he'd avoided love for so many years—it was a real pain in the butt.

He was peering out his cabin window when he heard Chloe's familiar knock on his door. "Come on in."

He hoped that the storm would hold itself at bay until they were finished talking. This conversation would be too important for him to be half-assed about it. She deserved his full attention. Still, he'd have to go to steering soon to help out Ace and Jose. The boat was already starting to toss in the larger-than-average waves.

Chloe was wearing a pair of low-riding jeans and a crop top, her cinnamon hair pulled up in a loose bun that let ringlets cascade around her face.

Stay focused, McCullough. This is important.

"I'm glad you're finally talking to me," he said. "I wanted to explain a few things."

Her smile was wistful, just this side of sad. "You don't have to explain anything," she said, her voice soothing and soft.

He sighed. "Actually, yeah, I do. I think you might've got the wrong impression from our conversation when you first got on the boat."

She sat down on the bed, and he started to take his customary position behind his desk when he was stopped by her words. "Jack…come sit here, by me."

He looked at the bed as if it was a booby trap. She was patting the mattress next to her, her eyes turning sultry. The sultriness that he remembered from their time together, on her ill-fated "honeymoon."

He knew it was stupid, especially when he was trying to keep focus, but he sat down next to her anyway, breathing in her perfume of vanilla and almond. The smile she wore now was much less sad and much more seductive.

He cleared his throat, ignoring his automatic bodily response at being in such close proximity to her. "I know I didn't say anything about wanting love or a wife or anything," he said slowly, concentrating as hard as he could. "But I've never met any woman who I would have considered worthwhile to stay with for life."

"Shhh," she said, and her fingertips stroked his arm. It was a simple touch, but he shivered slightly nonetheless.

"No, I need to say this." He plowed forward. "I know it seems like all guys have these commitment issues and crap like that, but in my case it's…well, I don't know if it's different or what, but it's a reason." He took a deep breath. "When I was a kid, my parents were strict. Insanely strict. They had my life planned out from my first breath."

Chloe's hand paused on his arm. He felt the warmth from her palm seep through his skin, comforting him.

Jack hadn't thought about this in depth for years—hadn't wanted to. He closed his eyes for a second, then felt Chloe's hand move, caressing the back of his neck…more to console than to seduce.

It was almost more than he could bear.

"They sent me to military school when I was ten," he said. "Totally regimented. My dad had been in the Army, in Vietnam. He wanted to train me to be disciplined. My mom wanted me to be successful and get married and carry on the family legacy. By the time I was eighteen, I knew I didn't want to do anything they wanted me to. Once I got out of military school, I just left them behind."

Chloe made a sympathetic noise. He glanced at her face. She was staring at him intently.

"I've been with plenty of women, I'm not going to lie to you," he said, his voice—his spirit—heavy with it. "And most of them have wanted to heal my past and give me something better. I enjoyed them, I cared about them, but I didn't want to take what they were offering. I didn't want the perfect life they wanted to give me. I wanted *my* life. My ship, my rules…"

"Your freedom," Chloe summarized.

He nodded, grateful. "Yeah. I wanted freedom more than anything."

"That's understandable," she said. "I'm not trying to take that away from you, Jack. You didn't have to tell me all of this…although I'm glad you did."

"I wanted you to understand that it wasn't about you," he said. He felt the need to hold her, to hug her, to believe that she really did accept all this about him and didn't want to press forward and "fix" him. "I know you want marriage and the whole nine yards. I never thought that way before. I always saw it as a loss of freedom."

"In a way, it is," she said. "But it doesn't have to be a bad thing. I always thought it was a trade of sorts. A partnership."

He sighed. "Honestly, I hadn't really thought of that, either."

"Your freedom again," she said.

"But it's different now," he said, putting an arm around her shoulders and squeezing gently. "I care about you. You know I want you and you know I want to be with you. I think maybe we could make this work."

She held him, and he felt her sigh against his chest. "Jack, I don't want you to force yourself into anything."

"I'm not," he said quickly. "I've been thinking about this…."

"But you don't sound thrilled with it," she countered. "This isn't what you want—it's what you think needs to happen. And that's not what I want."

He pulled back, huffing slightly. "Don't I get points for trying?"

"I love that you're trying," she said, and he felt some of his irritation back down. "But I…care too much about you to watch you tie yourself up in knots. It's not supposed to be hard, Jack."

"You have to work at any relationship," he argued.

"Yeah. But you don't have to fight to the death for it." That small, sad smile was back, and it was mirrored in the depths of her amber eyes. "At least I don't think you have to. And I've gone pretty far in my day."

He bit back a swear. "So where does that leave us?"

She didn't say anything. She simply leaned up and kissed him.

The feel of her soft lips against his was a balm—and also a torture. His emotions were already burning at a high level. He shouldn't be able to switch gears this fast—for the first time in his life, it seemed, he wanted to talk more than he wanted to have sex. But she was insistent and more temptation than his body or spirit could handle. He'd wanted her for too long, and when she started something, the woman damned well knew how to finish it.

He groaned against her mouth, succumbing to her. His hand threaded around the nape of her neck, holding her to him, and he heard her little cry of relief. He lowered them both to the bed, and her leg automatically hooked over his hip, bringing the heat between her thighs against his erection. His eyes went half-lidded in response as he kept kissing her.

He could do this forever, was his last coherent thought. He *wanted* to do this forever.

She pushed against him, to his surprise, laying him flat out on his back. Then she straddled him, and he mentally cursed the layers of denim between them.

"I want you," she said, looming over him, and shook her hair out of the bun, letting it tumble in cinnamon waves across her shoulders. "I've always wanted you. I don't care that it's not forever."

He wanted to protest, but she tightened her thighs and leaned down, crushing her breasts against his chest as she kissed him fiercely. It was almost more than his body could stand. He'd been dying, wanting her and not having her. Now she was seducing him.

He heard a boom and wondered for a second if it was his heart exploding. Then his brain registered a second loud noise

He sat up, holding Chloe to him.

"What was that?" she murmured, hugging him tighter, an edge of fear piercing through the desire.

"The storm," he said, glancing quickly out the window. "Damn it. I was hoping we'd avoid this."

He gently moved her from his lap, ignoring the throbbing ache of his groin. Outside the window it was dark…too dark. And loud. He had been too engrossed in his physical response to notice the increased tossing of the ship, the rolling pitch of it.

This was going to be bad.

"I have to go," he said quickly, turning to Chloe, whose eyes had widened. "Don't be scared. We've been through squalls before. I just need to concentrate on this."

She nodded.

Jose burst into the room, his clothes soaked. "We've got a wall of water coming at us, boss," he said, his voice grim.

"I'm on my way," Jack assured him. He turned to Chloe. "Stay belowdecks. Don't come up. I'll be back when everything's all right."

She nodded again, silent.

Jose was waiting for him, but he leaned down and kissed Chloe, hard. "I'm sorry," he murmured.

Then he walked out of his cabin, bracing himself for the storm.

"WHAT WAS THAT?"

Chloe heard Lily's shriek from her own cabin. Chloe had wondered the same thing; there were crashing noises of both surf and thunder, and the yacht was being tossed around like a sock in the spin cycle. Every sense was overwhelmed by the sheer magnitude of the storm: the deafening noise, the engulfing darkness shot through by flashes of lightning, the smell of salt water and rain, the raging feel of imbalance as bodies struggled for stability in a world that could not provide it. As for taste—everything tasted like fear.

In her cabin, bracing herself on whatever she could, Chloe felt as if she were going crazy. Jack had gone up to help Ace and Jose, presumably to steer while they did…something. Bail water? Fix machinery? She didn't know what exactly facing this storm entailed. It seemed more luck than anything. She realized just how little about this "business" she actually knew. She felt like a dilettante, a fraud. It was one thing to love boats when they were cruising on calm blue waves in balmy skies. But this?

She thought it might be exhilarating if she weren't so scared of dying.

Lily was crying by this point, loud, gulping sobs. Tom was trying to calm her, but his words were tinged in hysteria. "It's gonna be all right, honey," he yelled, but his words seemed more geared to convince himself first. "It's going to be all right…."

Chloe got up, lurching into the door of her cabin and throwing it open. She made her way down the hallway. She pounded on the door of the honeymoon cabin. Lily screamed in response.

"Tom! Lily!" she called. "It's Chloe!"

After a few moments, the door opened with some difficulty. Tom had opened it and he looked frantic. The evidence of Lily's sobbing was clear on her face: her pale complexion was splotchy, hectic with color. "Has something else happened? Are we okay?" Tom asked warily.

"No, no. Everything's fine." Or as fine as it could be. As far as she knew.

Tom looked puzzled for a second, his expression asking *Then why are you here?*

"I wanted to see how you were holding up," Chloe said slowly. "Sorry. That's stupid, considering. I mean, I wanted to see if there was anything I could do to help you two feel better."

That wasn't much of an improvement, she realized, since unless she had some godlike control of the weather, she could do exactly zip about their situation.

"Are we going to be all right?" Lily asked plaintively, curled up in a fetal ball on the bed.

Tom went back to Lily, and Chloe followed, sitting on Lily's other side. Tom was rubbing Lily's back with one hand and bracing himself with the other.

"We're going to be fine," Chloe said, packing as much reassurance into her voice as humanly possible.

"Of course we are," Tom echoed, sounding slightly more convincing than he had a few minutes ago. Apparently it was easier for him to comfort Lily with assistance, so Chloe felt better—she'd made the right decision. "Chloe's been on a ton of cruises with Jack and his crew. She knows he'll pull us through this."

Lily turned to Chloe, her eyes huge and imploring. "Is that true? Can Jack get us through this?"

Chloe blanched for a second. What could she say? She'd been on board for a month, and all of it in San Diego's temperate weather or up and down the coast. But Lily was pleading, and Tom was obviously expecting her to help out, not make the situation worse.

"Jack will get us through this," Chloe said.

"See?" Tom nodded like a bobblehead doll.

"But how do you *know*?" Lily's cry was almost a shriek.

Chloe watched the two of them, so terrified, trying so hard to cling to any kind of hope but still managing because the two of them were together.

Suddenly she felt calm, as if everything around them had gone quiet and still.

She took Lily's other hand, giving it a comforting squeeze to get her attention. When Lily focused on her, she said slowly and clearly, "I trust Jack with my life." The words rang with sincerity.

Lily swallowed, then some of the panic receded in her eyes.

"You can trust him, too." Chloe released Lily's hand, feeling more at peace than she had since this whole ordeal had begun.

Tom looked grateful. Lily turned to him, the worry lines in her face smoothing out a bit. She squeezed his hand with both of hers. "I love you, baby," she whispered.

He didn't say anything in response. He cradled her head in his lap, stroking her hair, then leaning down and kissing her temple. It was one of the most tender things Chloe had ever seen. It was obvious that Lily was his world.

Chloe felt her throat close up. *That's what I want,* she thought. Even with disaster looming all around them, they had each other. And it was enough.

She was in love with Jack McCullough. Whether or not he felt the same way, it was there. He might never be able to be in a committed relationship—he might never be able to fulfill her dreams. But for right now he was what she needed, and after a storm like this, she was beginning to realize there wasn't always going to be a future to plan for. Sometimes you had to take life moment by moment.

Now was one of those times.

She left Tom and Lily, reassured that they were going to be all right, and went back to Jack's cabin to wait. The storm dragged on for another two hours, and Chloe spent most of the time curled up, like Lily, in Jack's bed, waiting for him. She had faith that he would pull them through the worst of it.

She just knew that when he was finished, she wanted to be there. With him.

"LOOKS LIKE THE WORST is over," Ace said, relief thick in his voice.

Jack nodded, for a second too tired to speak. That hadn't been the worst storm he'd ever weathered, not by a long shot, but he wasn't quite as young a man and this time he had two charter passengers and Chloe on board, counting on him. His crew knew what they'd signed up for. Tom and Lily were probably still hysterical. And Chloe...

He smiled. Chloe was a trooper. She was tougher than anybody, certainly that pansy ex of hers, would give her credit for. He imagined she was probably in her cabin or at his desk, coming up with a list of things they'd need to deal with when they got to Oahu.

"We'll be in Hawaii in a day," Jack said finally. "Jose, you okay to steer from here?"

"I'm fine," he said. Thankfully, Jose was Zen-stoic. He could handle pretty much any crisis. He'd be a great captain of his own one day. "I'll just make myself a pot of coffee."

"Ace, you go get a few hours of sleep and then spell him," Jack instructed. "I'm going to grab a few hours, too, but if anything comes up—"

"I'll get you," Jose said as if it went without saying. Which, Jack supposed, it did. "Go get some rest, boss."

Jack nodded gratefully and headed down belowdecks to the cabins. He didn't hear Tom and Lily, so he hoped that, with the gradual calm, they were asleep. He also hoped it hadn't been too tough a trip for them. He knew this was Chloe's last trip with the *Rascal,* but that could only happen if she got enough money to pay her mortgage payment—and *that* could only happen if the Rorshans paid. Although, after a trip like this, if they complained and tried to cut their payment, he wouldn't blame them. Nobody signed on for a honeymoon vacation with a squall.

Maybe I can help Chloe pay for it, he thought, heading numbly back to his own cabin. He didn't want her to leave, not by any stretch of the imagination. But he wasn't bastard enough to ruin her credit and her plans just so he could selfishly spend more time with her against her will.

He might be commitment-phobic and have a boatload of issues, but he really did love her.

He opened his door, surprised to find the battery-cube lights glowing. And Chloe was in his bed, sleeping, looking like an angel in tangled sheets.

He stood there for a second, studying her. Her hair was loose, trailing across his pillow. The blanket was pulled around her, and she snuggled in. She had to have been scared, he thought, gently sitting down on the bed next to her. She was tough, sure. He never underestimated her on that front. But she was fragile, too. He remembered what he'd first thought the moment she'd walked onto the *Rascal* and into his life. She'd seemed so delicate she might shatter under one harsh look. He'd revised his assessment since then, but the delicacy was still a part of her, one he treasured.

She stirred, turning to look at him. "Jack," she breathed, sitting up and wrapping her arms around him. It wasn't sexual, at least not intentionally. She clung to him as if she couldn't bear to let him go, and that's when he realized he was holding her the same way. He'd had close calls before, but he'd never had someone waiting there when he came out on the other side…same as he'd never had someone he cared about so deeply.

He stroked the back of her head, smoothing her hair down her back. When his hand left her hair, he realized he had moved onto bare skin. She wasn't wearing anything beneath his sheet and comforter. She'd been waiting for him, naked, in his bed.

His hand froze on her hip as his mind and body temporarily shorted out in confusion on what to do next.

"Jack?" she asked quietly. "Are you all right?"

If he made the move on her, they'd have one fantastic night, he already knew that. But he also knew she was planning on leaving as soon as this trip was over. Did that mean she'd jump on a plane as soon as she got to Hawaii? Was this going to be a goodbye encounter? Or did this mean he'd have a chance to keep her and buy himself time to figure out his commitment issues? And maybe move on to something more meaningful?

And if it was a goodbye and nothing else, was he going to turn her down on principles or risk missing this last experience of her, something he'd probably regret for the rest of his life?

"Jack?" Chloe repeated.

The concern in her voice registered, and he sighed heavily, kissing her neck. "Sorry, baby," he murmured. "It's been a hell of a night."

"The ship's all right, though." It wasn't even a question. Her faith in him was mind-boggling.

"Yeah, the ship's all right," he repeated. "We'll get to Oahu tomorrow, and from all the reports, there won't be any more problems. Smooth sailing from here on out."

"That's good," she said, nuzzling against his chest. "I was worried about you."

He smiled, kissing her on the lips gently. "I was pretty worried there for a while myself," he admitted. Then he stroked her collarbone with one finger. "Thanks for waiting for me."

He didn't want to ask her point blank *What exactly are your intentions here?* But confusion warred with exhaustion, and when she stroked his shoulders and kissed him, he found himself unable to ask her anything. She reached for the edge of his T-shirt, pulling it over his head, and he let her. She unbuckled the fly of his sea-soaked jeans, and he stood up and peeled them off, his skin feeling clammy and numb. He kicked off all his clothes and left them in a pile.

She held the sheet open with invitation, and he wordlessly climbed in beside her. She made a little squeak of protest when she moved against him.

"Sorry," he said, referring to the cold state of his body. "God, you feel good. Warm."

She took a deep breath and then she climbed on top of him. He moaned, and not just from the naked contact of their skin but from the delicious feeling of calm seeping through his tired muscles. "That better?" she murmured against his ear.

"You are better to me than I deserve," he said with feeling, stroking her sides with his hands as their legs entwined. "This is heaven. I could fall asleep."

He could feel her tense against him. "Uh…okay," she said finally.

He laughed. "But I get the feeling I'm not going to."

She smiled down at him, her hair framing both of their faces. "Well, that's okay, too," she said, her tone wry.

His body was warming up—in more ways than one. He leaned up and kissed her more thoroughly now, and her breasts moved against his chest, her legs splaying outside of his hips. He reached up and cupped her breasts, and she made a low moan of pleasure. Her hips moved downward, and he could feel her wetness brush against his penis. The shudder that hit him was impossible to stop. All his feelings of fatigue seemed to burn away in the face of this, the two of them. He went rock-hard, his body straining to enter hers.

"Chloe," he breathed against her mouth. "I feel like I've wanted you forever."

"Then take me." She arched back, and he felt the tip of his erection dip inside her.

His hands shot down her body, fingers digging into the curves of her hips before cupping her buttocks. He wasn't wearing a condom...

"Wait," he started to say. Tried to say.

She was closing her eyes and moving rhythmically against him, teasing him. He dipped a little farther, the head of his cock disappearing into the juncture of her thighs. She paused, cradling him, and he felt her shiver against him. "Please," she whispered. "I've wanted you for so long."

Rational thought fled. He pulled her down as he pushed his hips upward and he slid inside her, feeling her tight, damp passage caressing the whole hard length of him. *"Chloe,"* he choked out. He couldn't remember the last time he'd had sex like this. Probably because it had *never* been like this.

"Oh, Jack!" she cried, twisting her hips in a circle that almost made him come right there. "It feels so *good*..."

He let her dictate the tempo, watching her ride him as he caressed her hips and thighs, gritting his teeth against the torrent of sensations burning through him. She moved with the grace of a dancer and the sensual skill of some legendary courtesan. His body was aflame, all memories of the cold and the damp and the fear disintegrated. All that mattered was being here, with her, now.

She started to pick up in speed, her breathing going to the telltale quickness of a woman on the edge.

"Are you close?" he asked, straining to keep his own need leashed.

She couldn't respond, only nodded and continued her relentless motions. He sat up, kissing her hard, and she kissed him back ferociously, their tongues intertwining as she moved to wrap her legs around his waist, bringing her clit in closer friction with the top of his cock. She threw her head back and cried out with pleasure, constricting around him as he drove higher and harder against her.

"Jack!" she shouted, shuddering against him.

His cock was throbbing painfully, his whole body clamoring for release, but he rode her through the waves of her orgasm and then held her gently as she held him, leaning her sweat-dampened forehead against his shoulder. He waited for her to look over, into his eyes.

"I think I love you, Chloe," he murmured.

She stared at him solemnly.

He didn't want her to answer or feel pressured, so he tenderly kissed her again. Then, with one fluid motion, he moved her to her back, staying buried between her thighs. She smiled at him then, her arms reaching out to his waist, her legs staying hooked over his hips as she tilted her pelvis up to receive as much of him as he could give her.

He moved slowly, savoring each sensation, and she moved with him. They were so close—it was cliché, but he felt as if they'd blurred boundaries, as if he couldn't distinguish between her body and his. He wanted her. He loved her. He had her.

She was moving in time with him, the two of them picking up speed, clutching at each other with a frantic passion that was impossibly intense, when he heard her let out a squeak of surprise before letting out a rippling cry. He felt her body clench around him again, the tremors of orgasm lapping at him, and he gave in to his own need. He moaned, shuddering, emptying himself in her, and he lost his mind in oblivion.

After long moments, he collapsed against her, feeling hot and wrung out and sated. And, above all, happy. He nuzzled against her neck, then kissed her face, gentle kisses that seemed silly and joyful after what they'd just done. Finally realizing he was probably getting heavy, he rolled off her but keeping skin contact. He didn't want to be apart from her. Not for a second.

She was quiet, only the uneven sound of her breathing could be heard.

"Are you all right?" he asked, grinning.

She turned to him, her eyes huge and round. "Jack," she said, hesitant. "What did we just do?"

He started as if she'd slapped him. When, in fact, reality had smacked him a good one.

Sex. Without a condom.

Oh, God, what did we just do?

9

"WELL, TOM & LILY ARE flying home instead of sailing." Jack spoke, standing on the deck of the *Rascal* in a sleeveless shirt and a pair of shorts. "I can't blame them, really. They are going to spend a couple of days here on the island, though, to make up for it."

"That's nice," Chloe said absently. "They probably want to replace some of the scarier moments with some pleasant ones. It's their honeymoon, after all."

"Exactly," Jack said. "They're great people. I offered to discount their cruise—it wasn't their fault, and they had a lot more traumatic time than Mrs. Newcombe. Tom said no, that there was nothing we could have done about a freak storm. He also said if it weren't for our crew, he and Lily might not have survived." Jack smiled. "They're just good people."

Chloe smiled, too, thinking of the couple in their cabin, hanging on to each other in the belly of the storm. "Yes, they are."

Chloe and Jack fell silent. It was an uncomfortable, awkward silence, and for them it was unusual.

Chloe looked out from the dock to the island. She'd never seen Hawaii before. The place looked like every single postcard she'd ever received from a vacationing friend or neighbor—only a lot more so. Aquamarine water rolling against white sand beaches under a perfect turquoise sky. She would've been gaping with awe if it weren't for her mind drowning out any other thought: *You might be pregnant.*

The island's beauty was lost on her.

After the trauma of the storm and her decision that she was falling in love with Jack—even after that short a time period, in such unbelievable circumstances—she'd made a rash decision. She hadn't slept with very many people, admittedly, and with those people she'd always been scrupulously careful. She'd enjoyed herself, but safety had always been paramount over sheer pleasure. Last night she'd been reckless. Stupid. So glad to be alive and with Jack that she'd let her body do what it wanted and the hell with the consequences.

Well, welcome to hell. Consequences coming right up.

"Ace and Jose are going out for the day—and most of the night," Jack said. "I doubt either of them will be back before morning. But by tomorrow afternoon or so, we'll probably head back to San Diego." He paused. "Is that okay? Did you want to stay longer? Or…hell, are you going to be okay crossing the ocean again? The weather reports are all clear for the week, but I wouldn't blame you…."

"No, I'll go back on the boat," Chloe said quickly.

They fell into that painful silence again.

Chloe finally cleared her throat.

"First of all," began Jack, "I am so sorry for not being more careful last night. I feel horrible."

She shook her head. "I was there, too," she protested. "I was just as responsible, trust me."

"I want you to know that I haven't done that before. With anyone." He grimaced. "It was incredible."

She closed her eyes. Yes, it certainly had been. Which was why the shock of it hit her so hard. She couldn't say she was entirely sorry that it happened, even though she knew it was ill-advised, to say the least, that it had happened at all.

"But it was still dangerous," Jack said.

She nodded, feeling weary. Of course, he was right—and more than that, he was logical. He was being rational and saying the right things. So why was she feeling so depressed?

It should have been beautiful, romantic. Uncomplicated. Now it sounded like a criminal case.

I thought love was supposed to be different than this.

She quashed the thought. "I agree. Of course."

He squinted at her. "Are you sure you're ready to talk about this now?"

Was she? "Of course," she demurred.

He put his hands in his pockets. "There is one other thing," he said slowly. "I don't suppose you're on the Pill or anything…."

Okay, she wasn't ready for this conversation after all. "I think I'm going to go onshore," she blurted.

He nodded in return, his eyes a little surprised. She wished he'd hold her, hug her, comfort her somehow, instead of being so bloody levelheaded. But no, he just said, "I'll have my cell phone on if you need me. We should get reception here."

"All right," she said numbly, then grabbed her purse and fled off the dock and up to the island itself. She didn't know where she was going and frankly she didn't care. she just needed to be away…away from the *Rascal,* away from Jack. Away from reality, if only for a minute or two.

She might be pregnant, she thought, looking over some skimpy bikinis and boxes of chocolate-covered macadamia nuts in a small shop. She loved Jack, but this…

I can't even get him to agree to work with me. How could I get him to be okay with this?

Her cell phone rang, startling her. "Hello?"

"Oh, good, you're able to answer." Her mother's voice sounded perky. "You're never going to believe what's been happening!"

I could say the same thing to you, Chloe almost said. "What's going on? Is something wrong?"

"Nothing's wrong." Her mother sounded downright gleeful. "First, we got a call from her."

"Her?"

"The mother. You know, Gerald's mother."

Chloe flinched. As if she didn't have enough problems. "What did she want?"

Her mother paused, obviously surprised by Chloe's uncharacteristic bluntness. "Uh…well, apparently she decided that Gerald ought to keep the house after all."

Chloe felt anger well up inside her like…like lava, she thought, seeing a miniature plastic volcano. "I told him. I warned him that this thing was going to be taken care of this month. If she's trying to jerk me around, I don't care how many lawyers they have, I'm going for blood."

"Good heavens, dear!" Her mother sounded truly shocked. "Actually, it's just the opposite. She's agreed to pay you back your half deposit and cover all costs of changing the deed, putting it in Gerald's name. So it would be off your hands."

Chloe made a *humph* noise. "Why the sudden change of heart, I wonder?"

"I think it's because she likes the neighborhood—and the school district." Her mother paused again. "I don't mean to upset you with this, but she did mention that Gerald was probably getting married. To that other woman."

Chloe gritted her teeth. Gerald's mother had deliberately dropped that in to hurt her, she felt quite sure. Well, she had bigger issues in her immediate future. "Fine. That's fine. Have her send over the check and any paperwork I have to sign. I should be back next week."

"But there's more." Her mother didn't gossip often, but when she did, it was with all the enthusiasm of a kid with a banana split. "Guess who else called?"

"Mom," Chloe warned, rubbing at her temple with her free hand. She thought Hawaii was supposed to be relaxing.

"Gerald called. Can you believe it?" Her mother all but crowed the announcement. "He said he had to talk to you, that it was urgent. I told him you were on another cruise and wouldn't be reachable. Can you believe it? The nerve of that wretch!"

"If it's so urgent, I'm sure his lawyers will call me," Chloe said, not caring at all about Gerald anymore. Which was a good sign, she supposed. "Anything else?"

"Are you all right, dear? You sound out of sorts."

Out of sorts? Didn't begin to cover it. *The man I'm in love with might or might not be in love with me but probably can't commit to me, and now I might be carrying a child that he doesn't want and which will doubtlessly push him over the edge.*

Out of sorts, indeed.

"I'm just tired, Mom," Chloe countered, her rote answer for when things were going wrong but she didn't want to discuss it.

"You're working too hard," her mother gave her pat response. "You'll be home, what, tomorrow?"

"No, this is a little longer cruise," Chloe said, then grinned. "I'm in Oahu, actually."

"Oahu?" her mother squeaked. "Hawaii?"

"That's the one."

"And you went in a boat?"

"People do it all the time, Mom," Chloe said.

"Oh, right." Her mother's voice crackled with awe and humor.

"I'm handling everything, Mom," Chloe said, her voice a shade too sharp. "I'll call when I get back to town."

For a second, Chloe wished she could spill everything, talk it all out. But would her mother be sympathetic? Or whip out her pen and organizer and write her a checklist of all her options and what she needed to take action on next? Chloe didn't need that, not right now. Right now, she needed…

Comfort.

She was crying before she realized it, and people were starting to stare. She mumbled a tearful goodbye to her mother and hung up. With blurred vision she retraced her steps and headed back to the *Rascal*. She rushed on board to find Jack still on deck, drinking a beer and looking out at the water.

"Chloe?" he asked, his voice filled with concern.

She waved him away with one hand and ran to her cabin, throwing herself down on her narrow cot. She cried herself exhausted, and then finally fell into a thankfully dreamless sleep.

JACK SAT IN HIS CABIN, feeling…well, feeling a lot of things.

Confusion probably topped the list, he had to admit. He rearranged things on his desk endlessly, as though he were playing a game of Tetris, moving folders and ledgers and his calculator with no purpose. He had had enough problems just dealing with the fact that he was falling in love with Chloe. He was wrestling with the dilemma of how to make this "partnership" work, as well—how much freedom to give up, considering he'd already be living with her and working with her. And now this.

She'd stopped crying, as far as he could hear, but he felt

wrecked. He hated seeing her hurt and hated more knowing that he was the cause of it.

How could you have been so stupid?

He'd known for a second that night that it was the wrong thing to do, but in that pivotal moment he'd ignored his conscience and gone for it anyway. And now…well, there they were.

Can you raise a kid on a boat?

For a second, he had a picture of himself with a son, standing on the bow. Jack could see himself teaching the kid how to steer, how to fish, swim. It was idyllic. A far cry from what he'd grown up with. He'd be damned if he raised his kid the way he was raised.

But then, he knew some things just happened. You went back to what you were used to. It was a big part of why he'd never thought of having kids. Now the possibility, the potential reality of it was staring him in the face. Maybe a more apt analogy was the possibility he had a laser sight aimed between his eyes. So right behind confusion, his next ranking emotion would have to be classified as fear. Plain and simple.

He wasn't proud, but he wasn't about to start lying to himself. Not with this much at stake.

The guys were still out, as he'd predicted. He glanced at his watch: ten o'clock. Chloe hadn't eaten anything since breakfast, as far as he knew. She had to be starving, upset or not, and she hadn't left her cabin since running on board early that afternoon.

He got up and headed for the galley. He cut up some fruit and cheese and got some of the crackers she favored and set it all out on a plate. Then he headed for her cabin and knocked on the door. She didn't answer, which worried him, so he opened it.

She woke up when he turned on the light and she blinked owlishly. "I'm sorry I woke you," he said, immediately contrite. "I just…I figured you hadn't eaten anything."

"You cooked?"

He grimaced. "Um, sort of."

He sat down next to her on her cot, taking as little room as possible—there wasn't much to the bed to begin with. She sat up, propped up on one elbow. "I don't know that I feel hungry," she said.

"You still should eat something," he pressed. "You're upset. You'll feel better after you've had some nourishment."

She sighed, then shrugged, reaching for a piece of apple.

"Let me do the talking," he said with more bravado than he felt. "We did something...well, probably not all that bright last night. But it's not the end of the world. It was really emotional, and I'm done beating myself up about it. And you should be, too."

She sat up at his stringent tone. "I'm not beating myself up about last night," she protested, then looked down when his stare bore into her. "Not as much as I was, anyway."

"Good, because it would be a waste of time. We did it, it's done. Next issue."

"It's the next issue that has me so..." She made a futile gesture with her hands, a spinning motion. "It's like being in that storm last night. Only about a thousand times worse."

"I know exactly what you mean," he said with feeling and then felt like a heel when her face crumpled with remorse. "But I steered us through that storm last night, remember? It's disorienting, but if you keep your head about you, you get through it. This is the same sort of thing."

"So, what, I should...buck up?" Her tone was incredulous.

"I'm not saying that," he said, putting an arm around her shoulders and squeezing her. She felt chilly to him. "I'm saying I got us through last night. I'll get us through this time."

She blinked at him.

"Good grief," he said, offended. "What did you think I'd do? Abandon you?"

"I...I guess I didn't really think at all," she said, then grimaced. "Lot of that going around."

"What did I say about beating yourself up?" he warned. "And, trust me, I wouldn't abandon you." He kissed her head, a quick buss. "I *won't* abandon you."

He pulled back enough to see the sheen of tears across her eyes.

"I mean it," he said, feeling his own heart beat heavily. "Why are you crying?"

"Because you mean it," she said, the edges of her words watery with emotion. "I...God, I can't remember the last time I could count on somebody to be there for me. I'm used to taking care of myself."

He realized from the way she said it that she meant it, too.

He stood up, ignoring her startled look. Then he scooped her up and carried her out of the cabin, down the hallway, to his cabin. He placed her gently on his bed.

"What are you doing?"

"You're going to stay with me tonight," he instructed. "In fact, I'm going to stay by your side all the way to San Diego pretty much."

She snorted. "Let's not get carried away here. I wasn't pleading for sympathy when I said I'm used to taking care of myself. I'm not a martyr and I believe I've already told you...I'm certainly not a victim. I take responsibility for my own..."

"Oh, shush," he said, and the look of utter shock on her face was enough to put a smile on his. "I know you're a woman who takes responsibility for her life. Well, fantastic. But you're the one who wanted to be partners with me, remember?"

"That's...that's a whole other issue entirely!" she spluttered.

"Yeah, well, this is part of that," he said. "It doesn't just mean that you become my Girl Friday. You're not signing on to take care of me. If you become my partner…or more…" The words made his stomach drop, like being on a free-fall roller coaster, but he plowed forward anyway. "That means you need to get used to me taking care of you, too. Equal partners."

She frowned, looking as if she was still trying to wrap her head around the concept.

Yet another reason for me to hate Gerald. Obviously the guy had simply used Chloe for years, as his secretary and his lover, and had given her exactly diddly-squat when it came to any kind of support.

"I…huh. I think I may need to get used to this," she said in a small voice.

"Yeah, well, I'll give you plenty of opportunities to adjust," he said, climbing into bed next to her. "So work on it."

She smiled reluctantly, and he felt the knot that had formed in his chest releasing slowly. Now that was more like it. Seeing her feel more comfortable was enough to ratchet his tension down a few notches.

He started stroking her hair, and her smile became more natural. "You want a back rub?" he asked.

"You don't have to…."

"You're not working on it."

She rolled over onto her stomach. "I feel a little ridiculous," she admitted, her voice muffled by his pillow.

He started rubbing her back gently, as nonseductively as possible. For once, sex with Chloe was the furthest thing from his mind. He felt her muscles slowly dissolve from the calcified knots of stress to a more smooth, jellylike state of relaxation. She sighed with pleasure, and he felt gratified. He kept working at her slowly, from the crown of her head to her toes.

"This is more than just helping me out," she finally said when he finished. "This is spoiling me."

"You're due," he said.

She smiled at him. "Is there anything I can do for you?"

He studied her. He guessed that she was offering something of a more carnal nature. And she was in his bed. All she had to do was be near him or on the same boat or possibly in the same state, and he'd want her, no question.

But she still had bruiselike smudges of darkness beneath those amber eyes of hers, and while she was now relaxed, he could still sense the fatigue coming off her. "We've got time," he said, kissing her gently on the mouth. "Let's take it slow tonight."

She sighed and took off her clothes, and he did the same, wondering if he was going to be able to keep his resolve when the two of them were naked under the covers. Still, when she curled up against him like a cat and almost immediately fell asleep, he knew he'd made the right decision.

At least he'd done *something* right, he thought as he lay in bed, sleep completely evading him. He talked a good game and he did want to help her. But he was still terrified of what was ahead of them—and he was not a man who scared easily. He would've loved to have talked it out with her. In fact, there really wasn't anyone else he could talk to as easily as he could to Chloe. She related. She made him feel like not only was anything possible but she believed that anything was possible *for him*. With her, he felt strong, heroic, invulnerable. Invincible.

Now she was the one who needed the strength and invincibility. And without her being his cheerleader, he was really lagging, trying to provide those things.

He had to figure out a way to make this work, he coached

himself. She was the big planner, granted, but he was a ship captain and he'd been running his own business for years now. He wasn't ready for this—for a kid, for a partnership or for whatever else might come up. But he'd have to get ready. And if it would be too upsetting for her to discuss his worries with...

Well, he'd just have to suck it up and get it done. No matter how he felt inside.

THEY TOOK ONE MORE day in Hawaii. Jose and Ace were in no hurry to get back to San Diego. After a night of partying, they really weren't in the best shape to man the crossing over the Pacific, so Jack had given them one more night. Chloe had spent the day happily distracted. Jack had been to Hawaii dozens of times, apparently, and he knew Oahu the way he knew his own cabin. He took her for a gorgeous walk through a tropical forest, took her to lunch at a great little café, and planned to take her to dinner. He even bought her a sarong in a bright red print. Now she was tanning on a towel on one of the beaches while Jack went and got her sugar cane and pineapple.

She'd never felt this taken care of before. It was an amazing feeling.

She rolled over onto her stomach, to ensure that she got even color on both sides, checking that her office-pale skin wasn't getting burned from the unaccustomed sun exposure. She'd become more tan as she'd worked on the boat, she realized, seeing the marks from her shorts and her T-shirts. Living and working on the boat was changing her life.

She rubbed absently at her still-flat stomach. Changing her life might be the biggest understatement of all.

Her cell phone rang in her purse, and she pulled it out, checking the caller ID. It was Gerald. She decided to ignore him. Within moments, the voice-mail alert came up. She listened to it, wondering if he was going to make her life worse and delay the house sale. His voice sounded reedy and somewhat whiny to her now. It also held elements of his sales voice, which immediately caused her guard to go up.

"Chloe, your Mom says you're working on a cruise ship of some sort. She mentioned that you'd probably be home by now, but I've stopped by their place and they haven't seen you and wouldn't tell me where you were."

Ha! She frowned. As if he had any right to know!

"We really need to talk. About the house sale, about the wedding…about everything. I can't let things keep going on this way. I feel like I'm going crazy."

Yeah, lot of that going around, pal. She shook her head. *Take a number. I'll get back to you at my earliest convenience, which may not be for a hellish long while.*

"I think I might be able to get you your job back, as well." This said in his superpersuasive voice. As if it was somehow an incentive. "And…well, I can't leave all this on a voice mail. I think we should meet. Face-to-face."

As if that was going to happen. Her mother was right. The nerve of this guy.

"Finally…I know how my mother's been bullying you. My lawyers have been giving you the runaround. I should've said something, but you know how my family gets. I couldn't stop them, but I can make this up to you. The money, the headaches…everything. Just give me a chance."

I almost married that guy, she thought with a sense of detachment. He'd made sense, in a lot of ways. He would've been like a business partner, except he was more her boss. Even though she'd run the show, he'd still taken the lion's share of the credit. And she had been okay with that. In fact, she'd been *proud* of being the silent partner, the one behind the scenes. She still could be, she sensed with a sense of distaste.

Jack walked up to her as she was putting her phone away. "Problems?" he asked, kneeling carefully beside her on the towel. "You don't look happy."

"That was Gerald," she said, and his frown looked like a thundercloud. "He left a voice mail."

"What does he want?" The suspicion and malice dripped from Jack's words.

She shook her head. "He seems to have developed an attack of conscience. Maybe he was visited by three ghosts or something. He wants to try to make things up to me. Yeah, I didn't believe it, either," she said in response to Jack's new expression.

"He must need something," Jack said, his tone curt and dismissive.

"I think he just wants me back," Chloe said, wondering if she should feel offended. She was pretty touchy, emotionally speaking. "Maybe he misses me."

"I didn't get the impression that he was that smart," Jack said, and Chloe smiled, feeling better. "And if he had any kind of conscience, he would never have put you through what he did. No real man would have acted like he did."

"What, by standing me up?"

"That and being a total coward," Jack said, his voice almost a growl. He was gripping the sugar cane so hard it actually dripped juice on the corner of the towel. "The guy sent a messenger to do his dirty work and his *mama* to bust your kneecaps. The guy's a jerk."

"No arguments here," Chloe said, comforted. "You're, uh, crushing my dessert there."

"Huh? Oh, crap." Jack quickly handed her the sugar cane. It was spliced at the end, dripping with gooey, clear sugar-juice.

She'd been watching kids devouring the stuff all morning, so she gingerly took a bite. "Oh! Yikes. This stuff is *sweet!*"

"Sort of the point, Chloe," Jack teased. "Incredible, huh?"

"I think I can feel my heart rate increasing," she laughed.

"Well, come on. There's more to do."

From there, they did another tour of the area, and dinner was lovely. Finally, they walked in the moonlight to the *Rascal.*

"Are Ace and Jose back?" Chloe asked.

"They're staying on the island tonight," Jack replied as they went into his cabin. "I told them I wanted you to myself tonight."

She blushed, wondering what they thought of the whole thing.

"Don't worry," Jack said, as if reading her mind. "They like you. And they don't know why you're settling for me, but they're glad we're together."

Together. The very thought made her insides turn to warm jelly.

She'd been so worried about falling for him. And he was being so supportive and kind and just *there* for her. She didn't know life could be like this. Now that she knew, she didn't know how she'd settled for anything else.

Jack latched the door and she smiled as she shrugged out of her sarong.

"We don't have to take it slow tonight, do we?"

She said it in her sexiest voice, even though she was nervous. He was being incredibly tender and sweet, but did he still want her? They were talking about being partners. She got the feeling that they were headed for more. And she knew that once she and Gerald had gotten engaged, sex had become a back-burner issue. She was sure there probably wasn't any logical connection, but still…

His smile was laced with heat. "Not if you don't want to, sweetheart." The light in his eyes was heart-stopping.

She shimmied out of her underwear and walked to him, her eyes never leaving his. "I don't want to go slow."

He nodded, then closed his eyes as she unbuttoned his shirt and undid his pants. She was moving slower, partially to make the experience last but also because it felt new. Now…it meant more than just sex and confusion. It was more than love, even.

It was *commitment,* she realized. And that put a whole new spin on things. This must have been what real honeymoons felt like, she thought with wonder.

As she eased his shirt off his shoulders, he turned his head to kiss her hand, and she felt a wave of warmth tumble through her. Finally, he was standing as naked as she was in the center of the cabin. "I wasn't sure if you'd still want me," she said, then winced. She hadn't meant to admit that, certainly not to him and certainly not right now.

"Are you kidding?" His voice was reassuring. "I always want you, Chloe. Even when I couldn't have you, I wanted you. Sometimes I think it was from the first minute I saw you. I've never felt like this before."

"I haven't, either," she said, running her hands down the smooth planes of his chest, down the hard muscles of his abs. His penis was almost in a full erection, and she circled her hands around the heated hardness. He groaned, his hips pressing forward involuntarily so her palms could grip him completely. "You're so amazing."

He didn't respond to that verbally. Leaning down, he kissed her passionately. Her body immediately kicked into high burn, a state that always seemed easy to reach when Jack was around. They kissed like that for long minutes as his hands stroked her shoulders, her sides, then moved forward to cup her breasts, causing her to gasp against his lips. "You're the amazing one," he whispered to her.

He led her to the bed. She leaned forward and took his cock into her mouth, savoring its textures. A guttural moan of pleasure ripped from him as she sucked gently, cupping his balls with her hand. She tickled the tip of his cock with her tongue, feeling it pulse beneath her. Then he pulled her up.

"You'll have me going too fast," he said in a choked voice. "I want to be inside you."

She watched as he got out a condom and put it on with shaking hands. The sight of it, the memory, caused her mood to darken a little. Of course, he was being careful, and she was grateful. But it did bring back everything she was trying not to think about now.

He reached for her, then paused, studying her face. "I lost you there for a minute."

"No," she demurred, but he was right. She was quite firmly in her logical mind at this point, rather than concentrating on what she was feeling.

"Allow me," he said, then nudged her onto her back. She giggled as he kissed the undersides of her breasts, then traced a ticklish pattern down to her belly button with his tongue. When he inched lower, she started to gasp. He put one finger inside her, gently, then used his tongue to work on her clit with sure, swift motions. Soon, all thought vanished, blown away by the sheer onslaught of physical sensation. By the time he sat up, there was a small, smug grin on his face, and she was begging for him, her body writhing for completion.

He turned her over, surprising her, then eased himself in, his hand reaching forward to manipulate her now-moist clit. She'd never gotten much out of the position before, the rare times

she'd tried it, but now she arched up, holding the headboard.
He glided inside her, circling his hips slightly, moving as surely
as he had moments ago with his tongue. The position made him
go deeper within her, and the pressure started to build.

"Oh," she moaned, bracing herself and pressing backward
as he pushed forward, the heat of him warming her, the strength
of him lifting her. Amazingly she felt orgasm blooming. He
reached with the other hand, cupping her breast almost roughly,
and her body shivered in delicious response. *"Ooooh—"*

"That's it, baby. Move with me," he muttered around
uneven breaths. He started to move faster, a bit harder, and
she was throwing herself against him, spreading her legs to
take him as far in as she possibly could. The slick pressure
of him, the intensity of his fingers moving her clit, the feel
of his cock pressing her spot was the perfect storm. She
screamed as the orgasm shot through her, almost passing out
from the force of it.

"Chloe!" He shuddered and lifted her with the force of his
thrust. Clutching both arms around her waist, just below her
breasts, it was as if he couldn't bear to be parted from her.
The two of them collapsed against the bed.

She felt spent. She felt *wonderful.* He was incredible, and
she couldn't believe that she was lucky enough to have found
him, even under the circumstances. He withdrew and she just
lay there, basking in the feeling. When he'd cleaned up and
returned to her side, she snuggled against him, kissing his chest.

"I love you, Jack," she said. "I could stay like this forever.
Thank you."

He didn't say anything, and she finally looked over at him.
He smiled at her, though she could've sworn she saw something, a pained expression cross his face.

She put her head against his shoulder. He loved her. He

wanted her. She knew all those things to be fact. And if it came down to it, he'd keep her with him. He was committed.

But something was still wrong.

10

THEY WERE WELL ON their way to San Diego. Out on the open ocean, the weather was pristine and beautiful. It should have been a pleasure—this was Jack's favorite kind of sailing, especially since there were no guests to attend to. Yet he couldn't help but feel a little cabin fever.

They weren't going to find out definitively if Chloe was pregnant or not until they got back to the mainland; apparently, you couldn't take the test the next day. The anticipation was beginning to wear him down. In the meantime, they talked about everything but the possible results. And "everything" included the partnership between the two of them regarding the *Rascal,* a subject that would have been difficult even if they didn't have this new added pressure bringing more significance to it. At the moment, he was standing up in the steering compartment, following the navigator and paying attention to the ship. It was as close to calm as he was going to get.

Chloe was so quiet walking up to him he actually jumped when she put her arms around his waist. "Good morning, you," she said, pressing a small kiss against his back.

"Hey, there." He shook himself mentally. He was getting far too wound up. She needed him to be strong, so he was being strong. He wouldn't dump his petty worries about all of this on her. After all, he wasn't going to be pregnant and possibly unemployed if all of this went kablooey.

"Are you going to be driving all morning?" she asked, her voice still light and happy.

"For another hour or two," he said, knowing that if he spent any longer, she'd know he was dodging her. "Then Jose will take over. Why? Did you want me for something?"

She hugged him again, and he felt guilt pile-drive him into the floor. "Nah. I've been thinking about marketing, that's all. Also, I wanted to run some invoice automation by you—the handwritten ones you've got could use work, and I think it'd make the process easier."

Jack frowned. "I don't have a computer."

"I thought we'd talk about that, too."

He grimaced. "How much is that going to cost me?"

"Well, it depends," she said. "And if I'm going to go in on this…well, if I'm a partner, maybe I could pay for it."

He bit back a sigh. "Let's talk about it," he agreed.

"Okay, I'll be sunning myself on the front deck."

He turned to see her smiling at him, looking like sunshine itself. He leaned forward and kissed her, marveling at the quickness of her response—the full sincerity and love he always felt when he kissed her. After a long moment, she broke off the kiss, her cheeks rosy, her eyes glowing.

"Don't be too long," she said with a wink. "Maybe we can fit in another kind of meeting."

His smile wasn't forced this time. "Count on it."

He watched her leave, then turned back to the steering wheel. Sex was the one uncomplicated thing in their relationship, in a way. He knew that they were phenomenal together and that it was the one place he was virtually guaranteed to make her happy and not screw up. Suddenly he remembered the condom incident, the thing that had forced all of this to a boil.

So it was *almost* the one place he didn't screw up. It was the one time he made up for everything else.

Jose walked in. "Hey, have you seen Chloe's bikini? Yow!"

Jack glared at him.

"Oops. Sorry. But, hey, your woman's hot," Jose said with a chuckle. "It's not like that's a secret."

Your woman. Jose and Ace had responded to Chloe's open status as his lover with aplomb. They liked Chloe and thought she was good for both Jack and the business. "Is something up?"

"I figured you'd enjoy the bikini rather than being stuck up here all day," Jose said. "The engine's going fine, although that pump will probably need some repairs. And we're going to want a tune-up pretty soon."

More expenses, Jack thought, nodding. "We'll get it taken care of as soon as we get a break. Anything else?"

"Nothing that can't wait," Jose said. "Go ahead. Have some fun."

"I think I'll keep driving for a while," Jack said.

Now Jose's eyes narrowed. "Uh-oh."

"Uh-oh, what?"

"Uh-oh...tell me you're not thinking of cutting bait with Chloe."

Jack gripped the steering wheel tighter. "It's not like that." He let out a deep breath. "It's...complicated."

Jose crossed his arms. "Really."

He couldn't tell Jose about the pregnancy stuff—sure, they'd been friends for years, but some things were just too personal. "I'm thinking of bringing Chloe on board as a partner," he said instead.

Jose frowned. "I thought you were hiring her as a marketing person."

"Well, yeah. Like that," Jack said.

"That's different than partner, don't you think?"

Now Jack frowned. "Actually, you're right." And that might've been part of the problem he was having with her.

"If you were going to have someone co-own the boat," Jose pointed out, "I've been with the *Rascal* for three years—and I've worked with you on different crews for longer than that. She's been here for—what—just over a month?"

Now guilt revisited Jack in spades. "I told you it was complicated."

"No wonder you're looking like you've got demons running after you," Jose said. "I wouldn't have pegged her to be someone power-hungry, honestly. Is she pressuring you into this?"

"No." He closed his eyes. Though he wasn't doing this entirely out of his own free will, either. "Not exactly."

"Damn." Jose shook his head. "This isn't good, pal. No wonder you're thinking of breaking it off."

"I'm not thinking of breaking it off," Jack repeated vehemently.

Jose quietly studied Jack for a minute. "I've never seen you like this with a woman ever, man. What's different about this one?"

What *was* different about Chloe?

"She's smart and funny and she genuinely gives a damn," Jack said slowly. "She cares about things. And people. She just wants to help. She's giving and generous and sweet."

"You mean, you'd take her on as a partner because you feel badly for her?"

"No," Jack growled. "I'd take her on as a partner because I'm in love with her."

That remark fell like an anchor. Jose whistled slowly.

"Wow. She *is* different."

"Tell me about it." Jack rubbed his hand over his face.

"That's an even better reason for why you look like you want to run," Jose said with a trace of amusement in his voice. "You take her on as a partner…that's like marriage."

"I know."

"After a month? Aren't you rushing it a little?"

"Maybe. Hell, probably." Jack felt like chewing on nails. "Here, take over the wheel. The way my head is this morning, I'll probably steer us to goddamn Fiji."

Jose took the wheel and clicked it on autopilot, then turned back to Jack. "You sure you don't want to think about all this, boss?"

"I have been thinking about it. I *am* thinking about it," Jack said wearily.

"What's she saying?"

"She seems to have no doubts whatsoever," Jack replied. "It's unnerving. She's so happy and certain, and it makes me feel like…"

"A piece of crap for not feeling the same way." Jose nodded sagely. "Man, if you don't tell her, it's going to come out later and it's going to be ugly. I know you. You mean well, but if you bottle stuff up, you snap."

"Thanks for the vote of confidence," Jack said drily. "But I think I know what I'm doing."

Jose shook his head. "Whatever you say, Jack."

He was still mulling Jose's comments as he walked to the front deck. The sight of Chloe momentarily knocked *all* thoughts from his head.

She was wearing a bikini, all right.

She turned, looking like a cover model, miles of tanned

skin stretching luxuriously over a white towel. There wasn't much to the midnight-blue suit, just a few strategically placed triangles of iridescent material. She smiled when she saw his expression. "Do you like it? I got it in Oahu."

He nodded, unable to speak.

"Come on down here," she said, patting the towel in front of her. "Enjoy the sun."

He stripped off his shirt and stretched out next to her. The sun heated him up in seconds. "This is nice," he said, still unable to tear his gaze from her body.

"Thanks," she said, grinning. "I would've never thought of this as work before. Thanks for introducing me to all of this, too."

He didn't want to pay attention to that, so he leaned forward and kissed her neck, enjoying her shiver of response.

"Not going to be a lot of time to sunbathe later on," she said with a reluctant sigh.

"Oh?"

"Two cruises booked back-to-back," she said. "I know it's a heavy schedule, but they went for the higher price. I figured we could use the money."

Jack frowned. "Well, we're going to have to cancel one of them," he said, remembering his conversation with Jose.

She sat up. "Why?"

"Engine needs a tune-up," he said. "And that pump's dodgy after the storm. I'm all for business, but not if we sink for it."

She bit her lip. "Damn."

For whatever reason—Jose's conversation, his general feelings of frustration—Jack took offense to that. "Listen, I know you've been great for business, but maybe you should be clearing more things with me before you book them."

She looked at him, startled, as if he'd just slapped her. "I was, generally. But you said you trusted me."

"I do, but you don't know about boats," he said. "There's more to running a cruise yacht than just answering the phone and plunking people in the calendar, you know."

She squinted at him. "I know that...."

"And after the storm, we really need to give the boat a checkup. Make sure the equipment's okay," he explained. He realized his voice was angry, and he struggled to keep it under control. "You don't know stuff like that."

"Well, I won't unless you tell me," she said, her voice tart.

"I am telling you!"

She stood up. "What is wrong with you? Why are you so mad at me?"

"I'm not mad at you!" he yelled. "I just...I think that you're great at sales and at administrative stuff and marketing. And I know you've enjoyed living on the *Rascal*. But it's not like this is one big floating holiday. This is serious. This is my life!"

Bam. There was the crux of it.

"Do you think I don't take this seriously?" she said, her voice incredulous. "That just because I don't know how to fix a bilge pump or steer the boat I'm not fit to be a sailor or, more importantly, a partner? That I'm a pretty damned good secretary, but that's about it?"

"I didn't say that," he snapped, knowing she was projecting.

"You haven't said anything!" She grabbed her towel, stalking past him. He got up and followed her. "I thought everything was fine...no, I knew something was wrong, but you were putting on such a brave face. I can't believe you're letting this out *now*. It's obviously been bothering you. When would you have told me, Jack? When we were signing paperwork to share ownership? When we were writing up business contracts? Or, worse, *after* we'd signed?"

"Damn it, Chloe…" He chased her toward the cabins.

She spun on him. "You once called Gerald a coward for not facing me. But what do you think you're doing?"

"That's not the same thing at all and you know it!"

She walked to her cabin. "You keep telling yourself that," she spat out, then slammed the door on him.

He let out a yowl of frustration then went back to the dock, ignoring Ace's curious face peering out from his cabin.

Jack went up to steering. Jose looked at him, cracking a grin. "What did I tell—"

"Not one word, Jose," Jack warned. "Not. One. Word."

LATER THAT NIGHT CHLOE was still reeling from her spat with Jack. Her instincts had been telling her, despite their Ozzie-and-Harriet domesticity, that something was wrong. That Jack wasn't quite as thrilled with the situation as she was. And she hadn't meant to barge in on him with the partnership.

She frowned. Had she?

Ever since her canceled wedding, her life seemed to have been spent on a roller coaster. She'd been reacting to frequent twists and turns, it seemed. She didn't have a job, Jack needed help, she loved her time on the *Rascal,* both for itself and for Jack. So it had seemed a natural progression to get a job on the ship—and then maybe making it more than just a job, if at all possible.

Then she'd fallen in love with Jack and things quickly spiraled out of control.

Maybe she should have known better. She paced the narrow confines of her cabin. She wasn't the type to fall in love quickly and she wasn't the type to act rashly. In fact, she was genetically predisposed to acting slowly and with lots of careful consideration. No wonder her parents and family members thought she'd blown a gasket. She wasn't acting like herself.

Why is that?

She didn't know. She rubbed at her temples with her fingertips. She honestly didn't know, although she suspected it had a lot to do with Jack.

She'd never met anyone like him, much less gotten involved with someone so laid-back. He took things as they came at him. He didn't plan. He barely seemed to care about anything, she thought with a wince, except for his freedom, which he equated with the *Rascal.*

And here she was, threatening the only thing he gave a damn about.

It wasn't like I planned all this myself, she thought bitterly. *It's not like I woke up and thought, gee, how can I ruin a man's life today?*

She'd sequestered herself in the cabin, irritated with herself and Jack, if not the whole situation in general. At this point, doing something little and stupid just to feel better had escalated to big and really stupid for the sake of fixing the little-and-stupid, and she was tired of it. She needed a plan. She needed to put her life back in order.

She grabbed her spiral notebook and a pen and headed for the galley. Her stomach was growling—she'd missed lunch. She needed to eat and to think.

She opened the galley door, and there was Jack, munching disconsolately on a sandwich. He swallowed hard when he saw her.

"Hey, there," he said in a subdued tone.

She nodded—rude, she knew. But she was still irritated and upset enough not to trust what might come out of her mouth. She put the notebook down on the table and rummaged through the refrigerator, deciding to make a sandwich for herself, as well. She threw together smoked turkey, Swiss cheese and avocado between honey-wheat bread slices slathered with deli mustard, and then grabbed a small carton of milk to go along with it. She sliced the sandwich in half and considered returning to her room, but the small table there was too tiny to fit both the food and her notebook. She bit her lip, then sat across from Jack.

"Did you want me to leave?" He'd finished his sandwich and was staring at her warily.

She shrugged. "Whatever you want."

He stared for a few minutes as she ate. She clicked the pen and started writing *Plan* at the top of the page. It was hard to focus with him looking at her.

Finally she looked up. "There are cookies in the cupboard," she offered. Maybe if he was eating, he'd be more distracted and therefore less distracting to her.

"I know," he replied. "I was afraid this was going to happen."

She sighed, putting the pen down. "Afraid what was going to happen?" she prompted, taking a bite of her sandwich. That would prevent her from making any untoward comments, at least.

"That I was going to screw up," he said, his voice glum.

She sighed and finished chewing. She said, "It would be better if you'd said something earlier, when things started to bug you."

"No, it wouldn't," he countered, as she took another bite. "It would've been the same thing, only earlier." He paused, then continued in a lower voice, "What kind of a jerk would I have to be, besides, to complain to you when you've got all this…you know, *stuff* going on?"

"We've both got *stuff* going on," she reminded him.

"Yeah," he said, though it didn't sound as if he believed it. "But it's worse for you."

She didn't know how he calculated that, but she wasn't going to argue with him. "So where does that leave us?"

"I don't know." He rubbed his hands through his hair in a gesture of frustration. "I honestly don't know."

She sighed again and finished the rest of her sandwich in silence. After putting her dishes in the sink, she grabbed her notebook and motioned to him. "Come on."

He looked at her as if she were holding a gun. "Where're we going?"

"To your cabin. We're having this out." She almost laughed at his expression—would have laughed if the whole thing weren't so depressing. "It's not a root canal, Jack. It's just talking."

He scowled and said something under his breath, but he followed her anyway. When they got there, she put her notebook down on his desk and then took off her clothes.

The look of stunned surprise on his face did make her laugh. "Uh…I thought we were going to talk."

"We are," she said, climbing into bed.

"So…" He paused and shifted his weight from foot to foot. "Okay, I'm an idiot. Why are you naked again?"

She smiled a little sadly. "Because sex is the one place we don't seem to have any problems," she said. "When it comes to sex, we're always good."

He nodded. "I noticed that, too." He paused again. "Are we having sex now, then? As a precursor to the talk?"

She shook her head. "No, we're going to have sex afterward. No matter what we talk about. That way, we'll have something good to shoot for."

"You can't honestly tell me you're going to want to have

sex after a fight," he said with disbelief. "Women never want sex when they're angry."

"If we're angry, then we're not done talking," she said reasonably. "We're going to hash this out, come to some conclusions, then we'll have sex. Work from there."

"This sounds nuts," he said but obligingly took off his clothes and clambered into bed next to her. "All right, we'll do this."

She couldn't help it, she chuckled. He just sounded so businesslike. "Why don't you start by telling me what you're feeling. What's *really* bothering you."

He squirmed uncomfortably. "This is very strange," he prefaced. "Let's see… What's really bothering me?"

She waited, ignoring the expanse of bare chest in front of her and looking intently into his eyes instead.

He took a deep breath, looking pained. Then he let out: "We've only known each other little more than a few months, we met because you were about to get married, I've never lived with anyone and I was just getting used to working with you when now I've found out that we're thinking of splitting my boat and possibly having a kid."

"Wow," she said. Then repeated. "Wow."

"Do you hate me?" He turned over, staring at her. "Like I said, you've got a ton on your plate. Am I a wretched human being for dumping all that on you now?"

"No," she said, still reeling from the sting. It wasn't as if he'd said anything she hadn't figured on her own. But hearing him put it out there so clearly, in such stark black-and-white detail… She shook her head. "You're totally entitled to feeling whatever you're feeling, Jack. You can't just keep quiet and hope for the best. We need to talk about stuff like this."

He sighed and then beamed at her. "This is why I fell in love with you," he said. "You understand. You listen to me.

You don't fly off the handle or fall apart when things get hairy. You're just *there*."

He leaned forward, nuzzling her shoulder. Her mind wasn't there, though—it was still mulling over what he'd said.

"Jack, would you say you're not quite ready for what's happening?"

He looked up, distracted from his caresses. "No, I'm not," he admitted. "But who is, right? We'll pull through it."

"Mmm." The sound meant nothing. Her brain continued to process.

He stopped, turning her face, forcing her to focus. "Were you really ready for all of this? Because you always seem so certain of everything. That was the other reason I didn't say anything."

She bit her lip. "I thought I was," she finally said, shrugging. "I mean, it's fast. And, yes, I was going to get married…"

She rolled over and muffled a growl of frustration into a pillow. "I don't know," she finished, rolling over again. "I don't know anything anymore."

"Shhh." Funny how he'd been the one who was freaking out that morning and now here he was comforting her as she fell apart. "It's going to be fine. I think our biggest problem was we were trying to figure out too much too soon. These things work out naturally. You'll see."

She felt her stomach clench. Living with the uncertainty for even longer? *That* was his solution?

They were very different people. No question about it.

He nuzzled more intently, his hand reaching up to cup her breast, and she felt her body start to respond, albeit less ardently than it would have if she weren't so preoccupied. "Are we done discussing, then? You're not angry with me?"

"I'm not angry with you," she assured him. "And yes…we're done discussing."

She let him take her then, moving slowly, bringing her body around and letting her mind float free of stress, if only temporarily. Afterward, he dozed, a smile playing around his lips. He had been given a temporary reprieve, she thought, from making any life-changing decisions. Now they'd have to wait until they got to San Diego before they sorted things out. She got the feeling he would shoulder his responsibility, not be a coward. If he thought what was best for Chloe was staying and giving her a share of his boat and his life, then he would do it.

She thought about her notebook, about the word scrawled at the top of it: *Plan*.

She sighed, leaning back.

The thing was, she now had a plan.

She had to leave Jack. For both of their sakes.

ONLY IN SAN DIEGO a few hours and Jack was already pacing a hole through his deck planking. Ace and Jose had gone home for a few days R & R, while he and Chloe had stopped by a local drugstore and gotten a pregnancy test. Now Chloe was belowdecks, divining his future with a small white stick. Depending on what showed up in the next five minutes, he'd know what he was in for.

Would it be so bad to spend the rest of your life with that woman?

No, it wouldn't, he thought. Especially after the past few days. After his little blowup and consequent confession, she'd gone from upset to calm and supportive. She hadn't breathed a word about future planning or the ship or anything else that was remotely stress inducing. Instead it had become very like their first week together, her botched "honeymoon." They'd fished, talked…made love.

No matter what she said in the next ten minutes, no matter what their future held, he knew that she was the perfect person for him. He'd never find another woman who understood and anticipated his needs as well as she did. He'd be an idiot not to snap her up. He'd just ask her to stay on board with him, and eventually they'd iron out the details.

It was, in his mind, a perfect plan.

"Jack?"

Her voice was tentative, but he sprinted down the corridor to his cabin. "Yes?" he asked, his heart beating rapidly in his throat even as his stomach dropped to somewhere near his feet. "What's the verdict?"

He'd meant for that to be a joke, of sorts, but the look on her face told him it wasn't funny, even if he hadn't already decided that for himself.

She looked…sad. No, heartbroken.

Oh, no, oh, no, oh, no…

"It's negative," she stated.

He tilted his head, not able to put together the words with the expression she was wearing. "Negative for what?" he asked, not sure he understood.

She rolled her eyes. "It's negative for pregnancy." And then, obviously seeing that he still wasn't getting it, she said more slowly, "I'm not pregnant, Jack."

He felt relief bowl over him like a tsunami. He let out a breath he hadn't even realized he was holding and said a heartfelt, "Thank God."

She smiled weakly.

"Not that…I screwed that one up, too, huh," he said, sitting next to her on his bed as he had countless times in the past. He put an arm around her shoulder. "I didn't mean…"

"I know, Jack."

She just sounded so melancholy. He squeezed her for a second. "You weren't ready for it, either," he said, then winced at the defensive quality of his voice.

She stood up, shrugging off his arm. "You're right. I wasn't. At some point, I do want a family, but this probably wouldn't be the best way."

Her voice sounded logical. Actually, for her, it sounded cold. Jack frowned. "It's not like you don't have time, Chloe," he said, wondering if that was what was bothering her—the biological-clock thing. She was only—what—thirty? Women were having kids practically into their fifties these days.

"I know that, too," she said, turning to look at him. "I completely agree with you, Jack, don't worry. This all happened so fast—this thing between us—and this would've just been throwing gasoline on a fire. We didn't need this kind of pressure."

"I'm glad you see that," he said, still tense. She wasn't smiling, she wasn't happy.

Something was very wrong.

She crossed her arms. "Just like you didn't need the pressure of me barging in and asking to take a partnership interest in the *Rascal*."

He nodded before he could stop himself. "I was in a bad way, financially speaking," he said carefully. "I'm sure I could've pulled it out in time, but you made it possible for me to get back on my feet, and I appreciate that. Your wanting to become a partner...well, you have a lot of things going on in your life. I can't blame you for seeing this as a way out."

"That's just the thing," she said. "I didn't see this as a way out. I saw this as..." She made an open gesture with her arms, as if she were trying to hug something enormous. "I saw this as *something better.*"

He smiled at the dreamy look in her eyes. "I don't think there's anything better than this."

"Yeah, but the problem is," she continued, "you don't see 'this' as anything but *yours*."

He stiffened. "It's been my boat and my business for the past five years."

"I know that," she said with a weary breath. "I am not trying to take it from you. But I am starting to realize that you're going to want everything on your terms. What makes it worse is, if I'd met you before I was engaged to Gerald, I would've thought that you had every right to have everything on your terms." She laughed. "Heck, I would've made it my life's work to get you everything you wanted."

He had already started scowling when she mentioned Gerald. Now his mouth dropped open. "Please tell me you're not equating me with him."

"No. Don't you see? I'm the common denominator here. *I'm* the problem."

Now he was flabbergasted. "What are you talking about?"

She looked frustrated and upset. He knew how she felt. "I've known we were going to have this conversation, no matter what," she said. "I love it on the boat. I love the ocean. I never realized I could have a life like this. I have you to thank for that, Jack."

"So what's the problem?" he asked with irritation. "I want you to stay here. We can keep working together. We can keep *being* together. What's wrong with that?"

"I need more than just being somebody's girl Friday," she said. "I want to be a part of something. I think that partnerships, in business or in love, have to be fifty-fifty, or no go."

Now he felt offended and a tinge guilty. "Are you saying I've just been taking advantage of you?"

"No," she assured him quickly. "Not really."

His hackles went up at the "not really" part of that sentence.

"What I'm saying is, you like having me help out the team. You like being my lover. And I love being yours," she said. "But…you don't want to think about any kind of future unless you absolutely have to. You don't want to lose your freedom or give up control. And I hate to be the one to break it to you, but to be in any kind of partnership, you need to do both, that is, let another person in."

"I've let you in, lady," he said, getting to his feet. He had to let the ferocious energy coursing through him out with some kind of activity or he'd explode. "I've changed plans and put up with things and altered my life because of you. You can't tell me I pushed you around and did nothing!"

"I know you have," she said, and now her voice was soothing. "I'm not saying you're a bad guy. You've been very kind. And I do believe you love me."

He swallowed hard, trying to dissolve the knot in his throat. "You're damned right I do," he said, stroking her cheek and catching the first tear that welled out of her eye.

"And I love you, too," she said, curving into his palm. "But…"

He sighed. "But?"

"But it's not enough," she said. "Sooner or later, I'll feel like I'm not getting enough or you'll feel trapped. I want to be a partner in something, not just the hired help. I thought I had that here, but it's still the Jack show, you know?"

"So what am I supposed to do, Chloe?" He felt despair swelling in him. He knew where this was going and for the life of him he couldn't figure out how to head it off. "What do you want me to do?"

"I don't think you can do anything," she said. "It's not your fault. You have really good reasons for not wanting to commit or give up your independence or your freedom. I can respect that. I used to be the same way."

He thought of her checklists and smiled. "I let things go more than you do."

"Yeah, you do," she said. "I learned that from you."

"So…you're letting this go," he said finally, pulling the trigger.

She pulled away from him, rubbing her arms as if she were cold. "Yes," she said in a quiet voice. "I think I have to."

He felt hurt and angry, so he hung on to angry. "You shouldn't let your experience with Gerald make everything a war," he said, his voice chill. "We could've had something really good here, and you're just walking away."

She spun on him, her amber eyes ablaze. "We do have something good here," she countered. "And you didn't want to think about any kind of future, not unless you had to. I deserve better than that. I deserve someone who loved me enough to want to share his future with me." She paused, taking a deep breath. "You were selfish, Jack. You're not a bad guy, but you have been selfish. And the worst part is, I've let you be."

He straightened. "You knew what this was…" And then he shut up, remembering that terrible fight with the honeymooning Newcombes.

You knew what this was!

"I didn't mean that," he said quickly, but she was already shaking her head and making her way to the door. "Come on, Chloe. You know it wasn't like that."

"Yeah, I know," she said. "But considering we were two people who were supposed to be in love…well, it wasn't like that, either."

He put a hand up, but she was already gone. He listened as she grabbed her luggage and walked off the ship.

He didn't even say goodbye, he thought, feeling completely adrift.

It's just as well. He couldn't bear to watching her leaving him forever.

11

"I'M SO GLAD YOU could meet me for lunch, Chloe."

Chloe looked around. The ritzy, upscale restaurant was on the marina in La Jolla. Taking a sip of her iced tea, she realized the place was probably one of Gerald's favorite eating spots—the crowd looked more interested in seeing who else was there and being seen by the other diners than they were in the magnificent view of the ocean that was right beyond their tables.

"You should try the crab salad," he said. "It's fantastic. My treat, of course."

She didn't even bother scowling at him for that one. *Damned right it's your treat.* After all the money he'd weaseled away from her and all the crap she'd taken from him, buying her lunch was the very least he could do.

"So how have you been?" he asked.

She stared at him, amazed at his nonchalant tone, as if they were high-school alumni having a reunion lunch. "I've been broke," she said flatly.

He winced. "I meant, what have you been up to?" His voice had a quality of injected cheerfulness about it, as if he could simply drown out anything unpleasant with a louder, slightly more perky question.

"I've been trying to recoup what I spent of my savings and

retirement," she continued. "Mostly I was working on a ship that was paying me to be a chef, maid and marketing assistant. It was really hard work." She sighed. Hard work that she'd really, really loved.

"That sounds fascinating," he said though clearly, he wasn't even listening to her, scanning the room. "But you're not going to keep doing that, are you? I mean, you're probably going to look for some real job now, right?"

"You mean, since your chiseling lawyers are finally giving me the money you owe me from what I contributed to the down payment of the house?" she asked.

He sighed, making an expression of distaste, like someone who'd just caught a whiff of an unpleasant odor. "You know, this would be a lot easier if you weren't quite so adversarial about the whole thing."

"Okay, *what* would be a lot easier?" She bit back on the desire to take a poke at him with her shrimp fork. "I thought you were here to give me my part of the down payment. If you want to make this *really* easy, you could just hand that over, and I could go and buy my own lunch, and you could enjoy the view by yourself. Why don't we just do that?"

"Chloe, this just isn't like you at all!"

She growled. "You don't know me," she warned him.

"Of course, I am partially to blame, I imagine."

Her mouth fell open. "You *think?*"

He grimaced again. "I should not have broken off our engagement the way I did. If anything, I should've broken it off weeks before."

"That probably would've been good," she noted, anger burning a hole in her stomach.

"I was under so much pressure," he said, and his blue eyes were imploring. He reached out and took her hand—or tried to. She jerked it away, tucking it under her other arm. "You know how my family is. How crazy they make me. My mother was convinced that you were no good for me."

"And you let her persuade you," Chloe said.

When he used to complain about his family, she'd always been so supportive. Now she felt all of that fall away.

"I didn't let her. She badgered me. She made everything more difficult," he said. No, he whined. "She called me all the time. She insisted that I might even get cut out of the will, Chloe!"

She knew that was a dire threat—the architectural firm depended on the occasional inflow of Sutton money. "But I'm curious, Gerald," she said, her voice deceptively casual. "How exactly did you screwing another woman come about, what with all this family pressure?"

She said it just loud enough to be heard by the tables surrounding her, causing a moment's lull in the conversation. Gerald's eyes bugged.

"Keep your voice down!" he begged, trying to smile it off as he surveyed the other customers. "I didn't mean to sleep with Simone. She's...well, she's a family friend, and she knew I was going through a tough time. And you were so busy with the wedding stuff I couldn't talk to you—"

"Of course. Somehow I got the feeling this would become at least partly my fault," she said.

"I didn't mean to hurt you, I swear to God," he said. "I feel terrible about the whole thing. I feel *wretched*. I'm...I'm slime."

Now her eyes widened. He was apologizing. He was accusing himself.

He was up to something.

"What do you want, Gerald?"

"Just to make it up to you," he said, and his handsome face was the picture of contrition.

"Handing over that check's a start," she said. "Writing another one for the balance of the wedding expenses that you agreed to pay for would probably go a long way, as well."

He winced, then nodded. "Of course. You're right."

He reached into his leather organizer and pulled out his checkbook. He had a check already for the house. When she told him how much the wedding expenses came to, he blanched, but he dutifully wrote out another check. He put them on the table.

This would put her back where she'd been, she thought. She'd be able to start fresh.

I could even invest in a boat...

She reached for the checks, and Gerald grabbed her hand. "I miss you," he said.

"Oh, Gerald." She crumpled the checks slightly, his grip was stronger. "Is that what this is all about? What happened to what's-her-name?"

"Simone," he said, and his voice was mournful. "I thought she was just a good friend, you know?"

"That you slept with," Chloe reminded him.

He frowned, obviously not interested in that detail. "So we've been seeing each other, and since my Mother loved her, I thought she'd be perfect. I mean, my family was off my back and, well, the wedding had been stressing me out terribly."

Stressing you out? Chloe thought, bewildered. She'd handled everything, from the planning to running defense against his psychotic mother. Exactly what had he been stressed out about?

"But once the smoke cleared," he said, "Simone started acting...different. She started expecting things. And then, out of the blue, she tells me that it's time I asked to marry her. Marry her!" He shook his head. "I had no idea she was thinking in those terms. I mean, she's…well, fun and a sweet kid. And that was just what I needed."

Now Chloe felt herself hitting the boiling point. "And what do you need now?" she asked in a cold monotone.

He didn't even pick up on the cue that she was upset. "I finally told my mother that I was doing things on my own," he said. "She can pull the family money if she wants, but I'm not going to be bullied anymore. I wasn't going to marry Simone, and that was that."

Aha, Chloe thought. So Mommy Dearest wanted someone "worthy"—aka handpicked and pliable—to marry her kid and help keep him in line.

"And I remembered how great you were," he said, his voice turning low and, she presumed, seductive. "How great we were together. And I realized I'd made the biggest mistake of my life when I sent that messenger to the church. When I didn't marry you."

Chloe couldn't believe it. He was actually saying what she'd once wanted to hear and what she knew in her heart.

"It wasn't a total loss," she said, her voice comforting.

"It wasn't?" His eyes lit hopefully.

"When you walked away," she said, "you showed me that I'd just dodged the biggest bullet of my life. So I guess from that standpoint, I owe *you* one."

He blinked, not comprehending, then shrugged. "I know it'll take some time, but I want to get us back to where we were."

He wasn't listening, she thought. He never listened.

"And you know what? Screw the partners and their snooty judgments," he said with a devil-may-care wink. "I've missed you at the office, too. Just because we're married doesn't mean we can't work together, right?"

"Are you kidding me?"

He smiled. "I never should've asked you to quit. It wasn't fair to you. I know how much you loved your job, how devoted you were to the firm."

"That was for *you*, you idiot!" she snapped.

His smile faltered, but he plowed forward. "And I value it."

"Certainly you do," she said, picturing throwing her iced tea in his face. She yanked her hand away from his with a vicious tug, stuffing the checks into her purse. "You probably can't even find your checkbook at this point. You don't have anybody running interference when the partners come down on you, you don't have anybody running your life and you've got your mom breathing down your neck. If I hadn't quit, we'd probably be married!"

"You know, I think that's right," he mused. "It wasn't until I had to deal with the office by myself, and my Mother had you all tied up with wedding stuff…"

"I wasn't saying that like—*grrrr!*" She rubbed her hands over her face. "I didn't mean that it was a mistake. I meant you just want me to keep your life tidy. You don't love me at all!"

"Now, that's not true," he reprimanded. "I love you a lot."

"No, you love what I can do for you," she said. "You've never once put my needs above your own comfort. And I am *sick* of it!"

She got up and then did what she'd visualized. She poured the iced tea on him.

"Hey!" he yelped, jumping to his feet.

"I am going to deposit these checks right now, and if you try to stop payment, so help me, Gerald," she said through gritted teeth, "I am going to drive over to your house and *kick your ass myself.* Do you understand?"

He nodded, looking at her as if she were a wild animal. Which, she supposed, she was.

"I'm through with being taken advantage of," she announced. "I'm through with rolling over. So go find yourself another girl Friday."

"Huh?" He looked wounded. Confused. Downright baffled, actually.

"Never mind," she said. "We're done, Gerald. Finally. From now on, just leave me alone."

And with that and her dignity, she turned and strode out of the restaurant, leaving him dripping wet.

"THIS IS A FINE SHIP you've got here, son."

Jack forced a smile. "Thanks. I like it."

The comment came from his charter passenger, a Roy Vicente, and his new wife Martha. The two of them were in their late sixties if they were a day. Yet they were cooing over each other like a couple of teenagers. Ordinarily, Jack would have found the whole thing kind of cute.

Lately, romance seemed to make his skin crawl. He spent as much time in his cabin or the steering compartment as possible and left the guests to their own devices as much as possible. He'd hired a temporary cook, a guy named Frank, who was quiet and adept and, other than getting seasick his first day, was handy enough.

Jose and Ace didn't like him, however. Which meant that he'd probably be looking for a new cook pretty soon.

"My wife," Roy continued with the amusement and pride that only a newlywed could infuse the words with, "has always loved the ocean and boats and stuff. This is a dream come true for her."

"Our pleasure," Jack said.

The guy leaned back in a chaise lounge, and Jack wondered if he could just skip out, when Roy continued. "Me," he said easily, looking like the king of the world, "I hate boats."

Jack blinked. "Beg pardon?"

"Don't like boats at all." Roy laughed. "Can't stand them. They're claustrophobic. And everything swaying all the time? I got drunk plenty when I was younger. I don't need all the effects of being off balance with none of the benefits, you know?"

Jack stared at him, incredulous. "Then...what, she's making you take this cruise?" He glanced around to see if she were there. She'd seemed like a nice woman, but then, even Mrs. Newcombe had seemed pretty sane when they'd started that cruise.

"No, no. She's belowdecks, taking a nap," Roy said with a wave of his hand. "Honestly, this is going a lot better than I thought. And of course she didn't force me. It was my idea. We got married at the justice of the peace, and I surprised her with it."

"You surprised her with something you hated?"

"She doesn't know how much I dislike boats," he said. "The important thing is I know how much she loves 'em. It's a gift, you know?"

Jack shrugged. "If you say so."

Roy looked him over with an eagle eye. "You've never been married, have you?"

"Is it that obvious?" Jack didn't mean for his tone to turn that sarcastic, but...

Well, damn it, since Chloe had left, he'd been bitter, snappy and pretty much a pain to be around. At least that's what Jose and Ace had told him. To make it worse, he was miserable. And even though he felt it was Chloe's fault for forcing the issue, it didn't stop the fact that he missed her terribly. If he had more of Chloe's spirit, he'd probably have come up with a solution to his problem by now, something neat, an action plan, a checklist of some kind. But he wasn't Chloe, so he'd wound up drinking when he wasn't ferrying passengers around. The boat was mostly booked, though, for the next month and a half with high-paying customers, thanks to Chloe.

It was a blessing and a curse.

"You know, I used to be like you," Roy mused. "This is my second marriage, did I mention that?"

"No," Jack said, growing more uncomfortable.

"It took me a while to get married the first time," Roy reminisced, and Jack sat down, feeling as if he wouldn't be able to escape unless he rode out this guy's story. "I didn't want to settle down, you know? Thought I'd be trapped. And, believe me, with most of the women I used to date, I would've been."

He laughed, not caring that Jack did not join in.

"Then I figured I was getting older, I should probably get my act together, start a family. Do the right thing. So I married a nice girl." He shook his head. "Big mistake. We both were getting married because we wanted marriage, not necessarily each other. She grew more pushy and I grew more distant. Thankfully we didn't have any kids. Still, it was a train wreck. We got divorced about three years later."

"That's too bad," Jack said, and he did mean it. Roy seemed like a nice enough guy.

"The worst part about it was I thought all women were going to be like that. I thought marriage *had* to be like that," he said, shaking his head as if surprised by his own stupidity. "Then I met Martha. She wasn't like anybody else I'd ever met in my life."

That's how I felt about Chloe.

Jack grimaced, forcing the thought from his head. That had ended as Roy had said, a train wreck. It was obviously different.

"She just..." Roy's smile was like sunshine after a storm.

"I felt comfortable when I was with her. Hell, I was happy when I was with her…and unhappy when I wasn't. She seemed to know me inside and out. She made my life sing." He laughed again. "That sounds completely corny, but it's true."

"Wow," Jack said, trying not to be sour. "You're a lucky man."

"Almost biffed it, too," Roy said. "I assumed we're both in our sixties so we've got nothing to prove to anybody, right? I'd done the marriage thing and it hadn't gone well. So this time I had the right girl and I wasn't going to…well, rock the boat, if you'll pardon the expression."

Jack's eyes narrowed. "Did one of my crew say anything to you?"

Roy paused, then started laughing. "Aha. Thought so. You had that look about you."

"What look?"

"The I'm-in-love-and-I-messed-it-up look," Roy said, laughing some more. "Which would explain why you've been glowering at me since I got on board."

Jack was torn between feeling offended and feeling aghast. "I didn't realize," he said lamely. "I mean…of course you and your wife are welcome on the ship…."

"Like I said, you remind me of me when I was younger. And dumber," Roy said, obviously not caring if he offended or not. Jack couldn't help reluctantly admiring the guy for being so forthright. "So, like I was saying, I wasn't going to marry Martha. Then one day we're out in the marina—'cause she loves boats, remember? We're having lunch at this nice restaurant. And she sees this couple getting married and she gets all weepy and emotional. Well, I don't like seeing her upset, so I ask her what's up."

Jack nodded, now completely drawn into the story.

Roy folded his hands behind his head. "She says that there's nothing more beautiful than two people who get married—who are completely devoted to each other. And there's this catch in her voice. So I try to joke it off by saying it's a whole lot of expense and nonsense for something that should already be there. And she turns to me—and I will never forget this to the day I die—and she says, Roy, it's more than that. It's not about the flowers or the dress or any of that. It's showing that you're willing to say to the whole world, officially, that you're going to make a go of it. That you're with each other to the end." Roy cleared his throat, obviously moved by the statement. "Well, in that moment I realized that I was willing to say that. That she needed—no, she *deserved*—to hear me say that to her and the whole damned world. So I asked her to marry me."

Jack didn't say anything. He frowned, thoughtful.

"And I took her on a cruise," he said, "because now that I'm in all the way, I know that she makes me happier than I've ever been in my life, every day of my life. If I can make her feel even a little bit the way she makes me feel, then I'm not a sorry son of a bitch just along for the ride."

"Now I know you've talked to my crew," Jack protested, then recalled that he hadn't even gone over the details of why Chloe had left with either Jose or Ace. "Damn it."

Roy shrugged. "Maybe she wasn't the right girl for you, whoever she was," he said with elaborate casualness. "You might've been totally on the mark and you're just riding it out. Maybe I'm simply a buttinsky in love for the first time in his life."

"Maybe," Jack agreed, and Roy chuckled. The guy was more cheerful than Santa Claus.

"But I know that if I met Martha earlier in my life and

walked away…" He shook his head. "I'd want somebody like me telling me I screwed up."

Roy stood, still grinning, then clapped Jack on the shoulder and headed belowdecks.

Jack sat there for a minute, contemplative.

She hadn't asked for the moon. She had just wanted to be more of his life. And he hadn't wanted to compromise an inch. He'd said he was in love with her, but he wanted to give what he felt he could give, and take what she had to offer.

She was right. He *had* been like Gerald.

He felt overcome with remorse. He'd been so intent on living his life on his own terms and never buckling to other people's demands and schedules that he'd practically run his business into the ground and driven off the one woman who made him happy.

He needed to fix this, he thought frantically. But what was he going to do? Strand his passengers? And there was still the partnership thing to work out. Just telling her he'd changed would not make a difference. He needed to show her that he was willing to be flexible in his life. And he couldn't keep living his life the way he had been.

He went to his cabin, and for the first time, he got out a notebook, one of the blank spiral-bounds she'd left behind.

On the top of the sheet he wrote the word: *Plan*.

Then he charted out what he was going to do next, step by step, right up to the point where he figured he would get Chloe back.

"I CAN'T BELIEVE IT," Chloe's mother said, leaning back in her chair at the kitchen table. "You dumped iced tea all over him?"

"Yup," Chloe said, feeling vindicated, if still a little sad.

"And he paid you for the wedding, as well?" her father asked.

Chloe nodded. "I'm right back where I was."

Her mother made a dismissive sound. "That…that *man* should've paid you interest. Or, better, his *mother* should have paid you!"

"I'm just glad the whole thing's finally done. I know it's cliché, but I feel like I finally got closure," Chloe said, swirling what was left of her coffee around in her mug.

"There is that," her father agreed.

"So have you decided what you're going to do next?" her mother probed gently, quickly adding, "You realize, of course, that you're welcome to stay here as long as you like."

"I'm still thinking about it," Chloe said evasively.

The truth was, since she'd stepped off the deck of the *Rascal,* nothing had sounded good to her and all her previous motivation seemed to have been sapped right out of her. She'd tried drawing up a plan but couldn't manage it. She'd kicked around the idea of working on another boat—maybe even buying a boat. But Jack was right about the fact that she didn't know anything about steering a boat or maintaining one. She had fallen in love with the lifestyle, but she had a long way to go before gaining the necessary experience to actually be a ship's captain. Besides, the fun part had been being a part of the crew. She liked booking passengers and promoting the cruises. She liked marketing. She didn't have any real interest in the inner workings of a bilge pump. So that idea had reached a dead end.

The idea of being a secretary again hadn't been very enticing, either. She'd applied for a few jobs in marketing, even one for a cruise line, but she hadn't had enough experience.

For someone as determined, optimistic and problem-solving as Chloe, the situation was shockingly bleak. And she couldn't seem to muster her usual energy to get herself back into the fray.

"It's that boat business, isn't it?" her father asked, his normally booming voice subdued.

She was surprised it was that obvious. Then, seeing her mother's look of compassion and her father's look of bushy-browed concern, she nodded.

"You could always get another job on a boat, if that's what you really wanted," her mother said with a note of hesitation. Chloe knew it was a huge concession for her—she didn't see it having any future, it was dangerous and it was highly unstable. But it cheered Chloe that her mother was so intent on seeing her happy.

"I thought about that," Chloe said. "But… I guess it's hard to explain. Working on the *Rascal* was the closest thing I've found to perfect."

"You enjoyed working at the architectural firm," her father noted.

"I did," she admitted. "But it was like all my hard work was going toward nothing. I never saw the results. I never saw people happy at the end product. It was always a matter of keeping Gerald out of hot water and keeping the place running. On the ship…" She smiled, thinking of it. "Seeing happy couples thanking me for their food or getting to be out on the ocean, knowing that every charter I booked meant another day I could be out at sea, in the sunshine, on the waves…"

She sighed.

Being with Jack, she added mentally. Spending every day with a guy who made her grin or taught her something and spending every night with a man who made her feel like the most precious, desirable thing in existence.

But, of course, she couldn't say that.

"So why did you leave?" her father asked, hunkering down. She could almost see his hands itching for pen and paper.

"It's complicated," Chloe deflected. "I don't want to get into it."

"Well, we're going to get into it," her mother said, surprising her with her insistence. "Because you've been wandering around this house like a ghost for a week and you're losing weight and your eyes look like your best friend died. I thought we should leave you alone, let you work it out, but it's obvious you're stuck. So…we're helping you."

"Whether I want you to or not, apparently," Chloe said. "You know, this is why I went on the honeymoon cruise in the first place." She winced. She hadn't meant that to be so rude. "I mean…"

"No, you're right," her father said. "Our family is notorious for plunging in and trying to solve everyone's problems. Usually everyone *else's* problems," he noted. "But you're our daughter and we love you. You don't have to take our advice or listen to us, but you can't sit here and expect us to be fine seeing you like this."

She sighed. "I understand."

In dribs and drabs, she wound up revealing that she'd gotten involved with the captain of the *Rascal*, editing it carefully so it was a lot less lurid.

"So…you asked to be a partner in his ship?" her father asked, surprised.

"I know it seems a bit risky," Chloe said quickly. "I mean, I hadn't even done due diligence or any research, so I suppose it was rash…"

"No, that's not what I meant," her father said. "What I meant was, you basically told this guy who had been sole proprietor of this place that you wanted to buy in, and that was that?"

Chloe frowned. "I don't think I put it like that…."

"And he lived there?" her mother interjected.

"So you were saying you not only wanted to own part of his business, you wanted to own part of his house," her father summarized.

"I didn't really put it that way…."

"After only knowing him for a month or so." Her mother shook her head. "Oh, dear."

"Listen, I know it sounds crazy, but I really fell in love with him," Chloe protested. "And it started out as just business. I needed money, he needed help. We helped each other."

"Yes, and then you wanted to take even more," her mother pointed out.

Chloe fell silent, feeling betrayed. "I thought you'd be on my side," she said. "After all I put up with Gerald…"

"Oh, you were right there," her father said, his eyes growing fiery at the mere mention of her ex. "He was beyond a jerk and you let him walk over you like a welcome mat."

"So I was trying not to do that again!" Chloe said sharply.

"I think you may have overcompensated a little," her mother said. "He sounds like a nice man. And, yes, he was being thoughtless. Of course he wanted you to stay. You were helping him, you made him happy just the way you were. Why wouldn't he want you to?"

"And…you don't think that's selfish?"

"Yes, it is," her mother agreed. "But I also think that you were being hardheaded."

"How?" Chloe said, then bit her tongue. That had sounded suspiciously like a whine, which reminded her of Gerald.

"You weren't giving him any time," she replied. "Men aren't perfect. He was being selfish, but he had also been open to helping you when you offered. He was caring and kind, you say—you wouldn't have fallen in love with him otherwise, would you?"

"I don't know," Chloe said doubtfully. "I fell in love with Gerald."

"That wasn't love. That was convenience," her father said. "And you made him wait for years before you two decided to settle down. Was this captain guy just a rebound?"

"No," Chloe said automatically. "I don't rebound, you know that. Normally I go into periods of hibernation when I break up with someone."

"So this guy was different," her father said. "What made you give him a chance?"

Chloe thought back to how kind he was to her during her honeymoon cruise. The way he was open to her suggestions in ways Gerald never had been. The way he was strong and tough but still very giving and gentle. He meant well, she knew it.

"Because he seemed to genuinely *see* me," Chloe said. "I don't think I've ever felt that with anybody before."

"And did you see him?" her mother pressed.

Chloe replied. "I thought I did."

"You understood why he was the way he was?"

"You mean commitment-phobic?" Chloe sighed, her mind starting to put together the pattern. "Yes."

"And you pushed him anyway," her mother continued. "You knew he had problems with giving up freedom, but you figured if he loved you enough, he'd be able to move beyond all that."

"Shouldn't he?" Chloe asked.

Her father let out a low, rumbling breath. Then he leaned over and took her mom's hand in a romantic gesture. Her mom smiled back at him.

"Men aren't perfect," he said. "We need time to work things out. I screwed up things plenty when I was still dating your mother."

"And I wasn't perfect, either," her mother added. "I used to worry him over every little detail—"

"And I used to tell her exactly how I wanted things," her father said, chuckling. "We had plenty of disagreements."

"Loud ones," her mother agreed, squeezing his hand.

"It's about compromise," her father finished. "I don't want you with someone who's going to use you. Of course not. But if you love someone, you have to give them the chance to meet you halfway. And you have to meet them there, as well."

Chloe went quiet, processing these thoughts. "Compromise," she said, rolling the thought over in her mind. "You guys have always compromised, then?"

Her mother's smile was wide and loving. "I don't want you on a ship for a living," she said.

"And I don't want you running off and falling in love with a man you barely know," her father added. "But we both love you and we want you to be happy. So we'll compromise, we'll tell you our thoughts and see where you go from there."

Chloe felt her throat choke with emotion. "Thank you," she said. "I lóve you guys."

"We love you, too," her mother said, rubbing at her own eyes with her fingertips. "Now go get a pad of paper. We're working this out."

12

"WHAT'S UP, BOSS?" JOSE asked, puzzled.

Jack cleared his throat. "I'm glad you two could meet with me today," he said, feeling like a complete doofus.

Ace and Jose exchanged glances, sitting in the two new chairs Jack had gotten for his "office" thinking it would be even worse if he asked Ace and Jose to sit on the bed. Still, their topic was too formal for him to sit out on deck and talk about. Besides, he had all of his notes at his desk. Man, did he have a lot of notes.

"Jose, you've been working with me for three years," he said. "Ace, you've been here over a year and a half. You've both busted your butts for me, and I appreciate it."

"Thanks," Ace mumbled, clearly confused and uncomfortable.

"Are we getting a raise or something?" Jose asked.

"Or something," Jack said, rubbing the back of his neck. "We're getting a lot of business. More business than I thought I'd see all year, actually."

"Yeah," Ace said. "I'm starting to get a little crispy, actually. I never thought I'd work this hard on this ship!"

Ace laughed after he said this, but Jack was thoughtful. He'd thought that initially, too, when he'd bought the *Rascal*—that it would be chartering a few drunk fisherman around and then spending the rest of the time kicking back, drinking beer, romancing the occasional lady. He'd learned quickly that it took a lot of time, effort and hard work to keep both boat and business afloat.

He was starting to learn that about relationships, too. And not just romantic ones.

"We've come close to going under a couple of times now," Jack said, "and you have stuck it out with me. That means a lot." He took a deep breath, frowning, trying to figure out how to attack the conversation. "I'm starting to notice that I may have been trying too hard to do things by myself."

"Hallelujah," Jose said half under his breath.

"So you're bringing Chloe back?" Ace asked eagerly.

"Huh? No. Well, yes," Jack said, "if she'll go for it. But that's the next part of the conversation. This is between me and you guys."

Now Ace seemed confused again, although Jose was looking keenly alert.

"I love the *Rascal.* She's been a good home for me for the past five years," he said with a feeling of pride. "But she's not enough to really make a good living on. Not to support a full crew, anyway, not the way she's built."

Jose nodded.

"If we really want to make a success out of this, we'll need a bigger boat," Jack said. "If we get enough business, we might want to expand."

"Expand?" Ace asked.

"Into a fleet," Jose said with a small smile. "A couple of boats, with more berths, more passengers. Maybe different kinds of charters."

Jack smiled, not surprised at all that Jose understood the concept. "I couldn't captain more than one boat," he said.

"And that sort of thing takes a lot of investment in time and money and planning. I didn't think I could handle all of that. And I can't…alone."

"Okay, what are you saying?" Ace finally asked, sounding bewildered.

"He's saying he wants to turn this from McCullough Charters into something a bigger," Jose said. "Isn't that right, Jack?"

Jack nodded gratefully. "I was wondering if you two wanted in on a partnership."

Ace blinked. "You mean, like, be an owner?" The thought obviously dazzled him.

Jose, on the other hand, grinned broadly. "About time," he said.

"Well, *you* could've brought it up," Jack said, grinning back at him.

"I know you," Jose said, shaking his head. "It takes a load of dynamite to get you going. I've been saving up for my own ship for years—and on your salaries, I gotta say it hasn't been easy."

"But you've been loyal," Jack said feeling even more grateful.

"It would've made leaving tough," Jose said, with a slow nod. "But you're my best friend, and I figured we'd just worry about that when I actually got enough money to buy my own boat."

"I don't have any money," Ace said. "Hell, I don't even have an apartment. I just have a storage unit and I crash at my brother's place or my parents' or some chick's. I don't want to be part owner in a business." He looked a little wild-eyed. "Can I still work here?"

"Yeah, you can," Jack said. "Of course you can. We'll probably hire some help, too, to give you more of a break."

"Man, that'd be nice."

Jack smiled. He'd made the offer. He was opening up. He was giving this whole thing a chance.

It was scary as all hell. At the same time, now that it had been, it felt pretty damned good.

"So is that it?" Ace asked, glancing at his watch. "I've got a hot date."

"Yeah, that was it," Jack said, smirking at him. "Go ahead."

He watched as Ace fled, thinking of how he'd been like that when he was younger. Jose seemed to read his mind.

"Kids," he said, shaking his head. "No concept of the future."

"Not like us old guys, huh?" Jack said, getting up and grabbing two beers from his fridge. He handed Jose one, and they clinked bottle necks. "Cheers."

"Back atcha," Jose said, taking a long pull from the bottle. "We're not old, man. We're *wise*."

Jack snorted.

"And you were just as bad as Ace was," Jose added, "until you met Chloe."

Jack didn't say anything. He took a long sip of beer before he nodded in concession.

"So you said if she was up for it, you'd get her back," Jose said. "She was the one you were thinking of going in with in the first place. That bugged me a bit, by the way," Jose said, "although I love the girl like a sister. So what's the deal?"

"I sort of screwed things up with her," Jack said, ignoring Jose's no-kidding expression. "I didn't want her to be partners."

"And she wasn't okay with that?"

"Well, I also said I wasn't into marriage," Jack said. "In my defense, we've only known each other for a couple of months now—"

"I can see how that might upset her," Jose offered. "So you told her you didn't want her working with you and you were leery about marriage, therefore she decided to stop seeing you. And now?"

Jack frowned. "I didn't say I didn't want her working with me."

"You didn't?"

"No, of course not," Jack said. "She did more for our business in a few months than I was able to do in a few years. So, yeah, of course I wanted her to stay."

Jose's eyes rounded. "So you said don't get any ideas about moving ahead, and I won't want to marry you...oh, but keep making me money?"

"I don't think I said that," Jack replied, feeling like an idiot.

"You weren't kidding," Jose said with a low whistle. "You screwed up *huge*. And I guess you still wanted to keep having sex with her, but she shouldn't think about marriage."

"I *know* I didn't say that," Jack said.

"You probably didn't have to." Jose leaned back, drinking more beer. "And you think she's going to come back *why* again?"

Jack sighed. "Hopefully, because I love her," he said. "And because I now *know* I was an jerk. And because she's got a big heart and she's good at fixing things."

"You've got a good point there," Jose agreed. "So you're giving her a chance to become a partner, too?"

"Yeah," Jack said. "If you're okay with working with her."

"Are you kidding?" Jose's grin almost split his face. "She's the best thing that's ever happened to you. And with this whole opportunity opening up, she's probably the best thing that's happened to *me*."

"Funny," Jack said. "Now I just need to get her to talk to me. If you've got any ideas on that, wise guy, I could use the help."

"Huh. Let's see..." Jose frowned. "I imagine groveling of some sort should be involved."

"I kind of figured that." Jack grimaced. "Anything else?"

"You could tell her she left something behind," Jose proposed. "And tell her to pick it up."

"No, no. Too juvenile," Jack said. "Besides, she'd just tell me to mail it."

"You could say you miss her, you screwed up, please come back," Jose said in an isn't-this-obvious? tone of voice.

"I don't want to do it over the phone," Jack said.

"You're a pain in the ass," Jose responded. "Okay. Then why don't you tell her you've got a gun to my head and if she isn't over here in an hour you're going to shoot me?"

"Do you really think that would work?"

Jose scowled. "She likes me, I think. And she's a soft touch."

Jack was about to make a sarcastic comment when his cell phone rang. "McCullough Charters," he said.

"Jack."

He sat up straight, almost falling out of his chair. "Chloe?"

"Listen, can I stop by the boat in an hour?" she said, her words almost tumbling over each other in her haste.

His mind went momentarily blank. "Uh…sure. Yes."

"Great." Without another word, she hung up.

Jack stared at his cell phone, hearing the dial tone before he snapped it shut.

"That was Chloe?" Jose said.

Jack nodded.

"So…what happened?"

"She's coming by," Jack said. "In an hour."

Jose laughed. "You have the devil's own luck, man," he said. "You do what you need to, but get her back. And this time, don't be a jerk, okay?"

"I'll try," Jack said. "Now get out of here. We'll talk more tomorrow."

He had an hour. And God willing, this time he'd be able to do things right.

CHLOE COULDN'T REMEMBER the last time she was this nervous. It had only been a few weeks since she'd been on the *Rascal,* but it seemed as though she'd been away from it forever. She felt a pang of nostalgia as she stepped on board. Jack was waiting there on the deck, just as he had been that first time she'd arrived, right after the disaster of her canceled wedding—the blessing in disguise in more ways than one. He looked good enough to eat, as usual, his hair slick-wet from a shower, wearing a T-shirt and a faded pair of jeans.

She paused, feeling awkward.

"Hey, you," she finally said.

He smiled back at her, and it felt as if she were basking in the sun. "Hey, yourself."

She wanted to run to him—to just burrow into his arms, say she'd been foolish, say she just wanted to feel happy again and beg him to take her back. But she wasn't going to do that.

Not right off the bat, anyway.

He had set out two of the deck chairs they usually used when serving dinner on deck. He also had a pitcher of lemonade. "Want to sit down?" he asked, pouring her a glass.

So. They were going to be civil. If anything, that made her more nervous. She sat down and accepted the beverage, taking a sip. "This is good," she said more for lack of anything to say.

"Yeah. I had to fire our last cook, but he did make some decent lemonade." Jack sat next to her with his own glass.

They were silent for a long moment.

This was your idea, Chloe chastised herself. *Say something!*

"So I guess you're wondering why I'm here," she finally said, then winced. *Okay, next time say something that isn't lame!*

"I am, a little," Jack said. "But I'm more glad that you're here at all."

She took a deep breath. "I shouldn't have left the way I did. And the things I said—"

"Were right," he finished, his voice low and comforting. "I was being selfish. I didn't mean to be. I just didn't want things to change."

"I know that," she said. "With your background…your parents…and we really haven't known each other that long…"

"Sometimes you don't need to," he said. "And don't make excuses for me."

"I'm not," she replied quickly. "I still want…what I want. A relationship that means something. A chance to work someplace and not just be an assistant or a gopher. But at the same time, I don't want to be out of your life completely."

"I know that," he said. "I want you in my life, too, believe me."

"So I drew up a list of options," she said, reaching into her purse.

She stopped when he burst into laughter.

"What?" she asked.

He leaned over and kissed her, and for a second her plan, her nerves, everything disappeared in the taste of that sweetness. She melted into him, putting her drink down on the deck and reaching for him. He pulled her into his lap, making the kiss more intent. Finally, after a long moment, he shifted the kiss to her neck, pressing against the pulse beating there.

"You aren't going to believe this, but I wrote up a list, too," he said.

She pulled back, floored. "You did? About what?"

"About how we can make this work," he said. "Come on."

He carried her, purse and all, down to his cabin in the way

that always thrilled her. His cabin had the little glow lights on again, she noted with a smile. He placed her gently on the bed, then went to his desk—which, to her shock, was still neat—and grabbed a sheet of paper.

"I came up with these," he said, and he sounded a little embarrassed—something that charmed her utterly. "I don't want to take advantage of you, so if you'd rather work, I would just see you between cruises. If you still wanted me to," he added, his voice tentative.

She nodded. She had that on her list, too.

"If you wanted to work as a chef and a marketing person or just one or the other, I could go with that," he said. "And if you wanted that more than you wanted the relationship…well, I didn't think that would work, but I'd help you find work with another crew, if that's what you really wanted."

Her eyes widened. That was thoughtful—and not on her list. But, of course, it left out the crucial element: him. She shook her head.

"As far as the two of us being together," he said, "I thought about it. I've been struggling with this on my own for a long time. You were right—I've been stubborn. So I will let you buy in as a partner if you want." He paused. "Except you've got to be okay with being partners with Jose, too, because I invited him to buy in, as well."

"I think that's a brilliant idea," she said.

"We've got a lot of ideas for expanding the business—some of them I got from your notes," Jack said, shifting his weight from one foot to the other. "And I know you could be a big help."

"But where would that leave us, Jack?" she asked finally.

He sighed. Then he knelt by the side of the bed, taking her hands in his. "I love you," he said. "You've opened my eyes to a lot of things. I'm sorry that I put you through all of this."

"No, I'm sorry," she said quickly, sitting up. "I rushed you and pushed you. I didn't think about how hard this was going to be for you."

"You shouldn't have to," he protested.

"If we're going to be partners, then we have to think about stuff like that," she said. "It's *compromise.* We each think of each other, and it makes it better for both of us." She leaned forward and kissed him gently. "I'm willing to compromise with you. I'll work with you in exchange for learning about the business. I don't need to buy into the boat until I know more about it."

"And...the other part?" he asked.

She smiled at him. "I love you like crazy," she said. "I'm not letting you go."

"I'm not letting you go, either," he said.

With that, he kissed her fiercely.

Before she knew it, they were tearing at each other's clothes, impatient to revive the closeness that they'd always felt. She tugged his shirt off. He unbuttoned her sleeveless blouse and tossed it to the ground. They kicked off their pants and shoes. Within minutes, they were naked and staring at each other, both breathing hard.

"I've missed you so much," she murmured, reaching for him.

He nuzzled against her, pressing heated kisses against every inch of her...her shoulders, the curve of her hips, the mound of her stomach. She kissed every part of him she could reach or stroked fingertips against his skin. It was like magic, she thought. Even when she wasn't sure of anything else, she could always be sure of this.

Minutes later, he rolled on a condom, his hands no longer shaking. She spread her legs, welcoming him.

He eased between her thighs, and she could feel the hard

length of him right at her opening. "I love you, Chloe," he said, and it sounded reverent. It sounded *right*.

"I love you, too," she murmured back, then gasped as he slowly entered her.

They just lay there for a minute, joined and still. The heat of their bodies between them. She felt like staying that way forever, no past, no future, only the two of them and all of that love.

Then he started moving with slow, sure strokes. She felt her heart rate increase and her body moisten in response as she lifted her hips to meet his every thrust. It was as soothing as the ocean, as exciting, as beautiful. She felt the pressure begin to build. She was breathing in soft pants, clutching him to her as he increased his speed.

"Baby," he murmured, "I want you…."

"Oh, Jack," she said. "Now…"

He pressed into her, and she felt the explosion of the orgasm. Shuddering against her, he responded in kind, holding her to him as if he never wanted to let her go.

When it was over, he turned, cradling her against him, refusing to release her. "You know something?" he said with a voice thick with emotion. "You're the best honeymoon cruise I've ever had."

She laughed, a delicious, free sound. "Get used to it," she said. "Because it's only going to be one long honeymoon from here."

Epilogue

"RIGHT THIS WAY, MRS. MCCULLOUGH," Jack said, carrying her into a palatial cabin on a brand new yacht.

"Jack! It's gorgeous!" Chloe marveled, looking at the wide windows, the gleaming furniture. The huge bed.

"And worth every penny," Jack said with a grin. "Jose loves being the captain of this thing."

Chloe smiled. It had taken them a year, but they'd finally added a ship to their fleet: the *Other Rascal*. Chloe wasn't sure about the name, but the guys had loved it. And they were having great success already. Chloe had managed to book several months in advance with a few wedding parties, a few fishing charters, even a business trip. It certainly seemed as if their business was taking off.

Still, Jack and Jose had insisted that the maiden voyage be for a very special honeymoon cruise.

"It still doesn't feel real," Chloe said, glancing at the ring on her finger.

"I hope you're okay with the fact that it was small," Jack said.

She smiled. "I hate planning big weddings," she said. "Besides, my parents were there, your parents were there, our friends were there. It was cozy."

"It was perfect," he said, kissing her. "You made it perfect."

"How's Ace handling his first time as captain?" she asked.

Jack laughed. "He's called me four times today. I told him I'm on my honeymoon and that I'm confident he can do the job." He shook his head. "He's a good kid. He won't crash the *Rascal* or anything. He'll manage."

"I never dreamed it would be like this," she said.

He stretched out on the bed next to her. "I didn't, either," he admitted. "Until I met you."

She kissed him and then smiled at him, winking saucily. "So. Want to break in the new bed?"

His grin back was pure pleasure. "Yes, Mrs. McCullough, I do."

* * * * *

Happily ever after is just the beginning...

Turn the page for a sneak preview of
DANCING ON SUNDAY AFTERNOONS
by Linda Cardillo

Harlequin Everlasting—Every great love has
a story to tell. ™
A brand-new line from Harlequin Books
launching this February!

Prologue

Giulia D'Orazio
1983

I had two husbands—Paolo and Salvatore.

Salvatore and I were married for thirty-two years. I still live in the house he bought for us; I still sleep in our bed. All around me are the signs of our life together. My bedroom window looks out over the garden he planted. In the middle of the city, he coaxed tomatoes, peppers, zucchini—even grapes for his wine—out of the ground. On weekends, he used to drive up to his cousin's farm in Waterbury and bring back manure. In the winter, he wrapped the peach tree and the fig tree with rags and black rubber hoses against the cold, his massive, coarse hands gentling those trees as if they were his fragile-skinned babies. My neighbor, Dominic Grazza, does that for me now. My boys have no time for the garden.

In the front of the house, Salvatore planted roses. The roses I take care of myself. They are giant, cream-colored, fragrant. In the afternoons, I like to sit out on the porch with my coffee, protected from the eyes of the neighborhood by that curtain of flowers.

Salvatore died in this house thirty-five years ago. In the last months, he lay on the sofa in the parlor so he could be in the middle of everything. Except for the two oldest boys, all the children were still at home and we ate together every evening. Salvatore could see the dining room table from the sofa, and he could hear everything that was said. "I'm not dead, yet," he told me. "I want to know what's going on."

When my first grandchild, Cara, was born, we brought her to him, and he held her on his chest, stroking her tiny head. Sometimes they fell asleep together.

Over on the radiator cover in the corner of the parlor is the portrait Salvatore and I had taken on our twenty-fifth anniversary. This brooch I'm wearing today, with the diamonds— I'm wearing it in the photograph also—Salvatore gave it to me that day. Upstairs on my dresser is a jewelry box filled with necklaces and bracelets and earrings. All from Salvatore.

I am surrounded by the things Salvatore gave me, or did for me. But, God forgive me, as I lie alone now in my bed, it is Paolo I remember.

Paolo left me nothing. Nothing, that is, that my family, especially my sisters, thought had any value. No house. No diamonds. Not even a photograph.

But after he was gone, and I could catch my breath from the pain, I knew that I still had something. In the middle of the night, I sat alone and held them in my hands, reading the words over and over until I heard his voice in my head. I had Paolo's letters.

* * * * *

Be sure to look for
DANCING ON SUNDAY AFTERNOONS
available January 30, 2007.
And look, too, for our other Everlasting title available,
FALL FROM GRACE by Kristi Gold.

FALL FROM GRACE is a deeply emotional story
of what a long-term love really means.
As Jack and Anne Morgan discover,
marriage vows can be broken—
but they can be mended, too.
And the memories of their marriage have
an unexpected power
to bring back a love that never really left....

The real action happens behind the scenes!

Introducing

SECRET LIVES OF DAYTIME DIVAS,

a new miniseries from author
SARAH MAYBERRY

TAKE ON ME

Dylan Anderson was the cause of Sadie Post's biggest humiliation. Now that he's back, she's going to get a little revenge. But no one ever told her that revenge could be this sweet...and oh, so satisfying.

Available March 2007

Don't miss the other books in the SECRET LIVES OF DAYTIME DIVAS miniseries!

Look for *All Over You* in April 2007
and *Hot for Him* in May 2007.

www.eHarlequin.com

HB314

This February...

Catch NASCAR Superstar **Carl Edwards** *in*

SPEED DATING!

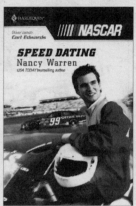

Kendall assesses risk for a living—
so she's the last person you'd
expect to see on the arm of a
race-car driver who thrives on the
unpredictable. But when a bizarre
turn of events—and NASCAR
hotshot Dylan Hargreave—inspire
her to trade in her ever-so-structured
existence for "life in the fast lane"
she starts to feel she might be
on to something!

**Collect all 4 debut novels in
the Harlequin NASCAR series.**

SPEED DATING
by *USA TODAY* bestselling author
Nancy Warren

*On sale
February
2007*

THUNDERSTRUCK
by Roxanne St. Claire

HEARTS UNDER CAUTION
by Gina Wilkins

DANGER ZONE
by Debra Webb

www.eHarlequin.com

HARLEQUIN® *Romance*®

What a month!

In February watch for

Rancher and Protector
Part of the Western Weddings miniseries
BY JUDY CHRISTENBERRY

The Boss's Pregnancy Proposal
BY RAYE MORGAN

Also in February, expect
MORE of what you love
as the Harlequin Romance line
increases to six titles per month.

www.eHarlequin.com   SRJAN07

Silhouette® Desire

Don't miss the first book
in THE ROYALS trilogy:

THE FORBIDDEN PRINCESS
(SD #1780)

by national bestselling author

DAY LECLAIRE

Moments before her loveless royal wedding,
Princess Alyssa was kidnapped by a mysterious man
who'd do anything to stop the ceremony. Even if that
meant marrying the forbidden princess himself!

On sale February 2007 from Silhouette Desire!

THE ROYALS
Stories of scandals and secrets
amidst the most powerful palaces.

Make sure to read the other titles in the series:
THE PRINCE'S MISTRESS
On sale March 2007
THE ROYAL WEDDING NIGHT
On sale April 2007

*Available wherever books are sold, including most
bookstores, supermarkets, discount stores and drugstores.*

Visit Silhouette Books at www.eHarlequin.com SDTFP0207

REQUEST YOUR FREE BOOKS!

2 FREE NOVELS PLUS 2 FREE GIFTS!

HARLEQUIN®

Blaze

Red-hot reads!

YES! Please send me 2 FREE Harlequin® Blaze® novels and my 2 FREE gifts. After receiving them, if I don't wish to receive any more books, I can return the shipping statement marked "cancel." If I don't cancel, I will receive 6 brand-new novels every month and be billed just $3.99 per book in the U.S., or $4.47 per book in Canada, plus 25¢ shipping and handling per book and applicable taxes, if any*. That's a savings of at least 15% off the cover price! I understand that accepting the 2 free books and gifts places me under no obligation to buy anything. I can always return a shipment and cancel at any time. Even if I never buy another book from Harlequin, the two free books and gifts are mine to keep forever.

151 HDN EF3W   351 HDN EF3X

Name	(PLEASE PRINT)	
Address		Apt.
City	State/Prov.	Zip/Postal Code

Signature (if under 18, a parent or guardian must sign)

Mail to the **Harlequin Reader Service®:**
IN U.S.A.: P.O. Box 1867, Buffalo, NY 14240-1867
IN CANADA: P.O. Box 609, Fort Erie, Ontario L2A 5X3

Not valid to current Harlequin Blaze subscribers.

**Want to try two free books from another line?
Call 1-800-873-8635 or visit www.morefreebooks.com.**

* Terms and prices subject to change without notice. NY residents add applicable sales tax. Canadian residents will be charged applicable provincial taxes and GST. This offer is limited to one order per household. All orders subject to approval. Credit or debit balances in a customer's account(s) may be offset by any other outstanding balance owed by or to the customer. Please allow 4 to 6 weeks for delivery.

Your Privacy: Harlequin is committed to protecting your privacy. Our Privacy Policy is available online at www.eHarlequin.com or upon request from the Reader Service. From time to time we make our lists of customers available to reputable firms who may have a product or service of interest to you. If you would prefer we not share your name and address, please check here. ☐

HB07

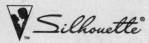

Romantic
SUSPENSE

Excitement, danger and passion guaranteed!

Same great authors and riveting editorial you've come to know and love.

Look for our new name next month as Silhouette Intimate Moments® becomes Silhouette® Romantic Suspense.

Bestselling author Marie Ferrarella is back with a hot new miniseries— The Doctors Pulaski: Medicine just got more interesting….

Check out her first title, HER LAWMAN ON CALL, next month.

Look for it wherever you buy books!

Visit Silhouette Books at www.eHarlequin.com

SIMRS0107

HARLEQUIN®

Blaze™

COMING NEXT MONTH

#303 JINXED! Jacquie D'Alessandro, Jill Shalvis, Crystal Green
Valentine Anthology
Valentine's Day. If she's lucky, a girl can expect to receive dark chocolate, red roses and fantastic sex! If she's not…well, she can wind up with a Valentine's Day curse…and fantastic sex! Join three of Harlequin Blaze's bestselling authors as they show how three very unlucky women can end up getting *very* lucky….

#304 HITTING THE MARK Jill Monroe
Danielle Ford has been a successful con artist most of her life. Giving up the habit has been hard, but she's kicked it. Until Eric Reynolds, security chief at a large Reno casino, antes up a challenge she can't back away from—one that touches her past and ups her odds on bedding sexy Eric.

#305 DON'T LOOK BACK Joanne Rock
Night Eyes, Bk. 1
Hitting the sheets with P.I. Sean Beringer might have been a mistake. While the sex is as hot as the man, NYPD detective Donata Casale is struggling to focus on their case. They need to wrap up this investigation fast. Then she'll be free to fully indulge in this fling.

#306 AT HER BECK AND CALL Dawn Atkins
Doing It…Better!, Bk. 2
Autumn Beskin can bring a man to his knees. The steamy glances from her new boss, Mike Fields, say she hasn't lost her touch. But while he may be interested in more than her job performance, he hasn't made a move. Guess she'll have to nudge this fling along.

#307 HOT MOVES Kristin Hardy
Sex & the Supper Club II, Bk. 2
Professional dancer Thea Mitchell knows all the right steps—new job, new city, new life. But then Brady McMillan joins her Latin tango dance class and suddenly she's got two left feet. When he makes his move, with naughty suggestions and even naughtier kisses, she doesn't know what to expect next!

#308 PRIVATE CONFESSIONS Lori Borrill
What does a woman do when she discovers that her secret online sex partner is actually her real-life boss—the man she's been lusting after for two years? She goes for it! Trisha Bain isn't sure how to approach Logan Moore with the knowledge that he's Pisces47, only that she wants to make the fantasy a reality. Fast…

www.eHarlequin.com

HBCNM0107